DARK
DESCENDANT

JENNA BLACK

Pocket Books

New York   London   Toronto   Sydney

Pocket Books
A Division of Simon & Schuster, Inc.
1230 Avenue of the Americas
New York, NY 10020

This book is a work of fiction. Names, characters, places, and incidents either are products of the author's imagination or are used fictitiously. Any resemblance to actual events or locales or persons, living or dead, is entirely coincidental.

Copyright © 2011 by Jenna Black

All rights reserved, including the right to reproduce this book or portions thereof in any form whatsoever. For information address Pocket Books Subsidiary Rights Department, 1230 Avenue of the Americas, New York, NY 10020

First Pocket Books paperback edition May 2011

POCKET and colophon are registered trademarks of Simon & Schuster, Inc.

For information about special discounts for bulk purchases, please contact Simon & Schuster Special Sales at 1-866-506-1949 or business@simonandschuster.com.

The Simon & Schuster Speakers Bureau can bring authors to your live event. For more information or to book an event contact the Simon & Schuster Speakers Bureau at 1-866-248-3049 or visit our website at www.simonspeakers.com.

Designed by Jacquelynne Hudson
Cover illustration by Nathália Suellen

Manufactured in the United States of America

10   9   8   7   6   5   4   3

ISBN 978-1-4516-0679-9
ISBN 978-1-4516-0689-8 (ebook)

"Why would the Olympians want to capture me?"

"Because Descendants of Artemis are exceedingly rare," Anderson explained. "She was a goddess of the hunt, and the skills her descendants possess would be of great use to the Olympians."

"Go on," I prompted.

"Because Descendants can potentially steal their immortality, the Olympians see them as a threat that needs to be eliminated. For centuries, they have hunted Descendants. They kill all the adults and all the children over the age of five. They then raise those youngest children themselves, indoctrinating them into their beliefs. If the children question the 'natural order,' they are disposed of."

I sank down, knees weak at the images Anderson's words brought to mind. "By disposed of, you mean killed."

Praise for the urban fantasy of Jenna Black

"Black seamlessly blends urban and fantasy elements."
—*Publishers Weekly* on *Glimmerglass*

"Black has done a remarkable job of taking an old myth . . . and spinning it into a fabulous new world."
—Fallen Angel Reviews

Dark Descendant is also available as an eBook

Enter the dark and seductive world of

JENNA BLACK

THE DESCENDANT SERIES
Dark Descendant

THE MORGAN KINGSLEY SERIES
The Devil Inside
The Devil You Know
The Devil's Due
Speak of the Devil
The Devil's Playground

GUARDIANS OF THE NIGHT SERIES
Watchers in the Night
Secrets in the Shadows
Shadows on the Soul
Hungers of the Heart

THE FAERIEWALKER SERIES
Glimmerglass
Shadowspell

WRITING AS JENNIFER BARLOW
Hamlet Dreams

In loving memory of Albert Barlow

DARK
DESCENDANT

ONE

My entire world shattered on a cold, rainy, miserable night in early December.

The evening started off depressingly normal with a blind date arranged by my sister, Steph. Now, I love Steph to death, and I know she means well, but her ability to pick just the kind of man I'm least likely to hit it off with is legendary.

My date *du jour,* Jim, was good-looking, unattached, and conspicuously charming, at least on the surface. In Steph's book, that made him perfect for me. Little details like his self-absorption and thinly veiled disrespect for women had apparently escaped her notice. They did not, however, escape mine.

When my cell phone rang, I practically dove into my purse to find it, praying the call would grant me a reprieve from the date from hell. I did a mental happy dance when I glanced at the caller ID and saw the name Emmitt Cartwright.

I gave Jim my best imitation of a chagrined expression. "I'm so sorry," I said, hoping I didn't sound relieved. "It's a client. I have to take it."

He indicated it was okay with a magnanimous sweep of his arm. His face conveyed another message—something along the lines of how much he loathed people who interrupted romantic dinners for something so crass as business. Considering some of the views he'd expressed over appetizers, I wouldn't have been surprised if he were a charter member of the "women belong in the kitchen, barefoot, and pregnant" club.

I dismissed Jim's disapproval and answered the call as I pushed away from the table, heading for a quiet corner near the back of the restaurant where I could talk in something resembling privacy.

"Nikki Glass," I said.

"Miss Glass," Emmitt said, sounding relieved to have reached me. I'd tried to convince him to call me Nikki, but he had the quaintly old-fashioned habit of reverting to "Miss Glass" whenever I failed to remind him. It made him sound almost grandfatherly, although he was younger than me. "I hope I'm not interrupting anything."

I smiled, glancing over at the table where Jim sat with his legs crossed and his fingers tapping impatiently. "Nothing that didn't badly need interrupting," I assured him. "Is everything all right?"

He hesitated a moment. "I . . . don't know."

I raised an eyebrow at that hesitation. I'd only met him in person once, but that was enough to leave a strong impression. He wasn't the hesitant type. The man practically had "alpha male" tattooed on his forehead.

"Maggie called me," he said quietly.

I leaned against the wall and bit my lip, trying to figure out what to make of this new development. Maggie was his ex-girlfriend, and he obviously hadn't gotten over her yet. He'd originally hired me to track her down after she'd left him for a guy he suspected of belonging to a weird cult of some kind. He'd said he was worried the cult was going to indoctrinate her.

"What did she have to say?" I asked, genuinely curious. I'd had very little luck in my investigations so far. Maggie and the other members of this so-called cult lived together in a massive mansion in Arlington, Virginia, and discreet inquiries in the neighborhood had revealed only that they "kept to themselves." Real helpful. All I had to show for my investigation so far were names and a handful of surveillance photos, and I'd been lucky to get those.

"She said she wanted out. She wants me to come get her."

I frowned. This seemed like exactly the kind of break Emmitt had been hoping for, and I wondered why he hadn't already whisked her away.

"She's going to wedge the front gate open, and I'm supposed to drive up to the back and pick her up," Emmitt continued.

Ah. Now I had a hint why he hadn't already run to the rescue.

"In other words, she thinks someone might try to

stop her, so she's trying to make a fast, quiet getaway."

"Yeah. Something like that. I'd like you to come with me. I want another witness there in case things get . . . weird."

All right, *that* I hadn't been expecting. "I'm not really sure I'd be much help," I said. Emmitt was about as imposing a human being as I could imagine. I'm five foot two, fine-boned, and female. Anyone not intimidated by Emmitt wouldn't even give me a second glance. " Maybe you should call the police."

"And tell them what? I have no proof of anything, and Maggie didn't even say she was being threatened. I'm probably just being paranoid, but I don't like the idea of going up there alone. Just in case. This cult believes some very strange stuff, and I don't think it's smart to expect them to act rationally."

Everything substantive I'd learned about the cult's beliefs had come from Emmitt himself, though he'd always been a little vague about how he'd learned the details. Apparently, they believed themselves to be descended of gods and therefore immortal. I didn't doubt that these nut jobs were dangerous, but my gut was telling me to turn Emmitt down. This wasn't a job for a private investigator. At least, not for *this* private investigator.

"I'll pay double your fee," Emmitt said, sounding almost desperate. "But I don't want to keep her waiting too long. I don't want to give her time to change her mind."

"Money isn't the issue," I assured him. "I just don't think . . ."

"Please humor me, okay? I don't have anyone else I can ask on short notice."

I glanced over at the table, where Jim's body language was screaming even more loudly that he resented me taking this call. The server had brought our entrees while I was talking. My stomach gave an unhappy grumble at the thought of going hungry, but I wasn't anxious to spend the next hour or so gnashing my teeth to keep from telling Jim exactly what I thought of him. Emmitt was giving me a perfect excuse to cut the evening short, and he was going to pay me, to boot.

I decided to ignore my gut instinct and agreed to meet Emmitt at the gate in front of the house.

I'm twenty-five years old and have been listening to my gut all my life. I should have known better than to ignore it.

A little more than half an hour later, my gut was insisting even more loudly that this was a piss-poor idea.

The skies opened up as soon as I left the restaurant, and by the time I pulled up to the gate in Arlington, the rain was mixed with sleet and the streets were growing slick. All the worst moments of my life have been associated with rain, so this should have been another clue it was time for me to turn around. My windshield wipers squeaked and squealed as they tried their best to dash the rain away. I'd meant to replace the wiper blades months ago.

The neighborhood was dark and quiet. Most of the houses were set far enough back from the road that they were hidden from view, and the streetlights were few and far between. Close to D.C. as it was, the neighborhood still felt distant from all the hustle and bustle, and I seemed to be the only person out and about in this weather.

I'd expected Emmitt to be waiting for me at the gate, but when I pulled up, I saw no sign of his car, nor of him. The gate stood open, however, making me wonder if Emmitt had gotten impatient and decided not to wait for me.

I pulled off to the side of the road, keeping the car running and the headlights pointing at the gate, then dug out my phone and called Emmitt's cell. There was no answer. A chill that had nothing to do with the frigid weather or the sleet crept down my spine. I knew he had his cell phone with him, since that was the number he'd called me from. So why wasn't he answering?

"Damn it," I muttered under my breath. This was *so* not my type of gig.

I sat there for a good ten minutes, debating what to do between repeated attempts to get Emmitt on the phone. The rain had turned to sleet, and icicles were forming on the gate. The branches of the trees beside the road hung low, weighted down by a thin coating of ice. There was no sound except the steady ping of the sleet bouncing off the windshield and the roof of my car.

Finally, I blew out a deep breath and put the car in drive. I couldn't sit idling forever. My choices were to turn around and go home, or drive through the gate and make sure everything was okay. Doing so was technically trespassing, but the gate *was* hanging open like an invitation. Emmitt had almost certainly gone in without me, and if he had, his failure to answer the phone was a bad sign.

"Screw it," I decided, and maneuvered the car carefully down the driveway, my tires struggling to find a grip on the ice-slicked asphalt.

I gave the ice the respect it deserved, driving slowly and trying not to make any sudden moves. Even so, my car slipped and slid, and I gripped the steering wheel tightly as I struggled to keep control. The damn driveway meandered through trees too evenly spaced to be natural growth. I wished whoever had done the landscaping had kept the trees farther back from the road. There wasn't a hell of a lot of room for error if I lost control of the car. Streetlights would have been a nice touch, too.

My nerves were taut, and I had to remind myself to breathe every once in a while. Driving in snow I can handle, but the sleet was a nightmare. I worked my way around yet another curve in the driveway, one that seemed specifically designed to send cars careening into the trees. I let out a sigh when the driveway finally straightened out, the lights of the house itself just visible in the distance. Anxious to find Emmitt and get out of there, I gave the car a little more gas than was strictly wise.

My only warning was a glimpse of movement in the trees off to my right. Then, as if he'd appeared literally out of nowhere, a figure stood in the middle of the road, barely two yards from my car.

With a shriek of alarm, I instinctively slammed on the brakes. If I'd had half a second to think about it, I'd have remembered that slamming brakes on an icy road was a bad idea. The wheels locked up, and the car skidded forward, the back slewing to one side.

The figure in the road made no attempt to get out of the way. At the last moment, he raised his head, and I recognized Emmitt's face in the glare of the headlights. His eyes met mine, and I'll never forget the small smile that curved his lips. Then the car slammed into him with a sickening wet thunk.

I screamed again, my car now spinning like a top as the airbag exploded out toward my face. The impact slammed my head back against the headrest. Though I tried to turn the wheel into the skid, I was so disoriented, I didn't know which way that was.

Out of the side window, I saw a tree trunk heading my way. The side of the car crunched with the impact, safety glass shattering and peppering my face as I held up my hand to protect my eyes. The car door crumpled under the pressure, and something sharp and hard stabbed into my side, the pain blinding. Even as my head snapped to one side, the car caromed into another tree. Something struck the other side of my head, and everything went black.

Two

When I came to, the engine was off and the air bag had deflated. My whole body hurt, and with the windows all broken, frigid air and sleet had frozen me to the marrow. With a groan, I looked down at myself to assess my injuries. My vision swam and my stomach lurched when I saw the huge gash in my side. Blood soaked my sweater and the top of my pants and coated the crumpled door.

My brain was working in slow motion, my head throbbing. I suspected I had a concussion in addition to my other injuries. Shivering, sick, and scared, I forced my nearly frozen fingers to release my seat belt. I didn't need a medical degree to know I needed help, but when I reached for my cell phone, I found it hadn't survived the crash.

The door was far too badly damaged to open, so I had to drag myself out the broken window. It hurt so much that I wondered if I wouldn't be better off just keeping still. Surely the people in the house had heard the accident. Someone would come to check it out, and then they could call an ambulance for me.

By the time this brilliant thought occurred to me, I was more than halfway out the window, and gravity took the decision out of my hands. I came close to blacking out when I hit the ground, but I fought for consciousness. I couldn't be *sure* anyone in the house heard the accident, and if I didn't find shelter soon, the sleet and cold would finish me off even if I didn't bleed to death.

I staggered to my feet, swallowing a cry of pain. Clutching my side, hoping I wasn't killing myself by making the wound bleed faster, I limped and stumbled back to the road.

Without the headlights, the dark was thick and oppressive, but the ambient light was just enough to illuminate Emmitt's body. He lay by the far side of the road, where he must have been tossed by the impact. He wasn't moving, and the angle of his neck was all wrong, but I had to check on him, just in case I was wrong and he was still alive.

My feet slid out from under me the moment they hit the icy road, and I slipped and slid the rest of the way on my hands and knees, leaving a trail of blood. In the distance, I could see three small yellow lights bobbing up and down from the direction of the house. Flashlights, I decided with relief. Good. Someone in the house *had* heard the accident, and help was on the way. I'd be a dead woman otherwise, because I didn't think I'd be able to make it to the house on my own before I collapsed and the elements had their way with me.

I came to a stop beside Emmitt's body and let out a sob at what I saw. His neck was obviously broken, his eyes wide and staring. The sob hurt like hell, but once I'd let go of one, I couldn't restrain the rest.

I was on my knees, clutching my side, which oozed more blood, and crying uncontrollably when the beam of a flashlight hit me square in the face. The light sent a stabbing pain through my head that almost made me vomit. My vision still blurred with tears, I held up one bloody hand to shield my eyes from the flashlight's glare. There were three flashlights, though only one was focused on me. The other two illuminated Emmitt's ruined body.

"Aw, shit," said a man's voice softly.

One of the men behind the flashlights knelt beside Emmitt. I recognized Blake Porter, one of the supposed cultists I'd been doing such a fabulous job of investigating. He was the quintessential pretty boy, though he didn't look so pretty now with his blond hair plastered to his scalp and the look of raw sorrow on his beautiful face. He brushed his hand gently over Emmitt's face.

"Keep your fucking hands off him!" one of the other two growled, the one who insisted on shining his light right in my eyes. He took a menacing step in Blake's direction.

Blake looked up at the speaker blandly. "I was just closing his eyes." He sat back on his heels and held his hands innocently to his sides.

My head was still spinning from a combination of concussion, shock, and blood loss, but everything around me had taken on a surreal quality that had nothing to do with my injuries. These men weren't acting at all like first responders to an accident. There was no sense of urgency or shock. No one had spoken to me, asked if I was all right. And the man who'd ordered Blake to keep his hands to himself had sounded distinctly protective. But why would the cultists—*any* of the cultists—feel protective of the man who'd been trying to lure one of their members away? Did they even know who he was?

My teeth were chattering, my feet and hands almost completely numb. The wound in my side was anything but. I didn't know how long hypothermia would take to kill me, but if I had to guess, I'd say I was halfway to the grave already.

"C-call an ambulance," I stammered, since it obviously hadn't occurred to these wingnuts that I was in need of medical assistance.

"Shut up, you fucking bitch!" roared Mr. Hostility, the flashlight in my eyes still keeping me from seeing his face.

"Jamaal, no!" Blake suddenly yelled, reaching out, but he was too late.

I didn't see the kick coming until the heavy boot connected with my face, and the world went dark again.

When I came to, I wished I hadn't. My side still screamed in pain. I was still freezing, and soaked, and light-headed.

And now my jaw felt not so much broken as crushed. I tasted blood in my mouth as I forced my eyes open.

I was lying on the road, being pelted by sleet. All three of the cultists' flashlights were on the ground. With none of the beams directly in my eyes, I could actually see what was going on around me.

The man who had kicked me—Jamaal—was being held back by a third man, who I recognized as Logan Fields, the man Maggie had run off with. It was hard to believe that Logan was physically capable of restraining Jamaal, who was even bigger and more imposing than Emmitt.

I had no idea what Jamaal had against me, but whatever it was, he was beyond livid. His face was twisted into a feral snarl, and he was struggling against Logan's hold with every ounce of strength, his head lashing back and forth, whipping the beads at the ends of his braids across Logan's face. Somehow, Logan held on, though his face was dotted with welts, and the uncertain footing should have seen them both sprawling on the ground.

"Take it easy, Jamaal," Blake said. He was standing between me and the two struggling men, but he looked even less able to hold off Jamaal than Logan did. "You're not helping Emmitt by acting like a mad dog."

That enraged Jamaal even more. His howl sounded scarcely human, sending a superstitious shiver down my spine.

Incongruously, Logan laughed, even as he struggled to hold Jamaal back. "You sure have a way with words, bud."

Blake looked sheepish. "Sorry."

Again, my sluggish brain struggled to make sense of things. Why were these guys talking about Emmitt like he was a friend of theirs? He was supposed to be the enemy. At least, that's what he'd told me. But I was beginning to wonder if anything Emmitt had told me was the truth.

"Jamaal," Logan said sharply, trying to get the other man's attention. "I don't want to hurt you, man, but I'm getting pretty damn tired of playing referee."

"Then let me go!" Jamaal snarled in reply, his eyes fixed on me with such hatred it was amazing I didn't go up in a puff of smoke.

"Enough!" Logan said, but Jamaal continued to struggle. Logan heaved a sigh, and then . . . I'm not really sure what happened. Maybe it was the multiple blows to my head, or the shock, or a cold-induced hallucination, but it looked to me like Logan shoved the bigger man forward so hard that he flew all the way across the road and slammed into the trunk of a tree on the other side. And when I say flew, I don't mean stumbled—I mean he flew through the air with the greatest of ease.

Impossible, of course. Even if the men had been more evenly matched, it wasn't possible for one human being to throw another human being that far and with such force. Icicles rained from the branches of the tree as it shuddered with the impact. When Jamaal collapsed to the ground over the knotty roots, he didn't get up.

Logan gave me a quick glance, his face registering

mild distaste—which I much preferred to Jamaal's rabid hostility—then turned his attention back to Blake. "Take her to the house. I'll hang out here until Jamaal comes to. And I'll try to talk him down a bit when he does."

Blake looked at Jamaal's crumpled form doubtfully. "I think she may have just killed the only person capable of talking him down."

Logan looked grim. "Maybe. But I might have a chance if you just get her out of sight."

Blake didn't look convinced. "Good luck with that."

I tried to form some kind of protest. I didn't need to go to the house—I needed to go to the *hospital*. I didn't know just how badly I was wounded, but I was sure it was pretty damn bad. Even before Jamaal kicked me in the face.

I doubt Blake would have listened to my protest, even if I'd managed to muster one. My jaw sent spears of agony through my head the moment I tried to move it, and I was now shivering so violently I wasn't sure I'd be able to get words out anyway.

Blake squatted beside me, slipping one arm behind my shoulders and one behind my knees. Then he rose easily to his feet, making no particular effort not to jostle me. I couldn't help crying out at the pain, but Blake ignored me.

Behind us, Jamaal let out a little groan.

"Shit," Blake and Logan said in unison. And then Blake began jogging back toward the house, slipping and sliding like mad, and I was in too much pain to think of anything other than how much I wished I would pass out for a third time.

Blake carried me all the way around the house to a back entrance. He knocked on the door with his foot, and moments later I heard footsteps approaching. The lights went on, and the door swung open.

I was barely conscious, my clothes soaked through with melted ice and blood. I felt I'd never be warm again, sure I was going to die if I didn't get medical attention stat. Through eyes narrowed in pain, I saw a few more cultists—including Maggie—standing in the hall with anxious looks on their faces.

"What happened?" one of them asked as Blake stepped inside.

He shook his head. "Emmitt's dead."

Someone gasped, and Maggie covered her mouth to stifle a cry. Even in my shocked, semi-lucid state, I was once again aware of how off everything seemed. Not only did everyone seem to know and care about Emmitt, but Blake was carrying the obviously battered body of a woman soaked in blood, and no one seemed to even consider calling an ambulance. What was wrong with these people?

My eyes finally adjusted to the brightly lit hallway, and I did a mental double take. Despite my distinct lack of success in investigating the cult, I had at least managed to identify and get photos of each member. In those photos, the only member of the cult who'd had a tattoo was Blake, who had a corny cartoon Cupid on his biceps. But as I blinked water out of my eyes, I saw that each person in the hall had a tattoo visible somewhere, mostly on their faces or necks.

The tattoos were like nothing I'd ever seen before. They looked like hieroglyphics or cuneiform or some other incomprehensible script, and though I stared, I couldn't for the life of me come up with a word to describe their color. In fact, the colors seemed to change with every minute shift of the light.

"What should I do with this one?" Blake asked, indicating me with a curl of his lip.

His question was directed at Anderson Kane, a man my observations had led me to believe was their leader, despite his laid-back demeanor; a suspicion that was even now being confirmed.

Anderson barely spared me a glance. "We'll deal with her later," he said dismissively. "Put her downstairs for now."

I voiced a protest at that, but no one listened to me. Oh, God. These guys were just going to dump me in a room somewhere and let me bleed to death!

I tried to find something I could say to persuade Blake he needed to call an ambulance, but if he heard a word I said, he made no sign of it. He carried me down a narrow flight of stairs into a huge basement, then into a drafty corridor punctuated with several doors, each of which came equipped with multiple deadbolt locks on the outside. None of those doors was locked, but the sight instantly called to mind a prison cellblock.

Blake stopped in front of the first door, pushing it open with his foot to reveal a small, barren room with a stone floor and a single thin cot in one corner. There was a sink and a toilet in another corner, but other than that, the room was empty.

Blake dropped me unceremoniously onto the cot, and I couldn't stifle a cry of pain as my side and my head both screamed in agony. Without another word, he turned his back on me and left the room, closing the door behind him.

With a moan of utter despair, I heard the dead bolts being thrown and realized that even if my wounds didn't kill me, I was still in big, big trouble.

THREE

I don't know how long I lay on that cot, shivering, bleeding, sure I was going to die. As far as I could tell, I didn't lose consciousness again, but my mind wasn't exactly all there. I suspected more time was passing than I could account for.

Feeling returned to my hands and feet, which was a relief. I'd been halfway convinced that even if I survived, I'd lose a few fingers and toes to frostbite. The pain in my side and my head faded to manageable levels, as long as I held absolutely still. The shivering didn't stop, but since my clothes were soaked through, that wasn't a surprise.

What the hell had happened out there?

I remembered my headlights illuminating Emmitt's face as he stood in the path of my car, remembered the little smile on his lips, and how he hadn't made the slightest attempt to get out of the way. The evidence suggested he had *wanted* me to hit him. But hell, if he was bent on committing suicide, surely he could have found an easier way!

After lying on that cot for who knows how long, I finally decided I couldn't stand the feel of wet fabric against my skin for another moment. Bracing myself for the pain, I made a tentative effort to push myself into a sitting position.

It was easier than I'd expected. Yeah, it hurt. My side screamed, and my head throbbed, and the whole room spun for a moment, but it was bearable. I glanced down at my sopping, bloodstained sweater and swallowed hard to keep from throwing up. Maybe moving around wasn't such a great idea after all. The blended scents of wet wool and coppery blood gave my stomach added incentive to rebel. I closed my eyes and breathed through my mouth until the nausea receded.

Wincing in anticipation, I grabbed the hem of the sweater and started slowly, carefully peeling it away from my skin. It stuck to my wound, but it was wet enough to come loose with little effort. I stifled a whimper, my stomach rolling again. I've never been that crazy about the sight of blood, especially my own.

Getting the sweater off over my head was pure torture; every movement of my left arm pulled on the muscles around the wound. Even so, I was determined to get the wet wool away from my skin.

Finally, I managed to drag the sweater off, dropping it to the floor with a plop. I sat still, breathing hard from the exertion. Each breath made my side hurt. I forced myself to open my eyes and examine the wound to see how bad it was and whether I'd started it bleeding again.

I expected to see a jagged, deep gash, based both on how much it hurt and how much I'd bled. The wound that met my eyes stretched from the bottom of my rib cage all the way down to my hip. Blood smeared my skin all the way around it, but the wound itself . . .

I blinked in confusion. The wound was an angry red seam, but the edges were kind of puckered together, as if there were a whole lot of invisible stitches holding it closed.

What the hell?

Gently, I touched the edge of the wound with one trembling finger, sure I must have passed out after all and been stitched up while I was unconscious. But I neither saw nor felt any stitches. Besides, if someone had stitched me up, they wouldn't have put the sodden sweater back on me.

I shuddered and decided to think about it later. I still had more wet clothing to get out of.

The pants came off more easily than the sweater. It was a relief to be out of the wet clothes, but I was still shivering in a residual chill, and there was nothing to wrap up in. The thin sheets of the cot were soaked and bloodstained and of no use. I wanted to take off the wet bra and panties, too, but there was no way I was sitting around this room naked. Bad enough that I was down to my underwear. At least I'd chosen a black satin matching set on the off chance Steph had set me up with a man I would hit it off with. Wishful thinking at its finest.

The date with Jim seemed so long ago, it had taken on an almost dreamlike quality. I checked my watch to get some feel for how long I'd been here, but the crystal was completely shattered, the hands bent so badly they couldn't move.

I looked across the room at the sink, thinking about running some hot water over my hands to warm up a little. Assuming there *was* any hot water in this dungeon.

I was trying to decide if it was worth the effort to drag myself to my feet to find out, when I heard footsteps approaching from down the hall. I quickly glanced around me, but no suitable cover-up had magically appeared. I settled for grabbing the soggy pillow, turning it so the dry side was against my skin and clasping it against my chest and belly. It wasn't much of a shield, but it was all I had.

My heart was in my throat as I heard the locks on my door clicking open. I sat up as straight as I could manage and raised my chin, hoping I looked braver than I felt.

The door swung open, and Anderson Kane stepped into the room, followed closely by Blake, who had changed into clean, dry clothes. The light revealed an iridescent tattoo beside Blake's left eye. The shape was vaguely phallic, and like the tattoos I'd seen on the other cultists, it hadn't been there when I'd taken the surveillance photos. Blake was carrying a chair, which he set on the floor before moving to stand in front of the door as if to block my escape.

Making a dash for it might have been tempting

if I'd thought I had the least chance in hell of getting to safety. But even if I could miraculously get by both Blake and Anderson, it was unlikely that I'd get past the other cultists and out of the house. And even if I did, running out into the sleet on foot wearing nothing but a bra and panties was somewhere between insane and outright suicidal.

Anderson adjusted the angle of the chair until it was squarely facing me, then sat down. He didn't speak, instead giving me a slow and thorough once-over. Not knowing what to say—I wasn't going to repeat the "call an ambulance" line yet again only to have it ignored—I followed suit.

At first glance, Anderson was unprepossessing. Medium height, medium build, medium brown hair. Not bad looking, in a bland vanilla sort of way. He wore a pair of tan cords with a slightly wrinkled blue Oxford shirt, and his hair was shaggy and past due for a cut. His five o'clock shadow looked scruffy, rather than sexy. He was the kind of guy you'd pass in the street without giving a second glance.

Except for the weird tattoo, that is.

It was on his neck, just above the collar of his shirt, and I still couldn't tell what color it was. Part of it looked kind of silver, another part flashed red, but then he tilted his head to the side and the silver turned green and the red turned gold. I blinked a couple of times, trying to clear my vision. The tattoo looked more like a hologram than ink, but I'd never heard of a wearable hologram.

"You're staring," Anderson said, his voice startling me so much I jumped and almost dropped the pillow.

I jerked my eyes away from the tattoo, which I had, indeed, been staring at. I swallowed and clutched the pillow a little more tightly against me.

I didn't know how to respond to his statement, so I didn't. "Is there some reason you're so dead set against calling me an ambulance?" I asked instead.

He raised his eyebrows. "I would think that's obvious."

I didn't like the sound of that. His reasoning was far from obvious, but nothing I came up with on my own—like he was going to kill me anyway—was in the least bit comforting.

"I was in a car accident and then kicked in the head," I said. "Even if it's obvious, I'm not getting it. Please humor me and explain."

He sat back in his chair, looking thoughtful.

Blake snorted, drawing my attention. He was leaning against the closed door, arms crossed over his chest. His blue eyes pierced me, his anger as cold as Jamaal's had been hot.

"Playing dumb isn't going to win you any brownie points," he said with a sneer. I'd never known a pretty boy could look that menacing. The sneer changed to a leer that was just as unpleasant. "Dropping the pillow might, though."

Blood heated my cheeks. It pissed me off that I was letting him get to me that easily, but I couldn't seem to help it. I dropped my gaze and held the pillow even more tightly.

Anderson sighed. "Please forgive Blake's bedside manner. Sometimes he just can't help himself when a pretty woman's around."

Anderson had his back to Blake and therefore couldn't see the look on the other man's face, but I didn't for a moment believe he hadn't heard the malice in Blake's tone of voice. Flirtation had been the furthest thing from Blake's mind, and Anderson knew that. Besides, I wasn't exactly a ravishing beauty, even when I wasn't wet, dirty, bruised, and bedraggled. I was kind of like Anderson, come to think of it—not bad to look at, but completely unremarkable.

"So you have no idea why we didn't call an ambulance?" Anderson asked, bringing us back on topic.

I shook my head. "It's generally what people do when there's been a car accident and someone's hurt."

"Oh, please!" Blake said. "Cut the bullshit."

"Ease down, Blake," Anderson said in a low, calming voice. "It's always possible she's telling the truth."

"Oh yeah, like this is all some big fucking coincidence."

"Blake!" Anderson said with a little more heat, and Blake shut up. Anderson smiled at me, but the expression didn't reach his eyes. "Do you still think you need an ambulance?"

The question stopped me cold. My sense of time was completely out of whack, but it couldn't have been more than an hour or so ago that I'd stumbled out onto the road, bleeding so badly I left a trail across the ice. Now I was still in pain and feeling badly beat up, but the wound seemed to have almost closed itself, and I seemed to be suffering no aftereffects from having lost so much blood. All of which was, of course, impossible.

Anderson didn't wait for me to answer. "What were you doing on our property?"

There was no heat or anger in his voice, and yet there was a studied intensity to his question. He looked at me like a lawyer might look at a witness he was sure was about to lie.

I wasn't sure what to say. The reason I was here was a long story, and one Anderson wasn't going to like. Plus, the more I thought about it, the more full of holes it sounded, especially if I accepted that Emmitt must have been lying to me about at least some of the stuff he'd told me.

"I was here to meet Emmitt," I finally said, deciding to keep my answer simple but true.

"Like hell you were!" Blake snapped. "Hey Anderson, maybe you should get her a towel or something to wrap up in. I'll stay here and keep watch." He gave me another creepy leer. His pants were so tight I couldn't help seeing the evidence of why he was really suggesting Anderson leave the room.

Anderson apparently didn't need to see Blake to know what he was thinking. He smiled that mild smile of his. "I'm sure the pillow will suffice." His eyes met mine, and there was no missing the threat in his next softly spoken words. "For now."

My gut cramped with fear as I recognized the

good cop/bad cop tactics. If you'd told me before tonight that Blake Porter would make an effective bad cop, I'd probably have laughed at you. He was just too goddamn pretty to be scary, with his smooth, flawless skin that probably never grew more than peach fuzz, and his Cupid's bow mouth. But right now, the absolute last thing I wanted was to be left alone with him. Unfortunately, my story sounded unbelievable even to my own ears, so why should these guys believe it?

"Why were you here to meet Emmitt?" Anderson prompted.

I decided that no matter how weird my story was going to sound under the circumstances, I had no alternative but to start talking and hope for the best.

Slowly, trying not to stammer, I told them a carefully edited version of how and why Emmitt had hired me, leaving out any mention of crazy cultists. Anderson's face gave away nothing, but Blake made repeated little snorts of disbelief and rolled his eyes a couple of times.

When I explained that Emmitt had asked me to meet him in front of the gates, and that I'd found the gates open and driven through, both men fell silent, the silence an oppressive weight that made me want to sink under the bed and disappear. I forced myself to keep talking, though I didn't want to relive the nightmare of seeing Emmitt standing there in the road with that little smile.

"So what you're saying is that it was an accident?" Anderson asked when I finished talking.

I blinked at him. "Of course it was an accident! At least on my part. Did you think I ran him down on purpose?"

"What do you mean, at least on your part?"

I was momentarily taken aback by the question. I thought I'd made it perfectly clear when I'd explained. But despite everything Emmitt had told me, I was now convinced these people were actually friends of his, and it must have been shocking for them to hear that he'd basically killed himself. Maybe they didn't want to hear it and had subconsciously filtered that part out.

"I mean he just stood there in the middle of the road, looking at me and smiling, waiting for me to hit him. I don't know if he could have gotten out of the way if he'd tried, but he didn't even try."

There was a howl of rage from just outside the room. The door slammed open with such force that Blake, who was standing in front of it, went flying. He hit the floor hard and came up cursing.

Jamaal stormed into the cell in the same towering rage I'd seen by the side of the road. If he was suffering any ill effects from his tussle with Logan, I saw no sign of them.

His eyes locked on me, and he came at me like a guided missile. Leader or not, Anderson scrambled out from between us, leaving me to fend for myself.

If Anderson was the good cop, and Blake was the bad cop, Jamaal was the complete psycho cop. I'm physically fit and fairly athletic. I also know enough basic self-defense not to be completely useless in a fight. But I would have been no match for Jamaal even without my injuries. I couldn't even manage to get to my feet before he was on me, grabbing me by the throat.

I dropped the pillow and tried to loosen Jamaal's grip, digging my fingernails into his hand as hard as I could. I'd have gone for his face, only his arms were longer than mine and I couldn't reach. When clawing at him didn't work, I tried to separate one of his fingers from the herd and throw all my strength into peeling it away, willing to break it if necessary. My efforts didn't bother him in the least, and he hauled me off of the cot until my feet dangled.

I stopped trying to loosen his fingers and merely held on to his arm, trying to pull myself up a bit so I didn't strangle. It was a useless effort, and his hand squeezed hard enough to cut off my air completely.

Still easily holding me off the floor, he stepped around the cot so he could slam me against the wall so hard I saw stars. Or maybe the stars were just because I couldn't breathe. My struggles weakened as my brain starved for oxygen.

Anderson came to stand beside Jamaal, his expression one of gentle concern. Concern for Jamaal, that is, not for me.

"She can't talk while you're choking her."

Jamaal bared his teeth in a feral smile. "That's a shame." He pulled me forward then slammed me into the wall again to show how heartbroken he was. I could hardly believe I hadn't passed out from lack of oxygen yet.

"We need to get answers out of her," Anderson said, still in that mild voice.

"You can get answers out of her when I'm finished!" Jamaal snarled, and the look on Anderson's face hardened.

"I'm giving you an order, Jamaal. Let go. Now!"

"Fuck you!"

Across the room, Blake cursed again. The whole mild-mannered leader act Anderson had been putting on suddenly dissolved. His back straightened, his eyes flashed with anger, and his face took on an expression that said someone was about to die—or *wish* for death.

"Wrong answer," Anderson said, his voice dropping about an octave and filled with a power that made my teeth ache.

My vision was beginning to fade around the edges, but I saw Anderson reach out and clap his hand on Jamaal's shoulder, right at the base of his neck. The hatred faded from Jamaal's face as his eyes widened in what looked like alarm, though I couldn't see why. Then suddenly, he let go of me and screamed.

My feet hit the floor. I crumpled to my knees, gagging and coughing as I tried to draw air into my lungs.

Jamaal collapsed, too, trying to pull away from Anderson's grip as he did. Anderson must have been stronger than he looked, maintaining his grip as he lowered himself into a crouch so he could keep his hand on Jamaal's shoulder. Anderson's face had turned to stone, all expression bleeding away as Jamaal continued to scream in obvious pain. In that moment, Anderson looked almost inhuman, an ice-cold predator who could kill without hesitation or remorse.

Blake appeared in the periphery of my vision. He moved with caution, but he didn't look scared or surprised by whatever Anderson was doing. "Go easy on him, boss," he said with a wince of sympathy. "He just lost his best friend."

The expression on Anderson's face thawed, a hint of humanity returning to his eyes, but he didn't let go. Jamaal's screams were weakening. What the hell was Anderson doing that caused such intense pain? His grip didn't even look all that tight.

"He'll pass out soon enough," Anderson said, and moments later Jamaal's whole body went limp. Anderson let go of his shoulder, and even on Jamaal's coffee-colored skin, I could see the bright red hand mark where Anderson had been touching him.

"Sorry, my friend," Anderson said so softly I barely heard him. The stone-cold killer was gone, and the mild-mannered human being was back. He stood up and looked at Blake. "Put him next door," he said. "Then gather the troops in my study."

Blake didn't look happy with the order, but he complied, gently picking up Jamaal's limp body and carrying him out of the room. Anderson looked down his nose at me. I was still coughing, but the gagging seemed to have stopped, and my vision had cleared.

"I'll be back in a couple of hours," he told me. "Think carefully about your story and whether you'd like to amend it. Unless you're a very skilled actress, I'm pretty sure you were not familiar with the power I just used against Jamaal. If I come back later and don't like your answers, I'll let you experience it firsthand."

I swallowed hard. So much for the "good cop" act.

Without a backward glance, he marched out the door, slamming it behind him. Once again, the locks clicked shut.

No doubt about it. I was in deep shit.

FOUR

My throat hurt every time I swallowed, but other than that, I didn't feel as bad as I expected after nearly being choked to death. Especially considering that beforehand I'd been seriously injured in a car accident, then been kicked in the face, then nearly perished from exposure.

Do you still think you need an ambulance? Anderson's voice echoed in my head.

Rubbing my bruised throat, I sat down on the edge of the cot and tried to absorb everything I'd seen and heard tonight.

Emmitt, appearing in front of my car from out of nowhere.

Logan, lifting Jamaal off his feet and flinging him all the way across the road and into the trees beyond.

My wound sealing itself with invisible stitches.

Anderson's fire-red handprint on Jamaal's shoulder.

I've never been much into all that woo-woo stuff, but either I was having the longest, weirdest dream in the history of mankind, or something decidedly woo-woo was going on.

I hoped for the former, but suspected the latter.

I looked down at the gash in my side and was only dully surprised to see the entire line scabbed over. I imagined the *Twilight Zone* music playing in the background, then shook off the thought before I made myself hysterical.

I decided to make a cursory examination of my cell. I tried the door, of course, but the sound of those locks clicking shut had been no illusion. I tried the sink and discovered that yes, blessedly, I could get hot water. I picked up my bloody, ruined sweater, rinsed out as much of the blood as possible, then used the sleeve like a washcloth to clean myself up.

I was painfully aware that Anderson was planning to come back and question me later. The kid gloves were going to come off, but I couldn't figure out what he wanted to hear. If I thought about how our next interview was going to go, all I would do was send myself into a panic. Instead I stripped the sheets off the cot and rinsed them in the sink. Then I flipped the mattress over and was relieved to find I hadn't soaked it through. With nothing left to do, I reluctantly lay down, terrified of being alone with my thoughts.

I hadn't been lying down for more than five minutes when I heard footsteps out in the hall again, and I was struck with a far more virulent terror. I shot to my feet, heart pounding and adrenaline flooding my system as I waited in dread for Anderson to finally carry out his threat.

But when the door opened, it wasn't Anderson after all.

The word that had first come to my mind when Emmitt had shown me a picture of Maggie Burnham was *statuesque*. I guessed her height at about five-eleven, and she was built like an athlete. She had absolutely gorgeous curly auburn hair, and a pretty, heart-shaped face.

She wasn't looking her best tonight, though. Not with those red-rimmed eyes and the sorrowful droop of her shoulders. I had no clue what her real relationship with Emmitt had been, but it was clear she was grieving.

"Hi," she said, smiling weakly. "I'm Maggie."

"Nice to meet you," I said automatically, though I mentally grimaced at the empty pleasantry. "I'm Nikki Glass."

She nodded. "I thought maybe you could use this." She held out a plush terrycloth robe, and I was so happy I could have hugged her. Considering that she was mourning Emmitt and that I'd been the instrument of his death, I wouldn't have been surprised if her first move had been to slap me.

"Thanks," I said, taking the robe from her outstretched hand. My voice came out a little scratchy. I told myself that it was an aftereffect of Jamaal's attempt to choke me to death, not a sign that I was about to burst into tears at the first hint of kindness. Cynically, I couldn't help wondering if she'd taken up the mantle of "good cop" now that Anderson had dispensed with it.

Maggie considerately turned her back as I removed my undies and slipped into the robe. I wouldn't have died of embarrassment if she hadn't, but under the circumstances, I was feeling vulnerable enough to appreciate the gesture. I had to take a deep breath to keep control of my emotions before I told her it was okay to turn around.

She took in the stripped bed and the wet, still-stained sheets that I'd draped over the sink to dry, and frowned.

"I see the boys are in major hard-ass mode," she commented in obvious disapproval. As far as I'd been able to determine, she was the only woman living here.

I crossed my arms over my chest, pulling the warm, soft robe close around me. "Yeah, well, they seem to think I killed Emmitt on purpose." The last word came out in something almost like a sob as the full weight of what had happened hit me.

I'd killed someone.

No, of course I hadn't meant to. And from where I was standing, it sure looked like he'd deliberately put himself in harm's way. But still . . . He was dead, and it was my fault.

To my surprise, Maggie stepped forward and gave my shoulder a warm squeeze. "It's all right," she said, though her own eyes shone with unshed tears. "Anderson told us your story. The boys are all huffing and puffing with conspiracy theories, but I believe you."

I had to swallow hard a couple of times before I found my voice. "You do? Why?"

She smiled sadly and gestured at the cot. "Why don't we sit down? This might take a few minutes."

We both sat, backs to the wall. I gathered the robe around my legs and wrapped my arms around my knees.

"You told Anderson that Emmitt hired you to investigate me," Maggie said.

I shook my head. "Not exactly. He originally hired me to find you, then he asked me to try to learn more about . . . um . . ." I'd kind of glossed over the whole cult thing when I'd explained to Anderson, and I didn't want to blurt out anything tactless now, either.

Maggie grinned at me, a surprisingly genuine expression, considering her obvious sorrow. "I can only guess what he might have told you. He claimed that I'd fallen in with a bunch of loonies. Is that the gist of it?"

I couldn't help returning her grin. "Yeah, basically."

"And then tonight . . . ?"

"Tonight he said you'd called him and were ready to leave. I was supposed to meet him here as an extra witness." I frowned as I realized how flimsy Emmitt's story had been. There was a reason my gut had been telling me to say no, but my desire to escape from my bad date had overridden my common sense. It would have been so much better if I'd told Jim I had to meet a client and then driven straight home. Why hadn't I thought of that?

"Then he surprised you on a dark, icy road when you had no time to stop or swerve."

I nodded, but couldn't find the voice to speak.

"The goddamn selfish bastard," Maggie said thickly, shaking her head as a single tear snaked down her cheek. She reached up and dashed it away angrily.

"Do you . . . Do you know why he did it?" I asked softly, wondering if it was any of my business.

She let out a heavy sigh. "He was getting old. Old and tired. I knew that, but he was too much of a tough guy to admit how bad it was."

"Old?" I cried, totally confused. "The guy couldn't have been more than twenty-five, tops." Truthfully, I thought he was closer to twenty-two.

Her lips twisted into a wry smile. "He was more than twenty-five. Trust me."

I gaped. "Even if I'm off by a bit, there's no way in hell he qualified as 'old.'"

"What if you're off by an order of magnitude?"

"I don't believe in woo-woo," I said, without great conviction.

Another wry smile. "You might want to start. I'm afraid right now you're neck-deep in woo-woo and still sinking."

I grimaced. Yeah, that was kind of what I was afraid of. "Where's a life vest when you need it?" I joked feebly.

Maggie reached into the back pocket of her jeans and pulled out a slim compact. "There's something I think you should see," she said, thumbing the compact open and then handing it to me.

Hesitantly, I took the compact from her hand. The makeup inside looked ordinary enough, so I guessed that the something I needed to see would be in the mirror. Holding my breath, I opened the compact all the way and looked at my reflection.

I looked awful. There was a big lump on my temple, and my right eye was thoroughly blackened. The entire left side of my face was one big bruise from where Jamaal had kicked me—though the bruise looked like it was about three days old. But clearly, that wasn't what Maggie had wanted me to see.

No, what Maggie wanted me to see was the iridescent mark on my forehead. It vaguely resembled a half moon with an arrow through its middle. My mouth dropped open and my eyes widened as I reached up to touch the mark that quite obviously was not a tattoo.

"What the fuck is that?" I whispered.

"It's a glyph," Maggie explained, holding out her hand so I could see the mark on the back of it. Hers looked like stylized circular lightning bolt. "It represents whose line you're descended from."

"Line?" My voice sounded hollow, and I stared intently at the mirror. The glyph wouldn't go away, no matter how many times I blinked or how I rubbed it.

Out of the corner of my eye, I saw Maggie run a finger over the glyph on her hand. "Mine represents Zeus," she said. "I've never seen one like yours before, but Anderson says it's Artemis. I didn't think she had any descendants—she was supposed to be a virgin goddess—but I'll take his word for it."

"Artemis." I sounded like a mentally challenged myna bird, but none of this was quite sinking in. My rational mind threw in the towel, deciding to go hide somewhere safe until the world returned to order.

"Emmitt was from Hades' line. Jamaal's a descendant of Kali, and he and Emmitt bonded like brothers because both of them possessed death magic. Emmitt was mentoring him, teaching him control, but Jamaal still had a long way to go. Without Emmitt to balance him, it's hard to know if he'll be able to hold it together.

"You also met Logan, right?" She didn't wait for my answer. "He's Tyr." She cocked her head at me. "Are you familiar with Tyr?"

Totally numb—and not comprehending a word of what I was hearing—I shook my head.

"He was an old Germanic war god. Descendants of war gods tend to be kind of cranky, but Logan is one of the most easygoing people I know. Oh, and I almost forgot Blake." She made a face, making it clear Blake was not her favorite person. "He's a descendant of Eros. Despite that cutesy Cupid tattoo he's got, there's nothing even remotely cherubic about him. He's easily as deadly as Jamaal. He's just not as in-your-face about it."

I remembered the way Blake had looked at me while he was playing bad cop. That was plenty in-your-face for me.

Maggie gave my shoulder another sympathetic squeeze. "I know this has got to be overwhelming, and you probably don't believe half of what I've said.

I'll give you the quick highlights and then give you some time to try to absorb it all.

"Anderson and the rest of us are what is known as *Liberi Deorum,* which means 'children of the gods' in Latin. A long time ago, when the ancient gods were still around, they had children with mortals. Before the gods left Earth, they gave each of their children a seed from the Tree of Life. This seed made them immortal, and the *Liberi* thought they were gods themselves as a result. The only limitation they had—as far as they knew—was that they couldn't make their own children immortal, because the gods took the Tree of Life with them when they left. What the first *Liberi* didn't know until too late was that anyone with even a drop of divine blood—in other words, all their children and descendants—could steal their immortality by killing them."

Wow. That was one hell of a detailed delusion. I had to admit, there was something decidedly weird going on. But come on, children of the gods? Really?

"The glyph on your hand marks you as a Descendant of Artemis," Maggie continued. "When you killed Emmitt, you also stole his immortality. Not on purpose, I know," she hastened to add.

"So I'm immortal now?" I asked, trying to hide my skepticism the best I could—which wasn't well at all.

"I know it sounds crazy. But yes, you are."

"Uh-huh."

"The guys—especially Jamaal—think you already knew all this and staged the accident to steal Emmitt's immortality deliberately."

Perfectly logical—if you bought into the craziness in the first place, which I wasn't about to do. "But *you* think Emmitt committed suicide, because he knew I was a Descendant of Artemis and was actually capable of killing him?" I was well aware of my tone of voice, that I was talking to her like I was humoring a dangerous psycho, but I couldn't help it.

Maggie nodded. "I don't know how he found you, but he must have seen the glyph on your face and decided to use you."

"But the glyph only showed up a little while ago!" Had I caught an inconsistency in her story?

"It's been there all along. It's just that only *Liberi* can see it."

Some of this was beginning to make a weird kind of sense, and I began to worry about my own sanity. Maybe the blows to my head had rattled my brain around more than I knew. But Maggie was the closest thing I had to an ally in this loony bin, and I needed to take advantage of that while I could.

"It's all a little much to take in," I said, because I didn't have it in me to actually say I believed her.

"I know," she said with a gentle smile. "And it's all right. You don't have to pretend to believe me. I'm not offended."

Maggie was definitely the nicest of the cultists. It was time to test just *how* nice.

"Thanks for being so understanding," I said.

"Hey, we girls have to stick together here in Testosteroneville."

"Yeah, about that . . ."

"I'm sorry, but I can't let you out," Maggie said.

"Please, Maggie. I think Anderson's going to . . . interrogate me. And I don't think that's going to go so well for me." I didn't have to force the shudder.

She gave me a sympathetic smile. "It'll be all right. I'd let you out if I could, but Anderson gave me an order, and disobeying his orders isn't such a great idea."

I remembered Jamaal's scream, and felt just a little guilty for asking Maggie to defy Anderson. Not enough to stop asking, though.

"Maggie, I—"

But she'd had enough, rising to her feet and cutting me off. "I can't, Nikki. I just can't. I'll get you some clean bedding, some towels, and some toiletries, but that's the best I can do."

She started toward the door, and I slid off the bed, wondering if I could barrel past her and escape. I didn't like my odds, but I might have tried it anyway if my wounded side hadn't screamed in pain. Apparently, I'd stood too fast. By the time I was able to breathe through the pain, Maggie was gone and the door was closed.

FIVE

Maggie brought the supplies she had promised. If I had been inclined to stick my head in the sand and pretend nothing out of the ordinary was happening, I might have been able to curl up on the cot in something resembling comfort and gotten some sleep. Of course, sleeping was the last thing on my mind; I kept thinking Anderson was going to come back to "question" me.

He never showed. Maybe Maggie convinced him that I was telling the truth. Or maybe he just thought the anticipation of pain would crack me faster than the pain itself.

Whatever the reason, no one came for me through the long hours of the night. For a while, I was treated to the comforting sound of Jamaal pounding on a door and yelling at the top of his lungs. Apparently, Anderson had locked *him* in one of these basement rooms, too, and he wasn't shy about letting everyone know he was unhappy about it.

Every time I heard his voice, I found myself self-consciously rubbing my throat, where I should have had bruises galore from his attempt to strangle me to death. I didn't have a mirror, but as far as I could tell by touch, there wasn't any bruising at all.

Of course, everything Maggie had told me had to be bullshit. Right? There was a perfectly rational explanation for everything that had happened tonight. Damned if I could figure out what it was, though.

Locked as I was in a room without windows, and wearing a broken watch, my internal clock was my only way to keep track of time. No matter how scared and freaked out I was, as the hours crept by, exhaustion sat more and more heavily on my shoulders. When the pillow started to look inviting, I forced myself to the sink and splashed some cold water on my face. It helped me feel more alert for all of about five seconds.

I never consciously made the decision to lie down and sleep, but when the door to my cell next cracked open, the sound of squealing hinges woke me up with a start. My heart instantly went on red alert, pounding adrenaline through my system. I leapt to my feet, wide awake. My side didn't scream at me for the sudden movement, but I was too alarmed to be relieved.

Standing in the doorway, grinning as if my terror was the funniest thing he'd ever seen, was yet another one of Emmitt's "cult members." This one was Jack Gillespie, and he looked a bit like a transplanted surfer-dude. His curly, dark blond hair was streaked with lighter blond—an effect that was probably supposed to look like sun-bleaching, but was a little too even to be anything but man-made. His skin was a deep, skin-cancer tan, and in the handful of times I'd seen him, he'd always been wearing torn jeans and a short-sleeved T-shirt, despite the cold.

I shook off my fear and narrowed my eyes at him. "Has Anderson ordered you guys to take turns coming to see me, or what?" I asked. Unless there was another cultist I wasn't aware of, I had now met all but one of the men Emmitt had had me "investigating."

Jack's grin didn't falter. "If Anderson had ordered me to come down here and talk to you, I probably wouldn't be here. I'm not too good with orders."

I rubbed my eyes. Now that the first surge of adrenaline had faded, I remembered how utterly exhausted I was. I had no idea what time it was, or how long I'd been asleep, but I felt like I could sleep another six or eight hours, easy. I wasn't in the mood for witty banter.

"Are you just here to stare at me like I'm an animal in a zoo, or is there something you want?"

He leaned casually against the doorjamb and crossed his arms over what his tight T-shirt advertised was a very nice chest. "I'll go away if I'm interrupting your beauty sleep. But I thought you might sleep better in your own bed."

My heart leapt at the thought, though my rational mind immediately proclaimed the suggestion too good to be true.

"So you're letting me go?" I asked, making no attempt to mask my skepticism.

"I'm going to do better than that. I'm going to

drive you home, seeing as what's left of your car has been towed. And there's not much in the way of public transportation out here even in the daytime."

I examined his words for hidden nuances, but couldn't find any. Still, there was something decidedly fishy going on. If Anderson had decided to release me, I was pretty sure I'd have been gone hours ago. Jack showing up here in what my body clock told me was the middle of the night or very early morning screamed of ulterior motives. Unfortunately, I had no idea what those motives could be.

"Why would you do that?" I asked suspiciously.

The grin came back full force. "Because it'll make Jamaal shit bricks." He rubbed the glyph on his forearm. "I'm of Loki's line, so making trouble is in my blood. And Jamaal is the easiest target ever."

I wasn't much of an expert on mythology, but if memory served, Loki was a Norse trickster-god. But since I didn't buy this whole descended-from-the-gods bullshit, I didn't buy Jack's explanation, either. Still, letting him drive me home sounded like an excellent idea.

"Real nice of you to pick on someone whose best friend just died," I said, deciding that even if he was letting me go, I didn't much like him.

"Isn't it, though?" he responded, unperturbed.

"And you're not worried about what Anderson will do when he finds out?" Maggie had seemed awfully sympathetic to me, but she had categorically refused to defy Anderson's orders.

"Descendant of Loki, remember? We tend not

to trouble ourselves about consequences. If I didn't piss Anderson off at least once a week, I'd feel like a disgrace to my divine ancestor."

I looked at him like he was crazy. Even crazier than the rest of the crazies here, that is.

He straightened up and gave an exaggerated shrug. "Hey, no skin off my teeth if you'd rather stay locked up down here. Make yourself comfortable. Anderson's going to come talk to you in the morning, and I'm sure that'll be just *loads* of fun."

I felt myself pale on cue, a hard knot of fear twisting in my gut.

"I won't look a gift horse in the mouth," I told Jack hurriedly, hoping I didn't look as scared as I felt. I'd never thought of myself as a shrinking violet, but I'd been scared so many times over the last few hours I might have to reassess my own toughness.

Jack nodded briskly. "I thought you'd come to see it my way." He reached behind him to pick something up from the floor. He held it out to me, and I saw that it was my pocketbook.

At least, it had been a pocketbook once upon a time. The tan leather was soaked through, turning it almost chocolate brown, there was a slash all the way across the front, and one of the straps was gone. I took a moment to mourn the loss—I love my bags, and this one had been my favorite—then took the ruined pocketbook from Jack.

"I couldn't get your car key out of the ignition," he told me, "but I got the rest of the keys off the ring and put them in the inside zipper compartment."

Numbly, I checked the pocket in question and was glad to see that my apartment keys had survived the crash. I was tempted to check the rest of the contents of the purse, but decided that might be rude, implying that Jack might have taken something. I didn't know why he was helping me—if that was really what he was doing—but if he was going to take me home, I didn't want to do anything to risk pissing him off.

"Ready to go?" he asked, stepping away from the door.

Way more than ready, I hurried out of the cell and into the hallway beyond.

Jack drove me home in a surprisingly bland black BMW. I'd have figured him for the red sports car kind of guy, but maybe he didn't like to be predictable. Or maybe he was "borrowing" someone else's car. I wouldn't have put it past him.

The clock on the dashboard informed me it was four A.M. I fought a yawn. God, I was tired! My body felt ridiculously good, considering the abuse it had taken, but if I really was now possessed of supernatural healing ability—a fact that I was going to have trouble continuing to deny—I must have burned extra energy to do it. I could hardly hold my head up.

The streets of Arlington were deserted at that time of night, and Jack made good time into Bethesda. He seemed to consider the speed limit merely a suggestion. Same with red lights and stop signs. If I weren't exhausted down to my bones, I might have been alarmed.

The good news was that we didn't get stopped by cops, and that Jack was blessedly quiet for the whole ride. I wasn't up to either an encounter with the police or another conversation that would make my head hurt. The bad news was that Jack never bothered to ask me where I lived. He drove straight to my apartment building, barely even looking at street signs.

The obvious conclusion was that even if he hadn't taken anything from my pocketbook, he'd obviously looked in it. My driver's license would conveniently provide my address, which made the fact that he was willing to let me go a little less surprising. As long as he knew where I lived, he—and his crazy friends— could get to me. The smirk he gave me as I dragged myself out of the car made me wish I had the energy— and the guts—to smack him.

"Be seeing you around," he said with a wave just before I slammed my door closed. The smile and the twinkle in his eye failed to hide the warning behind the words.

Moments later, I was safe inside my own home and could have wept in relief. My body still cried out for sleep, but I didn't have time for it. I had no illusions that the folks at Nutso Central were going to leave me alone, and that meant I had some preparations to make.

First, I had to get out of the apartment, much though it pained me to admit it. The feeling of safety that enveloped me when I stepped in the door was nothing but an illusion when Jack knew where I lived.

He might or might not have been releasing me behind Anderson's back, but either way, I knew he wasn't doing it out of the goodness of his heart. I also knew he wasn't going to keep my address a secret.

I went into the kitchen to brew a pot of coffee—I was never going to stay awake otherwise—while I tried to figure out where to go. The light on my answering machine was blinking, and I hit it by reflex.

"Hey there, Nikki," said Steph's perky voice. "You know I hate it when you keep me in suspense. How'd it go tonight?"

I groaned and pinched the bridge of my nose. The Date from Hell seemed like it had happened in another lifetime. And any date Steph arranged for me came with a mandatory debriefing afterward, one that I could have done without in the best of times. In my current state of mind, I couldn't bear to face it. The answering machine beeped, then moved on to the next message. Steph again. What a surprise.

"It's midnight, and you haven't called me back yet," she scolded. "I promise to forgive you, but only if you're not calling because you're in the middle of some hot and heavy sex."

I snorted, both at the ridiculousness of the idea of me having hot and heavy sex with Jim, and at the ridiculousness of my real reason for not having called.

"I wish," I muttered.

I briefly considered going to stay with Steph for a while, just until I got things sorted out. Unlike me, she was willing to dip into her trust fund, and her house was more than big enough for the two of us. Not that my condo was a humble shack. My adoptive parents, the Glasses, had set up a trust fund for me at the same time they'd set up Steph's. When I'd refused to touch it, they'd bought this condo and offered to rent it to me for a ridiculously small sum. I should have turned it down, but I'd fallen in love with the place. I assuaged my guilty conscience by paying them three times what they asked, although they didn't need the money.

Mr. Glass had built a start-up company into a multinational corporation when he was young, and he had money to burn. I know it bothers him that I won't use the trust fund—he'd grown up poor and always dreamed of giving his children a better life. But as much as I loved my adoptive family, I can't help feeling like an interloper who doesn't deserve a share of their wealth.

Frowning fiercely as I packed a small roll-aboard bag, I decided that although Steph had plenty of room, I didn't dare stay at her place. It wouldn't be hard for Anderson and crew to find her connection to me and to track me there. I didn't want to put her in danger. Which meant I couldn't stay at the Glasses' house, either, even though they were away on a round the world cruise and I'd have had the place to myself. That left a hotel.

I took a long, hot shower before I left. Afterward, I stood naked in front of the foggy, full-length mirror. The wound was nothing but a faint red line. I couldn't even find a bruise anywhere. I didn't know whether to be thankful, or just freaked out.

Worse, the glyph was still there, despite my

attempt to wash and exfoliate it away. Gone was
my hope that it had all been a frighteningly realistic
nightmare.

The sun was just beginning to rise when I
cautiously set foot outside my apartment building,
dragging the roll-aboard and carrying my laptop
in a backpack. Along with the laptop, the backpack
held my .38 Special and several boxes of ammo. I had
never once needed to use it in my line of work, but
I did sometimes have to venture into neighborhoods
where I didn't feel safe. Having a gun gave me a sense
of security. I wasn't a very good shot, and I wasn't
sure I'd actually be able to pull the trigger if I were
pointing it at a human being, but it was comforting to
know I had the option. Of course, since I was headed
for D.C.—the better to lose myself in the crowds—
carrying a handgun was risky. I had concealed carry
permits for Maryland and Virginia, but there was no
such thing available for a civilian in D.C. Still, given
the mess I was in, I wasn't leaving home without it.

I looked carefully up and down the street, but
didn't see anyone suspicious lurking around. I then
headed for the closest Metro stop and took the train to
Dupont Circle, where I took a room at the Holiday Inn.
The fact that no one on the train or in the hotel gave me
a second glance suggested that Maggie had been telling
the truth and ordinary people couldn't see the glyph. I
refused to allow myself to speculate about which of the
other outlandish things she'd said might be true.

As soon as it was late enough for businesses to
open, I located the nearest shooting range—which,

of course, was outside the D.C. city limits, making me thankful for our efficient public transportation. I had a feeling that with Anderson and his crazies potentially after me, I might need to use the gun whether I wanted to or not, and it wouldn't hurt to try to upgrade my shooting ability from "poor" to "okay."

I picked up a new cell phone to replace the one that was destroyed in the accident. Then I showed up at the shooting range by ten o'clock, my nerves taut with one hell of a caffeine buzz even while I found myself yawning every two point five seconds. There were three other people shooting—all men—and even through the earplugs, the sound of all those gunshots made me jumpy. Probably just the caffeine. Or the fact that the guy standing nearest to me was firing an assault rifle, which sounded rather like a cannon.

I figured with the exhaustion, the caffeine, and the way I jumped every time the assault rifle fired, I was going to have one of my worst shooting performances ever. I took aim at the target, taking a few slow, deep breaths in hopes that it would soothe my frazzled nerves. The guy with the cannon fired off a shot right as I was squeezing the trigger. My attempt to go Zen notwithstanding, my arms jerked as I jumped at the noise.

I almost laughed when I saw that my shot had hit the bull's-eye. Maybe I should take target practice while exhausted and jumpy more often. I took another couple of deep breaths to dispel the remainder of the adrenaline, then fired again. This time, my hands were steady.

And I hit the bull's-eye again.

Luck, I told myself. Even a bad shot had to hit the bull's-eye occasionally. That I'd just done it two times in a row was nothing more than a freaky coincidence. I lowered the gun so I could roll my shoulders a little bit to work out the tension. Then I took my shooter's stance again and squeezed the trigger.

I swallowed a yelp when I saw that for the third time, I'd hit the bull's-eye. If two times in a row was a freaky coincidence, what was three times in a row?

I lowered the gun again, this time looking it over as though I might find some magical can't-go-wrong gizmo had been attached while I wasn't looking. Of course, there was nothing different about the gun. I couldn't help remembering Maggie telling me that my glyph meant I was a descendant of Artemis, the Greek goddess of the hunt. Crazy talk, right? But if it *was* crazy talk, then it seemed like an awfully strange coincidence that suddenly I seemed to have become a sharpshooter.

Telling myself three bull's-eyes in a row was statistically within the realm of possibility even for a lousy shot like me, I raised my shaking hands and took aim again.

I was considerably less surprised this time when I hit dead center.

I took about twenty shots after that, experimenting. I tried aiming at things other than the bull's-eye. Being nowhere close to ambidextrous, I tried firing with my left hand. I even tried shooting with my eyes closed.

Whatever I aimed at, whatever crappy technique

I used, I hit my target one hundred percent of the time, once and for all dismissing the statistical realm of possibility.

There was no more denying that I'd become a supernaturally good shot.

I headed back to the hotel in a daze, spaced out enough that I missed my stop on the Metro. I decided to walk the rest of the way, figuring the fresh air might do me good. I'm generally pretty good at denial, but the evidence was piling up too high. I might have been able to talk myself out of believing the things I'd seen the cultists do last night. They could have been tricks, after all, though who would go through such elaborate lengths to pull a trick like that on me? But it was much harder to explain away the glyph on my face, or the way my body had healed overnight, or the way I had suddenly become an expert marksman.

What am I talking about, "much harder"? It was *impossible* to explain away.

Much as I tried to convince myself that there had to be a rational explanation that didn't involve woo-woo, I failed. I didn't know where that left me—except with an aching head and an urge to give in to hysteria—but I'd had to learn to accept some very unpalatable truths in my life, so I would eventually find a way to accept this one.

I was in too much of a stupor to pay attention to what was going on around me, so at first I didn't notice the black Mercedes with the tinted windows that was pacing me. Even when the car behind it started honking indignantly, it barely registered on my conscious mind. Then, the Mercedes sped up a little, getting ahead of me and pulling into what would have been a parking space if it weren't for the fire hydrant.

The Mercedes's door opened and a man in an expensive charcoal gray suit got out. I froze in my tracks when I saw the stylized lightning-bolt glyph on the back of his hand.

SIX

He was not one of Anderson's people. He was a complete stranger to me, and the warm smile that curved his lips as he looked me up and down did nothing to ease my instant, instinctive dislike.

Many women would find him handsome. I supposed that objectively he was—tall, nicely muscled, manly square jaw softened by dimples when he smiled, and lovely gray-blue eyes. But the way he carried himself reminded me of every arrogant, entitled, self-centered country club asshole Steph had ever introduced me to, all rolled up into one pretty package.

I considered trying to walk past him, but the look in his eye told me he had no intention of letting me ignore him. There was nothing overtly threatening about him, but my gut was screaming "danger, danger" even so. I'd ignored my gut instincts last night, and look where it had gotten me.

"What do you want?" I growled at the stranger.

He blinked in what I suspected was surprise. I bet that smile of his had charmed every woman he'd ever used it on, but I was made of sterner stuff.

The smile flickered for a moment, then came back at full force as he took a step toward me. "My name is Alexis Colonomos," he said, holding out his hand for me to shake.

Instead of shaking his hand, I stepped backward, trying to keep a safe distance between us. I had no idea what a safe distance might be, however. Despite my recent skepticism, I had no doubt Alexis Colonomos would turn out to have supernatural powers of some sort.

"Nice to meet you," I said, making no attempt to sound like I meant it. "Now what do you want?"

The smile flickered again, and his eyes narrowed in what might have been anger as he let his hand fall back to his side. When he put the smiley face back on, it had lost some of its wattage, and there was a hard glint in his eye that suggested he was a man used to getting what he wanted.

"I just wanted to introduce myself," he said, and there was an edge in his voice that hadn't been there before. "And have a little talk." He gestured toward the open door of the Mercedes.

"If you think I'm going to get into a car with a total stranger, you're nuts." I took another step back, prepared to turn and bolt if he made a hostile move.

He didn't, but his smile lost even more wattage, until it started to look more like a snarl. "You're

Liberi," he said from between gritted teeth. What were the chances he and Maggie would use the same unusual term to describe what I apparently was if it were all some freaky cult delusion? Yet another nail in the coffin of denial. "I couldn't hurt you if I wanted to." And everything about his body language said he wanted to very much.

Personally, I didn't think I'd been rude enough to warrant the level of hostility that radiated from this guy, but based on the behavior I'd witnessed last night, either it didn't take much to set a *Liberi* off, or I just had a natural knack for it.

"You can't kill me," I clarified, though I felt ridiculous making the claim. It was one thing to almost kind of believe it, and quite another to truly *accept* it. "That doesn't mean you can't *hurt* me." I'd seen evidence enough of that last night.

The smile turned into a sneer. "Cowardice isn't becoming to a Descendant of Artemis."

I guess I was supposed to be so insulted by the suggestion I was a coward that I would meekly climb into the car. "There's a difference between cowardice and caution," I told him. "If you want to talk to me, then do it. If you don't want to do it standing here in the street, then offer to buy me a cup of coffee. I might take you up on it."

Maybe the smartest thing for me to have done was to turn around and run away. The vibe I was getting off this guy was anything but friendly. But I didn't know what he wanted from me, and I wasn't sure that ignorance was bliss. Plus, I had no idea how he'd found me. Even if he was some friend of Anderson's—a friend I'd never seen hanging around the mansion—he shouldn't have been able to locate me when I was nowhere near any of my usual stomping grounds.

Obviously, he *could* find me, and if I ran off now, he'd probably be even less friendly the next time he did. Which was why I was prepared to at least listen to what he had to say.

"Then may I buy you a cup of coffee?" he asked, and it looked like it physically hurt him to concede.

"I'd love one. How 'bout we head over to that diner?" I pointed at a greasy spoon on the opposite side of the street. It was doing a brisk business, so I figured it had good bad food and served bottomless cups of coffee.

Alexis looked at the place and curled his lip in disdain. I pegged him for the kind of guy who thought he was slumming it if he ate in a restaurant that charged less than five bucks for a cup of coffee. "Fine," he said, then slammed the door of the Mercedes with more force than necessary.

I hate sore losers.

I kept just enough space between us to be out of arm's reach as we crossed the street and headed to the diner. He probably wasn't going to try anything in broad daylight, in front of tons of witnesses, but you can never be too careful.

When he reached the diner, he pushed the door open and held it for me. It meant I had to brush by him to get inside, and I didn't like it. I reminded myself once again that he wouldn't dare try anything on a crowded street. His expression darkened as he noticed my hesitation, but I went inside before he could make an issue of it.

A waitress was clearing a table for two just as we walked in the door. The hostess directed us to that table with a wave of her hand, and we slid into the booth in silence while the waitress gathered up the remains of the previous patrons' meal.

"Be right back," she said with a distracted smile, then carried her loaded tray to the kitchen. As far as I could see, there was only one other waitress in the whole place, which explained why they were both moving so fast and looked so wild-eyed.

There were crumbs all over the place, and a smear of ketchup looking rather like a bloodstain threatened to drip over the edge and onto my lap. I grabbed a napkin from the dispenser to wipe it away, watching Alexis surreptitiously as I did. His lip remained curled in that singularly disdainful sneer, and his arms were crossed over his chest as if he were trying to minimize contact between himself and the diner. To say he looked out of place was an understatement. No one else was even wearing a dress shirt, much less a suit and tie.

The waitress came back and wiped off our table with a damp rag, but she had a harried look and wasn't very careful about it. A couple of crumbs tumbled off the table and onto Alexis's lap. His face reddened and his eyes sparked and I thought sure he was about to make a big scene. He restrained himself, however, and settled for staring daggers at her. It was all I could do not to smile.

Have I mentioned that this guy rubbed me the wrong way?

"What can I get you?" the waitress asked, pulling out her pen and order pad without making eye contact.

"Two cups of coffee, please," I said, because I was afraid that if Alexis opened his mouth he was going to be a total asshole.

"Anything else?"

"That'll do it," I said, and Alexis didn't contradict me. I suspected he'd rather starve to death than eat anything served at this place.

She was walking away before the last word left my mouth. If I couldn't see with my own two eyes how overworked she was, I'd have thought she was being rude.

I leaned back in my seat and eyed the dangerous-looking *Liberi* who sat across from me. I got the distinct impression that he'd been planning to charm me when he'd stepped out of that car, but I figured my attitude had killed that plan by now. Maybe I shouldn't have come on so strong right from the start, but I had a right to be grumpy after everything that had happened.

"So, what was it you wanted to talk about?" I asked as the waitress put two ceramic cups on the table and filled them with dark-as-pitch coffee. She reached into her apron and pulled out a handful of creamers, leaving them in a pile in the center of the table. She opened her mouth—I think she was going to ask if we needed anything else—but shut it again when she saw the forbidding expression on Alexis's face. He waited until she'd walked away to answer me.

"You're new in town," he said, and it wasn't a question.

I raised my eyebrows as I took a sip of coffee. "I am?"

He frowned at me, dark eyebrows forming a severe V. "You have to be. You're not one of ours, and you're not one of Anderson's." He said Anderson's name with another one of those little sneers of his.

I sipped my coffee, wishing I'd been able to believe Maggie last night so I could have asked her a lot more questions. There was a hell of a lot I didn't know about being a *Liberi*. For instance, I had no idea what Alexis was talking about when he referred to "one of ours." Nor did I have any idea what—if anything—I should tell him about myself.

"Let's say for the sake of argument that I *am* new in town. What's it to you?"

He leaned forward, resting his elbows on the table and pushing his untouched coffee out of the way. "You'd best have a care how you talk to me," he said in a menacing whisper that carried just fine even in the noisy diner. "Descendants of Artemis are rare, and therefore valuable to us, but that will protect you only so far."

Ah, we'd reached the threat-making stage of the conversation. I'd had a feeling this was coming. Maybe if I hadn't just had the scariest night of my life, I'd have been more intimidated. Maybe it would have been *smart* to be more intimidated.

I let my hand slide under the table and smiled broadly—not the reaction Alexis was hoping for, if his scowl was anything to go by. "You know what I was doing before you ambushed me?" I asked, keeping my body language completely relaxed as I unzipped the front compartment of my backpack. I rested my hand lightly on the .38 Special. "I was at a gun range, polishing my skills. Turns out I'm a very good shot. Feel like giving me some more target practice?"

I had no intention of actually shooting the guy, or even taking the gun out. I wasn't even sure I'd be able to shoot a person in the heat of battle, much less in cold blood, and I sure as hell wasn't waving a gun around in a crowded D.C. diner. Felony charges and a prison stay would *not* improve my situation. But part of being a good P.I. is being a good actress.

I was a good P.I.

"You wouldn't dare," he growled at me.

I blinked at him innocently. "I wouldn't? How the hell would you know that? You don't even know my name, do you?" I'd seen no reason to introduce myself, and if he'd already known my name, I suspected he'd have flaunted the knowledge by now. "I could be sweet as sunshine or a total psycho bitch for all you know."

I leaned forward till I was almost nose-to-nose with him, meeting his glare with a good bit of steel. "Back the hell off, or you're going to find out the hard way," I said as I cocked the gun, making as much noise about it as possible. The diner was kind of noisy, but not so much that Alexis couldn't hear and recognize the sound.

I got the feeling Alexis desperately wanted to come across the table at me, but he just sat there glaring instead. Then his gaze flicked to something over my shoulder, and his eyes widened.

It was a classic distraction technique, but I couldn't help taking a peek over my shoulder anyway.

Alexis hadn't been trying to trick me. Standing in the doorway, giving me a decidedly neutral look, was Blake.

The hostess—who had to be pushing fifty—was giving him goo-goo eyes, and practically every adult female in the place, not to mention a few men, were surreptitiously looking him over. There's nothing like a well-built pretty-boy to get the hormones working overtime.

Blake ignored all of them—even the hostess, who was trying to direct him to an open seat at the counter—and started toward our table. I uncocked the gun, then scooted over in my seat so I could have the wall at my back while keeping an eye on both men.

Blake had been only slightly less hostile than Jamaal last night, but he was barely paying attention to me today. He and Alexis engaged in a hot and heavy alpha-male staring contest. I could practically smell the testosterone in the air, even over the bacon grease and coffee. I'd have liked to get out from between them, but there wasn't anywhere to go.

When Blake reached the table, he casually leaned

against my side of the booth, never taking his eyes off Alexis.

"She's one of ours," Blake said, his voice as challenging as his stare. "Tell Konstantin to mind his own business."

Konstantin? Who the hell was Konstantin? And what was this "one of ours" crap?

Alexis raised his eyebrows. "If she's one of yours, then why are you letting her wander around the city unaccompanied before notifying Konstantin about her?"

"Get out. And leave her alone."

I'd have snapped at Blake for trying to protect the "little woman," only I wasn't sure that was what he was trying to do. It felt more like he was claiming his territory.

"I don't answer to you," Alexis countered. "And if she really belonged to Anderson, I'm sure she would have mentioned the fact by now."

"For the record," I said, though I wondered if drawing attention to myself was a bad idea, "I don't belong to anybody, especially you assholes."

Both men ignored me.

Blake shrugged. "Anderson has already decided she belongs to him. He sent me to fetch her, so that's what I'm doing. You have a problem with that, take it up with him."

Still barely sparing me a glance, Blake reached out and grabbed my arm in a bruising grip. I, of course, tried to pull away. But he was damn strong.

Alexis leaned forward, putting both his hands on

the tabletop, his eyes practically glowing with menace. "Let go of her and get the fuck out of here, or you'll be sorry," he growled. "Konstantin wants to talk to her, and only a fool would get in his way."

Blake let go of my arm and smiled. He, too, leaned forward and put his hands on the table. He was crowding my personal space, but he was doing the same to Alexis. If this went much further, people around us were going to notice and try to break it up or call the cops.

I was considering how I might bring the tension down a notch when I felt a change in the air. The diner suddenly felt about ten degrees hotter, and the crowd and traffic noise became muted and dull.

Blake ran his tongue over those full, sensual lips of his, and even though I'd never been particularly attracted to him, I felt a tug of desire in my nether regions. My pulse kicked up and my breath hitched. The air filled with the musky scent of sex, and I pressed my thighs together in hopes of erasing the ache that had built without warning.

Across from me, Alexis's eyes darkened, and his mouth fell open. His breaths came in excited little puffs, and sweat dewed his face. The look he was giving Blake screamed of something very different from anger, and I'd bet anything he was sporting quite a tent pole under the table.

"Don't ever forget who I am," Blake said in a chilling croon as he leaned in even closer to Alexis. "Zeus's line may be powerful, but even Zeus was helpless against Eros. Unless you'd like me to take you into the men's room and fuck you till you scream for mercy, you'd better go tell Konstantin that this one is ours. Understand?"

Whatever Blake had been doing, he stopped abruptly. The temperature dropped, the musky scent evaporated, and the crowd noise returned to normal.

Across the table from me, Alexis recoiled, his back slamming against the backrest as he tried to put distance between himself and Blake. There was a wild look in his eyes, the lust that had been there only moments ago completely gone.

"Konstantin would have your balls for a trophy if you tried it," Alexis whispered, but though that was supposed to sound like a threat, it wasn't very effective when his face was so white, and his eyes so wide.

Blake smiled easily. "Wouldn't do *you* any good, now would it? Besides, you'd have to tell him what happened, and I don't see you admitting it. Now get out. If you're still here when I've counted to five, we'll be partying in the men's room, and that's a promise."

Alexis made a hasty exit before Blake got to two.

I'd have liked nothing better than to follow Alexis's example, but I was under no illusion that Blake would let me go that easily. He slid into the booth across from me. He beckoned to the harried waitress, and she stopped everything to bring him a fresh cup of coffee.

"Would you really have done it?" I found myself asking, not sure why I cared one way or another.

"Hell yes," he answered with a sharklike grin as he poured an indecent amount of sugar into his cup. "I've always hated that holier-than-thou bastard. He'd have loved every minute of it, too, until his head cleared."

I sure as hell didn't like Alexis, but I couldn't help thinking that what Blake had planned to do to him was downright evil. I guess that thought must have shown on my face.

"Oh, please. Don't feel sorry for him," Blake said. "The Olympians have embraced rape and torture as a goddamn art form, and he's totally on board with that. As long as he's not the victim, of course."

"The Olympians?"

"A bunch of descendants of Greek gods. They envision themselves as some kind of master race. They also consider themselves to be the ruling body for all the *Liberi*." He flashed me a sarcastic smile. "Not all of us see it that way."

"And who's Konstantin?"

"Their leader. He styles himself as their king, but I refused to call him that even when I *was* an Olympian. I'm sure as hell not going to call him that now."

My mind boiled with an endless stream of questions. I settled for the one I decided was of most immediate importance. "How did you find me? And how did *he* find me?"

Blake leaned back in his seat. "I'm guessing he found you because their Oracle had a vision. And before you ask, the Oracle is a descendant of Apollo, and she sometimes sees the future. Most of her visions are so vague and confusing you can't understand what they mean until whatever it is has already happened. But every once in a while, she sees something clearly."

I nodded, swallowing my skepticism for the millionth time. "That doesn't explain how *you* found me."

He smiled and didn't answer. He was definitely being less hostile now than he had been last night, but there was a hint of malice in his eyes; he wanted the mystery of how he had found me to creep me out. Unfortunately, I was giving him exactly what he wanted.

"All right," I said, trying not to show my discomfort, "*why* did you find me?"

"Anderson promised you a follow-up conversation, remember?"

I had a feeling my effort to hide the chill that ran through me was in vain.

"Jack merely delayed the inevitable when he pulled his juvenile little trick and snuck you out," Blake continued. "I'll give you a ride back to the house. You'll be safer there anyway. It's off-limits to the Olympians."

Another conversation with Anderson was not on my to-do list, and no matter how much I'd disliked Alexis, I couldn't imagine feeling "safer" at Anderson's mansion. "What if I decide to decline your generous offer?"

"I know you caught the edge of my aura when I used it against Alexis," he said, his nostrils flaring as if he scented my weakness. "The effect would be a hell of a lot more intense if I directed it at you. You'd follow me anywhere, begging me to fuck you. I wouldn't do it, but I'd magnanimously offer to let you suck my cock during the ride to the house. You'd have a grand ol' time." He smiled pleasantly.

I was sick and tired of being scared. The threat made my stomach do flip-flops, but I did my best not to let my face show it. "Is threatening people with rape your answer to every problem?"

"I do find it's remarkably effective," he responded with a dry edge in his voice. "And it's far less ostentatious than grabbing you and dragging you kicking and screaming out the door."

I hated being bullied, but I didn't have much choice but to give in—for the moment. "Fine," I said. "Let's go see Anderson."

Blake fixed me with a long, penetrating stare. I had a feeling he knew I wasn't the type to give up so easily. I gave him my best innocent look. I had no intention of setting foot within ten miles of Anderson and his Hand of Doom, but I didn't want to give Blake an excuse to practice his unique method of coercion on me. I'd never realized sex could be so effectively weaponized.

I don't know if my feigned innocence convinced Blake, or if he merely decided he was in too strong a position for me to give him trouble. Whatever the reason, he slipped out of the booth, and I was mildly surprised to see him throw a ten-dollar bill on the table. He hadn't struck me as the generous type, but not only was he paying for my coffee—and Alexis's— he was leaving the waitress a sizeable tip. He reached for my arm as I stood up, but I quickly danced out of reach.

"Keep your hands to yourself," I warned. "I'm coming with you peacefully, but you touch me and all bets are off."

He gave me one of his malicious grins. My threat was an empty one when he could use his creepy power to force me to come along, but I didn't want him touching me if I could help it. Getting away from him was going to be hard enough without having to break free of his grasp.

My threat might have had no teeth, but Blake didn't try to grab me again. He led me out of the diner and onto K Street, keeping a careful eye on me. I hoped he wasn't parked too close, because I needed some time to come up with an escape plan. The gun was in my backpack, so even if I were willing to wave it around on a crowded street, I couldn't. He was walking close enough that I doubted I'd have the foot-speed to just bolt and hope to outrun him. Which meant I needed a distraction of some kind. Something to keep him busy long enough to give me a sizeable head start.

I scanned the streets and sidewalks for something that could help. Finally, I caught sight of two tough-looking black guys leaning against a wall as they eyed Blake's approach. Both were big and imposing, and at just the right age to be eager to prove their manhood. There was a predatory light in their eyes as they looked Blake up and down.

Like I said, Blake was a pretty boy, his hair moussed to look casually tousled, his clothes obviously expensive. The classic metrosexual. To a bigoted young punk looking for trouble, "metrosexual" meant "gay." Despite the fact that he'd used his aura against Alexis, I was pretty sure Blake didn't swing that way.

Blake didn't seem to notice the punks, not even when one of them whistled at him and the other made kissy noises. From their body language, I doubted they were planning to do anything more than harass Blake, unless he was hot-headed enough to engage with them. But I suspected they would be just the kind of distraction I needed.

I looked straight ahead, pretending not to pay any attention to them. There was a dangerous glitter in Blake's eyes, one that said he was seriously considering stopping to teach the punks some manners. I didn't know if he had any powers beyond lust, but I suspected he was more than a match for these two, despite appearances. I also suspected he was going to control his aggressive urges, knowing full well that I'd make a run for it if he tried anything. So I decided to take the choice out of his hands.

Timing my move carefully, I waited until we were just a couple feet short of the punks. Then I slung my backpack off my shoulder and swung it as hard as I could at Blake's back.

Since I hadn't wanted to leave my expensive laptop sitting around the hotel, there was plenty of oomph behind the blow. Blake grunted in surprise as he flew forward—right into the two punks.

I didn't wait to see what happened. I whirled around, shoving my arms back into the straps of my backpack, then ran for all I was worth. There was a lot of yelling behind me, but I ignored it, my arms and legs pumping for maximum speed. I probably should have dropped the backpack so it wouldn't slow me down, but it had my wallet, my gun, and my laptop in it, and I wasn't willing to part with it.

I whipped around the nearest corner, sneaking a glance behind me as I turned. One of the punks punched Blake right on that luscious mouth of his, but it didn't seem to bother him much. He shoved the guy away hard enough to send him to the pavement.

I kept running at top speed. There was a parking garage a few yards ahead of me and another street a few yards past that. If Blake managed to get away from the punks—which I suspected he would soon, if he hadn't already—he was going to catch up with me quickly. I'm a relatively fast runner given my size, but at five-two, my stride is pretty short.

I ducked into the garage, hoping Blake would assume I'd run all the way to the corner before turning.

My breath was coming in frantic gasps, the muscles in my legs burning like hell. There was a fair amount of activity on the ground level of the garage, people cruising for spaces or trying to remember where they'd parked. A few of them glanced at me curiously as I blew past, but no one seemed particularly alarmed.

The muscles in my legs complained even more as I forced them to carry me up the ramp to the next level of the garage. I was still hoping Blake would run right past the place, but with my luck these days, I wasn't counting on it. If he found me, he could use his special power to force me to go with him, right under the noses of any number of witnesses, and they would never know anything was wrong. I, however, would need my gun to defend myself, and that meant getting away from potential witnesses.

There were fewer cars on the second level, but there was still enough activity that I didn't dare draw the gun.

My pace wasn't much faster than a brisk walk as I forced myself onward, climbing the ramp to the third level. There were only a handful of cars up there, and no people.

Finally allowing myself to slow down, I examined my options as I sucked in air. If Blake managed to follow me up here, I'd pretty much run myself into a corner, but that wasn't entirely by accident. Best to be in a place where I could keep an eye on all the entrances.

There was a bank of elevators to my right, and a stairwell to my left, but other than the ramp, those appeared to be the only two ways up to this level. If Blake was following me, he'd have to use the ramp, otherwise it would be too easy for him to go right past me in the enclosed stairwell or the elevator.

I crossed the garage at a halfhearted trot, my legs feeling like they weighed about ten tons each. I can jog for miles if I have to, but the all-out sprint with the extra weight of the backpack had exhausted me.

When I reached the cluster of cars near the stairwell, I ducked down between them and crept forward until I was crouched between one car's bumper and the wall. I then quietly unzipped my pack and pulled out the gun. If Blake cornered me up here, I'd have to find the guts to shoot him. I didn't *want* to shoot him, but I doubted I'd have a lot of options if he found me. I couldn't risk letting him use his nasty special power on me.

I crouched in the shadow of the car for what felt like forever, my body practically vibrating with tension. The day wasn't particularly cold, but the air still felt icy against my sweaty skin. I was finally beginning to catch my breath after the long run, but my heart was still tripping on adrenaline.

It was all I could do not to groan when I saw Blake's silhouette as he stalked through a patch of sunlight. Goddammit! Why couldn't he have just kept on running? Or better yet, given up the chase? I should theoretically have had enough of a head start that I could be anywhere by now, so why was he *here*?

I carefully slid over so that I was in the deepest pool of shadow available. I kept my entire body hidden behind one front wheel—the driver hadn't bothered to straighten out once he'd pulled in, so the wheel gave me a gratifying amount of cover—and peeked from under the bumper to monitor Blake's progress as he approached.

He was moving slowly, staring at something in his hand. At first, I had no idea what he was doing, but when he got closer, I could see he was looking at the screen of a phone. I didn't think he was checking his email or surfing the Internet.

I mentally let out a stream of curses as I

remembered Jack handing me my pocketbook. The purse itself had been ruined, but when I'd gotten home, I'd transferred its contents into my backpack. Evidence suggested there'd been something in that purse that wasn't mine. Like, say, some kind of tracking device.

I was sure the jig was up, but even so, I remained stubbornly hidden. Blake was so close now I could see the thin, angry line of his lips, and the dangerous intensity of his eyes. He stood at the top of the ramp and turned a full circle, looking back and forth between the phone screen and his surroundings.

Maybe the smart thing to do would have been to leap to my feet the moment his back was turned and fire. I would have to take Maggie's word for it that he was immortal and I couldn't kill him by shooting him. I urged myself to do it, picturing myself as an action movie heroine blasting away, but the mental picture was so absurd it almost made me laugh.

It would have taken at least an hour for me to talk myself into shooting, and I had about two seconds. Blake had finished his circle before I'd gotten through preliminary arguments. I thought sure the tracker was going to lead him straight to me, but he just stood there, scowling and shaking his head in frustration.

Blake hit a button on his phone, then held it to his ear. I took a wild guess that he was calling Anderson, and that guess was confirmed by the conversation I overheard.

"She's in here somewhere," he said into the phone.

"Or at least her bag is. The tracker can't tell me which floor she's on. Jack gave you a cell phone number for her, didn't he?"

Oh, shit! My heart shot into my throat, and I reached for my backpack. I tried to hurry, but I was hampered by having to hold on to the gun and by having to be quiet. If I just yanked open the zipper, that sound would give me away just as effectively as the stupid cell phone.

I didn't make it.

Before I'd even gotten the zipper halfway open, my cell phone played the opening riff of George Thorogood's "Bad to the Bone." It had been Steph's idea of a joke, but I kinda liked it. At least under normal circumstances.

There was no point in hiding anymore, so I stood up and pointed the gun at Blake, praying that no one else would come along and become an inconvenient witness. I'd be in deep trouble if I got caught carrying a gun. Blake's expression was somewhere between a sneer and a grin. I guess the lighting was kind of dim and he didn't see the gun at first. When he did, the grin disappeared.

Half a second later, heat suffused my body. My nipples hardened to aching peaks, moisture flooded my core, and my eyes started to glaze over.

The effect was almost instantaneous. One moment, I was staring down the barrel of my gun trying to work up the nerve to pull the trigger, the next, I wanted to fling the gun to the ground and tear off my clothes. I had only an instant to realize what was happening before I was under his spell, but that was enough.

Desperation gave me the will I needed, and my finger squeezed the trigger.

The tide of lust stopped as fast as it had started, and my vision cleared as Blake clutched the bleeding wound in his chest, gave me a wide-eyed look, and fell to the floor of the garage.

SEVEN

To say I was shocked by what I'd done was an understatement. For a long, breathless moment, I just stood there and stared, hardly believing I'd actually shot someone. Blake's face was squinched in pain, and his hands were stained crimson as he tried to stanch the flow of blood.

My hands were shaking as I lowered the gun, and I blinked furiously to hold back tears. I couldn't afford to wallow. A .38 Special isn't exactly a quiet gun, and people on the lower levels of the garage had to have heard the shot. Maybe they'd assume it was just a car backfiring, but I couldn't count on it.

I grabbed my backpack and shoved the gun back inside. There was a tracker in my pack somewhere, but I didn't have time to look for it now, and all the reasons I'd had previously for not dropping the backpack still applied.

Heart in my throat, I stepped around the protection of the car, keeping a wary eye on Blake. His face was still tight with pain, and his skin was a bloodless shade of white, but he was conscious. I hoped that meant he wasn't going to die.

"I'm sorry," I said lamely, then rolled my eyes. What kind of action movie heroine apologized to the enemy for hurting him? If I was going to play the part of a badass, I was going to need some serious practice.

I slung the backpack over my shoulder and opened the door to the stairwell. Blake's eyes glittered as he glared at me, but when he tried to stand up, his face went even whiter and I thought he might pass out. I bit my tongue to stave off another apology, then slipped into the stairwell and let the door slam behind me. The echoing sound made me jump, and it took a healthy dose of self-control to keep myself from running down the stairs, which would only draw attention. I had enough people chasing me without adding the police to the list.

I hurried to the nearest Metro station, and got on the first train that arrived, not caring where it was going as long as it was away from the scene of the crime. Once the train was moving, I sat down and started examining the contents of my backpack— making sure the gun stayed safely concealed, naturally.

Eventually I found the tracker. Jack had done an impressive job of hiding it. I'd gone through every-thing twice and was beginning to think I'd have to dump the whole backpack after all, when I finally noticed that my purse-sized package of tissues weighed more than it should. I pulled out the first few tissues, then found a white, rectangular device, about two inches long, tucked into the center of the pack.

I left the tracker on the train—that ought to keep Anderson and crew occupied for a while—then got off at the next stop and took a cab back to my hotel.

Just in case the tracker had allowed Blake to figure out which hotel I was staying in, I decided to get out of there. My cell phone rang while I was packing. I checked caller ID: Steph. I groaned. There was no way I could talk to her now without her figuring out something was wrong, and I couldn't explain my situation without sounding like a lunatic.

I was going to have to talk to her eventually, but I couldn't handle Steph now.

Deciding I'd call her in a couple of hours, I checked out of the Holiday Inn and found myself a new hotel halfway across town. I took a hot bath, hoping that would calm my nerves, but nothing short of a horse tranquilizer could have done the trick.

I had no idea what my next step should be. Apparently, I had two factions of *Liberi* after me, and they had the financial and magical resources to make my life really difficult. I couldn't evade them forever, not unless I decided to run away and make myself disappear.

I'd had enough experience tracking people who didn't want to be found to cover my own tracks if I needed to. I could disappear from D.C. and create a new identity for myself somewhere else. But I'd spent most of my childhood being shuffled from foster home to foster home, and here in the D.C. area with the Glasses, I'd experienced the only true stability I'd ever known. I couldn't face the prospect of digging up my roots and leaving everything and everyone I'd come to love behind. Not unless it was absolutely the last resort.

Which meant that somehow, I was going to have to find a way to convince both factions of *Liberi* to leave me alone.

To be perfectly honest, I already had a sinking feeling that life as I had known it was over. I didn't have a clue how to get the *Liberi* to back off, and even if I did . . . Let's face it, I wasn't the same person I'd been just twenty-four hours ago. I believed in the supernatural. I'd become immortal with supernatural powers myself. And I'd shot a man. In cold blood.

I have to admit, I was wallowing. But then, who could possibly argue that I didn't have the right?

My phone rang again, and I snapped out of my funk enough to check caller ID. A nervous shiver ran through me when I saw the name Anderson Kane.

Naturally, my first instinct was to ignore the call, just as I'd ignored Steph's. I had, after all, gone to rather extreme lengths to avoid being forced to talk to him. But I was desperately in need of more information, and my available sources were pretty limited. Anderson couldn't hurt me over the phone—at least I hoped not—so I answered.

I'm not much of a badass. Hard to be, when you're only five-two. In spite of that, I've never been one to let people push me around and I'd had enough pushing already from the various *Liberi* I'd met, so instead of answering with a pleasant or neutral greeting, I said, "How's Blake?"

My stomach flip-flopped at the memory of Blake clutching his bleeding chest, at the memory that I'd actually pointed a gun at another human being and pulled the trigger. Good thing Anderson couldn't see my face, or he'd have known how much I was bluffing with my tough girl act. Hell, maybe he knew anyway.

He was silent for a long moment, and I wondered if he was more surprised or angry at my bravado.

"He'll recover," Anderson finally said, his voice perfectly neutral. "I suppose sending him after you was a miscalculation on my part. He has a unique ability to get under people's skin, and he still believes you killed Emmitt on purpose."

I raised an eyebrow, though of course he couldn't see. "You say that as if you *don't* believe it anymore."

He sighed, and it may have been my imagination, but I heard a world of sorrow in that sigh. "I don't know," he admitted. "Maggie is convinced Emmitt had grown weary and set you up, and I was beginning to agree with her. Then you up and shot Blake. I have to say that seems more like the act of a cold-blooded schemer than an innocent victim."

Internally, I cringed at the accusation in his voice. I didn't want to feel guilty about shooting Blake, but I couldn't help it. I'd already killed a man last night, and the fact that it had been an accident on my part didn't do much to ease my conscience. I couldn't help wondering . . . If I hadn't sped up when the driveway had straightened out, would I have been able to swerve in time to avoid hitting him? I hadn't thought I'd been going that fast, but the airbag *did* deploy, which suggested I'd been going faster than I'd realized.

I tried to summon a surge of anger to counter the guilt. "What was I supposed to do? Let him use that creepy power of his to violate me and then drag me to you so you could torture me? Are you suggesting only a cold-blooded schemer would do everything in her power to avoid that?"

There was such a long silence on the other end of the line I thought I might have lost the signal on my phone.

"I'm sorry," he finally said, and he actually sounded like he meant it. Whether he *did* or not was anyone's guess. "I don't suppose any of us are thinking as clearly as we should at the moment, especially me. Emmitt was my friend for a long, long time. I should have—" His voice cracked, and he cleared his throat.

My own eyes stung at the pain in Anderson's voice. I'm such a bleeding heart. But I couldn't help mentally putting myself in his shoes. I'd stolen his friend's life and immortality. Worse, I claimed that friend had used me to commit suicide. If I were in Anderson's shoes, I'd probably lash out at me, too.

"If he was really weary enough to end his life," Anderson continued, his voice steadier, "I should have seen it. I should have been able to help him. I'd much rather you were lying about it than to accept that I was so blind."

I took a deep, quiet breath, trying to distance myself from Anderson's pain. Yes, I could understand he was grieving for his friend, and I could even understand why he didn't want Emmitt's death to have been suicide. But none of that could forgive the threats and the strong-arm tactics.

"But the reasons for my behavior don't matter much to you, do they?" Anderson asked as if he'd read my mind. "I treated you like your guilt was a foregone conclusion last night, and for that I'm sorry. From now on, how about I presume you're innocent until proven guilty. And if you really are innocent, then we need to talk. There's a lot you don't know."

I resisted the urge to snort at the understatement. "I'm happy to talk on the phone for as long as my battery holds out."

"In person would be better."

I laughed. "Maybe for you."

"For you, too. Nikki, you have no idea the kind of danger you're in. I know I haven't exactly come off to you as one of the good guys, but I am. At least in comparison to Konstantin and the rest of the Olympians. They will stop at nothing to get their hands on you. You can't go up against them alone; and I promise you, you wouldn't like what would happen if they captured you."

"Why would they want to capture me?"

"Because Descendants of Artemis are exceedingly rare. Contrary to popular belief, she wasn't literally a virgin goddess, but she bore only one child, and her line has nearly died out. She was a goddess of the hunt, and a lot of the skills her descendants possess would be of great use to the Olympians."

"Go on," I prompted. "Prove to me that you're a good source of information."

"I believe in the proverb that with great power comes great responsibility. The Olympians believe that with great power comes great privilege and no responsibility whatsoever. From their perspective, they are better than everyone else, and that's the natural order of the universe. They are selfishness incarnate, but as reprehensible as I find that, it's not why I oppose them as I do.

"I understand that Maggie explained the origins of the *Liberi Deorum* last night."

"Yeah," I said, swallowing hard. Even after all I'd seen, there was a part of me that desperately wanted to deny I believed what Maggie had told me.

"So she explained that anyone descended from the ancient gods can steal the immortality of a *Liberi*?"

"Yes."

"Because Descendants can potentially steal their immortality, the Olympians see them as a threat that needs to be eliminated. For centuries, they have hunted Descendants. Generally, when they find a family of Descendants, they kill all the adults and all the children over the age of five. They then raise those youngest children themselves, indoctrinating them into their beliefs. If the children show any signs that they question the 'natural order,' they are disposed of."

I sank down onto the edge of my bed, knees suddenly weak at the images Anderson's words brought to mind. "By disposed of, you mean killed."

"Yes. Remember, as far as the Olympians are concerned, they are the pinnacle of perfection, and everyone else is expendable. Even children they have raised themselves."

"Why do they raise the children at all? Why not . . ." I let the question trail off because I couldn't put the horror into words.

"Because only a mortal Descendant can kill a *Liberi*. The Olympians can't kill rival *Liberi* themselves, so they need pet Descendants to do the dirty work for them. That's how they raise these children—with the philosophy that if they are good enough, the Olympians will one day give them a sacrificial *Liberi* so they can become immortal themselves.

"And if you don't find all of this distasteful enough, know also that only those descended from the *Greek* gods are considered worthy to become *Liberi*. If the Olympians find a family descended from one of the other pantheons, they leave no survivors.

"They want you to join them because they believe they can use your skills to help them hunt down and slaughter more Descendants. Without a Descendant of Artemis in their employ, the Olympians have to hunt Descendants using only conventional methods. They're always on the lookout for unfamiliar people with visible glyphs. If they find a Descendant, they'll extract a family history and go looking for all the relatives. If you join them, they'll use your powers to track down the ones they can't find."

"That's never going to happen," I said immediately. "I wouldn't help them kill *anyone,* much less helpless children!"

"That's what you think now," Anderson countered, "but the Olympians are very good at . . . persuasion. Come back to the house. You'll be much safer with us than you would be out on your own."

I laughed briefly, then swallowed it before it could turn into hysteria. "You've got to be kidding me! You let Jamaal practically choke me to death last night, you yourself threatened to torture me, and then you sent Blake with his slimy lust power after me, and you expect me to just hand myself over because you claim the other guys are worse?"

"I realize that—"

"You don't realize a goddamn thing!" I squeezed the phone so hard I accidentally hung up on Anderson. Then I decided my subconscious had the right idea, and I turned the phone off.

Maybe he was telling me the truth. But I had no way of knowing. And even if he *was,* I saw no reason why I would be better off hanging out at Psycho Central. Jamaal had made it crystal clear that he wanted to make me suffer, and Blake no doubt hated my guts after what I'd done to him this morning.

Geez, I was just making friends all over the place.

I lay down on my bed and closed my eyes, pinching the bridge of my nose where an exhaustion headache was starting up. I might not be willing to hand myself over to Anderson, but I was no closer to figuring out what I *should* do.

As a child, I'd been a real pro at getting into trouble. There was a good reason I'd been bounced from foster home to foster home so often before I'd landed with the Glasses. I couldn't blame the other foster families for getting rid of me. I'd been well on my way to becoming a juvenile delinquent, getting angrier and angrier each time a family gave up on me, my behavior worsening each time. But as much trouble as I'd gotten into, as close as I'd come to spending some quality time in juvie, none of it came close to preparing me for the trouble I was in now.

Between the physical exhaustion and the sense of hopelessness that enveloped me, I couldn't help curling up on my side, clutching a pillow to my chest. In no time, I was fast asleep.

The dream was familiar, one that I'd had countless times over the years. More a memory than a dream, really, though I wasn't sure how much of the memory was real, and how much was pieced together by my subconscious. I'd been awfully young at the time, but in my dreams, at least, the memory was crystal clear.

It was a nasty, rainy day, the air so thick with moisture you could drown in it. The rain should have made it cooler, but instead it merely made it feel like we were walking through a steam room.

I don't know where we were, exactly, except that it was in the South somewhere and that it was a long way from home. My mom was carrying my baby brother, Billy, his chubby little arms lost under her thick hair as he wailed and tried to hide from the rain. Momma murmured assurances, shielding his face with her other hand. Until Billy had started to cry, she'd been holding my hand. I kept plucking at her sleeve, wanting her to take my hand again, but she was too busy with Billy.

We'd been walking for what felt like miles, after having spent a day and a night riding on a stinky, crowded bus. I was hungry. I was soaked through. My feet hurt. And I wanted to curl up to sleep in my cozy, comfortable bed at home.

"Momma! Pick me up!" I whined, at the end of what little patience I had at the age of four. "My feet hurt."

"Hush, sweetheart," she said, absently reaching down to brush a dripping lock of hair out of my eyes. The stupid baby cried even louder once Momma wasn't holding him with both hands. I hated him for it even though I knew I was supposed to love him. "We're almost there."

I didn't know where "there" was, but I didn't see anything familiar on this run-down city street, so I knew "there" wasn't home, and home was the only "there" I wanted.

"Wanna go home!" I yelled, stamping my foot. Then I decided to see if I could out-wail my brother. If I was loud enough, maybe Momma would give me what I wanted. It always seemed to work for stupid Billy.

Momma closed her eyes in pain and weariness when I started to cry, but she didn't take me home. Instead, we continued to trudge through the rain. I tried going on a sit-down strike, but Momma grabbed my hand and dragged me along. I was too old to be carried, she informed me, so I was just going to have to walk.

Finally, when I was sure I couldn't walk another step even with Momma pulling on me, we climbed a set of weathered stone steps. Momma pushed open a door, and I followed her into a cool, dark entryway. It seemed we were finally "there."

I wiped my dripping hair away from my face as my eyes adjusted to the low light, which seemed to come almost entirely from candles. Ahead of us, a pair of doors were propped open to reveal a long aisle with rows of pews on either side. The rain had darkened the afternoon skies so that only the faintest glow of light shone through the stained glass windows, but a discreet spotlight illuminated a gruesome statue of Christ on the cross.

I shivered in the air-conditioned breeze. Seconds ago, I'd have done anything to get inside out of the rain, and to sit down, but I didn't like this church. Maybe it was a premonition. Or maybe it was just that I was reliving the memory/dream from my adult perspective, knowing what was going to happen.

Momma led me down the aisle, to a pew in the middle of the church. There were a couple of old ladies sitting at the very front, but other than them we were the only people in the place. Our footsteps echoed, despite the strip of carpet down the center of the aisle. It was then that I realized the baby had finally stopped crying.

Momma nudged me into the pew, and I sat down gratefully, no matter how uneasy the church made me. I thought she'd sit next to me, but she didn't. She knelt in the aisle, still cradling Billy in her arms. He made a little sound of protest, like he was about to start screaming again, but then stuck his thumb firmly in his mouth instead. The quiet made the patter of the rain on the windows seem loud.

Momma let go of Billy with one hand, and he was too busy sucking his thumb to complain. She brushed my cheek with the back of her hand, and the light glinted off the moisture in her eyes.

"I want you to sit here and be a good girl, Nikki," she said in a low whisper, the sound barely loud enough to hear over the patter of the rain. "I have to go change Billy's diaper," she continued, and her eyes shone even brighter. "I'll be right back, okay?"

A tear escaped her eye and trickled down her cheek. I didn't know why she was crying now that both Billy and I had stopped. I knew it was a bad sign, but I didn't know what to do about it. Momma was supposed to comfort *me* when *I* cried, not the other way around. The confusion was more than I could deal with, so I just nodded and didn't ask why she was so sad.

"I love you so much, baby," she said, leaning forward so she could plant a soft kiss on my forehead. "Never doubt that. Never."

When she pulled away from me, tears were streaming down her cheeks. And there was an iridescent glyph on her forehead.

She stroked my wet, tangled hair one last time and stood up. Then she wrapped both arms around Billy, and hurried down the aisle.

I never saw her again.

———

I awoke with a start and a gasp. I'd dreamed of my abandonment about a zillion times. The details varied here and there, which was what made me wonder how much was really memory, but never before had the dream included a glyph on my mother's forehead.

I sat up slowly, my head foggy and confused. The bright sunlight of the afternoon had faded to blue twilight while I'd slept, leaving the room in shadows. Still groggy, I reached over and switched on the bedside lamp, squinting in the sudden brightness.

Of course, it made sense for me to dream about my mom having a glyph on her forehead after all I'd gone through in the last twenty-four hours or so. Surely it was nothing more than the power of suggestion.

But what if it wasn't? Anderson said the Olympians hunted down Descendant families and killed them. What if I'd gotten my divine heritage through my mother's side of the family? And what if she'd found out the Olympians were after her? Could that explain why she'd abandoned me?

We'd been on that bus a day and a night—if my memory was accurate—which meant she'd traveled hundreds of miles away from our home, before she left me sitting on that church pew. When I'd finally realized she wasn't coming back and the old ladies at the front of the church had called the police, I was so hysterical I couldn't even tell them my own name, much less my mother's. Nor could I tell them where I lived. My mom had made me memorize our address and phone number once, but I didn't remember it.

Eventually, I calmed down enough to remember

the address, but it was just the street address—no city or state. The street name was common enough—Main, or Broad, or something like that—that the police were able to take me to the address, but since it was the wrong city, it didn't help.

My mother had not only abandoned me, she'd severed all ties to me. I was found so far from where I'd grown up that no one could possibly recognize me, and I was young enough to think my mother's name was "Momma." There was no way anyone could identify me, or associate me with my mother in any way. And if anyone was hunting her, if anyone *found* her, they'd still never have found *me*.

Most likely, it was just wishful thinking that built this scenario in my mind. After all, my mother hadn't left *Billy* at the church. Maybe she didn't think the old women at the front would have let her leave a crying baby and a four-year-old alone in the pews. Or maybe she'd left Billy somewhere else, hiding her tracks even more.

"Or maybe she just abandoned you because you were too much damn trouble," I muttered, disgusted with myself for the stupid fantasy. Odds were, my mom had known nothing whatsoever about the Olympians. I couldn't fathom why she was so desperate to get rid of me—I didn't become a hellion until I started living in foster care—but there is, sadly, no shortage of women who abandon their children, one way or another. There was no reason to believe my own mother wasn't just one more.

EIGHT

I felt even more tired now than I had before I'd taken my unintentional nap. I brewed a pot of the terrible in-room coffee, made even more terrible by non-dairy creamer. Then I took another shower, hoping it would clear my head.

It didn't.

Afterward, I reluctantly turned my phone back on and checked messages. As I'd expected, Anderson had tried calling back a couple of times, though he hadn't left any voice mails. Also as expected, I had a couple of messages from Steph, wondering where the hell I was and why I wasn't calling her back. Her third message revealed that her slight concern was well on its way to becoming full-out worry.

"Nikki. I talked to Jim, and he said you ducked out early last night. No one has seen or heard from you since. Please call me back as soon as you get this.

If I don't hear from you soon, I'm going to call the police. Please call."

I winced in guilt as I heard the quaver in my sister's voice. It wasn't like me not to return phone calls, and after what must have seemed like a somewhat mysterious exit from the restaurant last night, I couldn't blame Steph for being worried. I might not run into the kind of daily danger that cops did, but my profession was not without its risks. She'd probably come up with a boatload of worst-case scenarios already. I prayed to God she hadn't gotten worried enough to try to call the Glasses yet. Surely she wouldn't interrupt their cruise unless she were *certain* there was something wrong. At least, I hoped not.

Knowing I could put it off no longer, I put on my big-girl panties and called Steph's house. She answered on the first ring, like she'd been hovering over the phone willing me to call. Maybe she had.

"Oh, thank God!" she said in lieu of a greeting, then immediately burst into tears.

Another wave of guilt rolled over me, even as I was momentarily annoyed at the melodrama. Steph bursts into tears at the drop of a hat. Which is probably healthier than my stoic reserve, but it gets on my nerves anyway.

In a lot of ways, it's a minor miracle that Steph and I are so close, seeing as we're polar opposites. Steph is a true blond bombshell, the kind that makes anyone with a Y chromosome start drooling. She's perky as hell, and everyone seems to like her. She'd always run with the popular clique at school—naturally, she'd been a cheerleader—but she'd been friendly with just about everyone, even the kids at whom cheerleaders traditionally looked down their noses. Steph may have been a card-carrying member of the popular crowd, but behind the frothy façade, she had a backbone of steel. No amount of peer pressure was going to make her be cruel to people who were outside her usual social circle. And heaven help anyone who dared to be cruel to her adopted little sister, even when said little sister made being an outsider a point of pride.

"I'm sorry I worried you," I told Steph as she fought to control her tears. I hadn't yet figured out what I was going to tell her—if I'd waited until I dreamed up the perfect explanation, I'd never have gotten around to calling—but I knew I had to come up with something fast.

"I'm fine," I continued. "I promise. Not a scratch on me. But I was in a car accident last night."

"What?" she shrieked, and I had to hold the phone away from my ear.

"I'm fine!" I repeated. "My car has gone on to its heavenly reward, but I'm not hurt, so please don't be upset."

"Don't be upset? You're joking, right?"

Please, please, please let her not have called the Glasses yet. Mrs. Glass was the quintessential overprotective mother hen, and she mothered me every bit as thoroughly as she did Steph. Dealing with Steph's distress was enough already—I couldn't bear the thought of having to call and reassure Mrs. Glass afterward.

"If you were in an accident last night," Steph continued, and there was a hint of anger seeping into her voice, "then why am I just hearing about it now? Why haven't you answered any of my calls? You *knew* I was going to call to ask you how things went, and you had to know I'd get worried when you didn't call back."

I sighed and wished I'd forced myself to call earlier. I couldn't blame her for being upset with me. If the situation had been reversed, I'd have been furious.

"I'm sorry," I said again. "I wasn't hurt, but I was pretty badly shaken up. I haven't been quite myself, and I just didn't think. My phone was turned off all day, and I didn't even notice until just now."

"Have you eaten yet?"

I blinked and shook my head at the non sequitur. "Huh?"

"Meet me at Angelo's at seven. A phone call doesn't cut it for this conversation, kiddo."

I groaned, thinking I should have drunk more coffee before picking up the phone. If my brain had been fully awake, I'd have known Steph wouldn't settle for a phone call. Angelo's was her favorite Italian restaurant, a real dive that served great food and mediocre wine. My body was too confused to know whether it was hungry or not, but I knew I wasn't up to the level of scrutiny I would undergo over dinner.

"I'm really not up to——" I started.

"Be there at seven, or I'm going to call Mom and tell her you totaled the car."

"You bitch!" I cried. "Don't you dare!"

I knew Mrs. Glass would have to find out about it eventually, but the more time that passed before she heard about it, the less chance that she would become hysterical.

"Show up for dinner, and I won't have to," Steph said, sounding smug. "You owe me for scaring the life out of me."

I considered trying to argue some more. There was no way I could behave as if nothing was wrong if I talked to Steph in person, and I still had no clue what I could use as a convincing cover story. But as I mentioned, Steph has a quite a backbone beneath her deceptively sweet exterior. If she was determined to talk to me in person, nothing would change her mind. And if I didn't show up, she really would call her mom and rat me out.

"Fine," I said with poor grace. "I'll see you at seven."

I almost decided to skip the dinner, despite Steph's threat. I didn't like the idea that I might lead that creep Alexis right to her, and I didn't want him anywhere near my sister. However, Blake had told me that the Oracle's visions were rarely clear, so I figured the odds that Alexis would find me twice in one day were low. The odds that Steph would rat me out if I didn't show up were a hundred percent. Besides, I couldn't avoid her forever.

I pushed open the door to Angelo's at 7:15, and the scent of garlic and tomatoes set my mouth to watering instantly. A quick glance around the chipped Formica tables showed me what I'd already expected to find: Steph wasn't here yet. She is biologically incapable of showing up anywhere on time, despite all Mrs. Glass's best efforts to train her to punctuality. She also has a sixth sense about what time I'll arrive. Even when I specifically try to be late enough for her to get there before me, she's always just a little bit later.

The hostess led me to a table for two near the back. There was no longer any smoking allowed inside, but the walls themselves must have absorbed the stink of cigarette smoke over the years, because I could still catch a whiff of it in the air. Or maybe it was just because I'd been coming here so long I knew the table was in the old smoking section.

Steph made her grand entrance about five minutes later, rushing through the door and scanning the restaurant anxiously, like she was afraid I'd have bolted by now. I waved, and saw her sigh of relief.

The Glasses had already made their fortune by the time Steph was in her formative years, so she'd grown up with the best fashion sense money could buy. She was wearing perfectly tailored slate gray slacks and a luxurious red cashmere sweater that clung to her near-flawless figure. She'd finished the outfit with a black swing coat and a pair of stiletto-heeled boots that I'd have broken my neck trying to walk in.

As usual, every male over the age of twelve gave her at least one or two appreciative glances as she snaked her way through the tables toward me. I told myself I was *not* jealous, but it was a lie. She was just so damn . . . perfect. If only she were a bitch, so I could hate her like she deserved to be hated . . .

Steph's mischievous smile said she had an inkling what was running through my mind. She draped her coat over the back of her chair, then sat across from me and gave me a penetrating stare. It took every ounce of my willpower not to look away.

Steph leaned back in her chair and crossed her arms. "Something happened," she said with great authority. "Something other than a car accident. What is it?"

Great. I hadn't even opened my mouth yet, and already Steph saw through me.

I considered trying to bluff my way through it. When I was on the job, people always seemed to believe whatever pretext I made up, but Steph and her parents knew me too well, and I was rarely able to slip a lie past any of them.

"Yeah," I admitted. "I've got some stuff going on. But it's not anything I can talk about." Not without getting carted off to the loony bin, that is.

Steph uncrossed her arms and began tapping the table with her perfectly manicured nails.

"I mean it, Steph. I can't talk about it. I'm not willfully holding out on you." Well, not too much, anyway.

She continued tapping her fingers and staring at me, not saying a word. I recognized the ploy for what it was: she was hoping that the pressure of her silent scrutiny would make me blurt something out. It was a tactic she'd learned from her mom, and under normal circumstances, it might even have worked.

The waitress interrupted our silent standoff to take our orders. Neither one of us had even consulted the menu, but then we'd memorized it years ago.

"Are you in some kind of trouble?" Steph finally asked when the waitress was out of earshot.

"I can't—"

"Talk about it. Yeah, I heard you. I'm not asking for details. I just want to know if you're in trouble, and if there's anything I can do to help."

My throat tightened briefly. There were times when Steph bugged the hell out of me, but she was one of the nicest people I'd ever met. She could have resented me for inserting myself into her family when she'd had thirteen years of being an only child, but she'd been nothing but supportive even from the very beginning, when I'd been a sullen, sulky troublemaker.

"Thanks, Steph," I said, my voice a bit gruff. "But there's nothing you can do." I forced a grin. "Except stop setting me up on blind dates with assholes."

For a moment, I thought she was going to resist my attempt to deflect the conversation. Then her shoulders slumped in defeat.

"What's wrong with Jim?" she asked, though her heart wasn't in the question. "He's nice, he's handsome, he's successful, and he's single."

I rolled my eyes. One of the reasons everyone likes Steph is that she's so good at turning a blind eye to peoples' flaws. Which is why I should know better than to let her set me up with anyone.

"You honestly think he's a nice guy?" I asked. "Have you ever *talked* with him?"

She looked annoyed. "Of course I talked with him. I wouldn't set you up with someone if I didn't know him well enough to think you'd get on."

I bit back a caustic response, realizing that Jim might not have shown Steph the side of him I'd seen at dinner. After all, Steph was a sexist jerk's idea of feminine perfection, so she wouldn't have elicited the kind of reactions I'd gotten. She was beautiful, and put a lot of time and effort into keeping herself that way. She was sweet-natured enough that people who didn't know her might think her weak or submissive, though they'd be wrong. And because she didn't have my hang-ups about living off her trust fund, she'd never had a career to inconvenience a man who wanted her full attention.

"The problem with you," I told Steph, "is that you like everyone. I'm a little more particular."

She laughed. "To put it mildly."

"No more blind dates, okay? It never turns out well."

"You never give it a chance to."

"Please, Steph," I said, suddenly feeling exhausted again. "I don't want to fight."

Steph leaned across the table and squeezed my hand, smiling gently. "We're not fighting. I'm trying to give you sage, older-sister advice."

The advice might have been more convincing if Steph's love life had been any more successful than my own. Beauty and wealth attracted a lot of men, not all of them for the right reasons. Not to mention the men who made the mistake of thinking that because she was nice, pretty, and blond, she'd be a pushover and put up with crappy behavior. The door hit those guys on the ass pretty hard on their way out.

"Since when has giving me advice been a productive use of your time?" I asked, returning Steph's smile with a wry grin.

"Good point."

The rest of the meal was much more relaxed. Steph and I stayed away from sensitive subjects and just enjoyed our food. Steph talked about her upcoming charity project, a dinner and auction to support the American Cancer Society, and extracted a promise from me that I'd be there. Steph might not work a paying job, but with the stable of charities she actively supported, she worked a hell of a lot more than most of the nine-to-fivers I'd ever met.

Things didn't go to hell until we were sipping our after-dinner coffee and picking at the remains of the slice of cheesecake we'd shared. Steph's phone rang, and she frowned in annoyance.

"I should've turned the damn thing off," she mumbled, but I knew she couldn't quite bear to do that. The big auction was less than two weeks away, and she had to be available for crisis management at the drop of a hat.

I smiled as I took another sip of my rich, dark coffee. "Don't mind me," I assured her. "It could be important."

She acknowledged my point with a nod, then dug

her phone out from her tiny designer handbag. She looked at the caller ID and frowned.

"I have no idea who this is," she said, but she answered anyway.

Her frown deepened at whatever the caller said. I don't know what it was about her expression that made me sit up and take notice, but the hair on the back of my neck prickled.

"Who is this?" Steph asked, her voice tight with what sounded like alarm. Our eyes met over the table, and the prickle at the back of my neck turned into a chill of fear.

Steph lowered the phone and covered the microphone with her thumb. "He says his name is Alexis, and he wants to talk to *you*."

My hands clenched so hard it was a wonder I didn't break the coffee cup I was holding. How dare that bastard drag my sister into this? Even without talking to him, I knew his decision to call on Steph's phone had been a deliberate threat. I used my cell phone for business all the time, so if he'd learned my identity—which he obviously had—he'd have had no trouble finding my number.

I put my cup down so hard that coffee sloshed out and spilled on the table, but I didn't care. I reached for the phone, ignoring the combination of alarm and curiosity on Steph's face. There wasn't anywhere I could talk truly privately, but I got up from the table and moved a few paces away anyway. I was painfully aware of Steph's eyes boring through the back of my head as I tried to calm myself down enough to talk.

The last thing I wanted was to let Alexis know he'd gotten to me.

"What do you want?" I asked, and despite my best efforts, no one could have missed the fury in my voice.

"We didn't get to finish our conversation this afternoon," he said, and I could hear how much he was enjoying my reaction.

"I was finished with it even before Blake showed up."

"But I wasn't, and that's all that matters. You are not living in Anderson's mansion, therefore you're not covered under our agreement with him. I tried playing nice with you this afternoon, but you made it clear that playing nice wouldn't work.

"Meet me tomorrow at twelve noon in the lobby of the Sofitel. Konstantin requires your services. If you cooperate, you'll be rewarded more than generously. I doubt you've ever had a client who can pay you the sums we can.

"But make no mistake, Nikki Glass: you *will* do what we ask, whether it's to gain the financial rewards of cooperation, or to avoid the consequences of refusal. Are we clear?"

I wanted to crawl down the phone line and kill him right then and there. This afternoon when I'd shot Blake, I'd felt bad about it even though Blake was a jerk. Right now, I wouldn't have hesitated a moment to shoot Alexis. And no, I would not have felt bad.

I couldn't help sneaking a quick glance over my shoulder at Steph. She was chewing her lip with worry as she watched me. If Alexis or one of his cronies laid so much as a finger on her . . .

I must have been taking too long to answer, because Alexis spoke again.

"Your sister is truly a lovely woman," he said, his voice oozing slime. "I'm sure Konstantin would be delighted to make her acquaintance. He can be a little rough with his women, but I'm sure she'll still be at least marginally attractive when he tires of her and passes her on to me."

My blood boiled in my veins, and I bit down, hard, on my tongue to keep from giving him any more satisfaction than I already had.

"I'll see you tomorrow at noon?" he asked, back to using the pleasant, friendly tone he'd first tried on me, as if he hadn't just made such an ugly, revolting threat.

"Yes," I said through gritted teeth, because what else could I do? I had no clear picture of what Alexis and the Olympians were capable of, but I knew they had more power and resources to draw on than I did. I was under no illusion that I could single-handedly protect Steph.

"I knew you would make the right decision. I'll look forward to chatting with you again, without the interruptions."

Luckily for me, he hung up before I said any of the stupid, vitriolic things that came to mind.

Nine

I stood with the phone against my ear, my back turned to Steph, long after Alexis hung up. I needed time to regain control of myself, to tamp down the toxic combination of rage and fear that bubbled in my gut. I wished the earth would open up and swallow every one of the *Liberi*. With the exception of myself, of course.

Eventually, I could stall no longer, and I turned around to face Steph.

What the hell was I going to tell her? I couldn't possibly pretend nothing was wrong, but I couldn't tell her the truth. And I knew there was no way in hell Steph was going to let me go without an explanation of some sort.

I returned to the table and sat down, handing Steph back her phone. She took it from me in silence, tucking it back in her bag without looking. It must have taken a lot of willpower, but she managed not to question me, instead giving me a little more time to pull myself together. She could obviously see I wasn't ready to talk yet.

The problem was I would *never* be ready. I usually think pretty fast on my feet—again, an important trait for a P.I.—but I couldn't think fast enough to keep up with this mess.

"I'm . . . sorry about that," I said, figuring that was a safe place to start.

Steph raised her delicately curved brows. "Care to tell me who that was? And why he was calling *me* when he wanted to talk to *you*?"

Steph sometimes likes to play the spoiled, rich socialite, but there is a sharp mind under her fluffy exterior. I could see in her eyes that she'd made a number of assumptions—including the one that she'd just been subtly threatened. I didn't want to scare her, but I supposed it was better that I tell her something so she'd be extra careful. Alexis obviously knew Steph and I were together right now. I was damn sure no one had followed me here, so either someone had followed Steph, or the Oracle was more reliable than Blake had led me to believe.

"It was a wannabe client," I told her, which I supposed was something close to the truth. "I turned down his case, but he's not taking no for an answer."

"Have you called the police?"

I swallowed the urge to laugh. Somehow, I didn't think the police were going to be much use against the *Liberi*.

"He hasn't done anything the police would be

interested in." Which was also true, even if it wasn't really the reason I didn't call the cops.

Steph frowned and chewed her lip. "You could report him as a stalker, couldn't you?"

I dismissed that with a wave. "He's being a pain in the ass, but he's not technically stalking me."

She leaned forward, resting her arms on the table and dropping her voice. "I know you're not telling me everything, Nikki. Come on. Spit it out."

"I told you before, I can't."

Anger sparked in her eyes. "That man just threatened me, didn't he? That's why he called my phone instead of yours, right?"

I winced, which pretty much precluded the possibility of bluffing my way out of this.

"If people are threatening me, I have a right to know what's going on, don't I?"

I rubbed my eyes as a headache threatened to form behind them. "It's complicated, Steph. Please trust me that I have good reasons for not telling you more." I forced my hand back down to my side and met my sister's angry stare. "I won't let anything happen to you. No matter what."

She shook her head and looked disgusted. "That's not good enough."

"I'm sorry, but it's the best I can do."

Steph glared at me, but I was unmoved. I wasn't in a position to tell her the truth, and in all honesty, I didn't know if the truth would have done her any good. I didn't know a whole lot about the *Liberi* and what they could do yet, but if even half of what I'd been told was true, Steph was no match for them. Hell, *I* was no match for them, and I was supposedly one of them.

I walked Steph to her car on the pretense of being sociable when in reality I was looking for lurking *Liberi*. I didn't spot anyone, nor did I see any mysterious cars following when Steph pulled out of her parking space. I returned to my hotel, still trying to figure out how I was going to keep Steph safe. Too bad I didn't have the faintest idea how to go about it.

A good night's sleep failed to miraculously solve my problems, although I did feel fresher and more optimistic when I woke up the next day. For all that the *Liberi* were dangerous, and for all that I had no idea what their range of power was, they operated in secret, doing their best to blend in with the mortal population. That had to put some limits on their actions, and it suggested I'd be relatively safe meeting with Alexis in a public place later. Not that I was looking forward to it by any stretch of the imagination, but maybe when I talked to him again and got the details about what he wanted me to do, I'd be able to form a plan.

I'd turned off my phone for the night, but when I switched it back on in the morning, I found that I'd received another couple of calls from Anderson. I briefly considered calling him back and giving him an update on my upcoming meeting with Alexis, but thought better of it almost at once. I had no more reason to trust Anderson and his people than I did to trust Alexis. Though I might at some point find it to my advantage to play one against the other, right now I wanted to face one problem at a time.

I arrived at the Sofitel an hour before the appointment with Alexis. Not because I was anxious to meet him, of course, but because I wanted to give myself every possible advantage. I'd never been inside before, but I knew it was one of the more luxurious hotels in D.C. Of course, Alexis struck me as the kind of man who insisted on the best of everything.

I'm sure Alexis picked the place specifically for its lavish décor, but if he'd been looking for a place ideally suited for surveillance, I'm not sure he could have done better if he'd tried. The lobby was large, but there were a number of secluded nooks that were almost cozy. There were also a fair number of rectangular pillars, greatly cutting down on visibility, especially for someone coming in the front doors.

I took a seat on a not particularly comfortable sofa in one of the sitting areas. My seat was in a corner, where a pillar conveniently blocked me from view. Alexis would have to walk down a long hallway past the elevators before he'd be able to see me. I then pretended to drop something—not that anyone was paying particular attention to me—and positioned a small spy camera under the legs of the chair across from me. The camera gave me a perfect view of the hall leading up to the front desk.

Sitting once again in my secluded position, I opened my laptop and pretended to work as I scrutinized the feed from the camera. I watched every person who came in the front doors, without ever having to lift my head from my computer screen. If I saw anyone who tweaked my radar, there was room for me to retreat down another hallway, and I could leave another spy camera right next to my current position so I could keep up my surveillance. But carefully though I watched, I saw no sign that anyone was getting into position for an ambush.

At noon exactly, Alexis strode through the front doors of the hotel. He was not alone, although I didn't recognize his companion, a tall, imposing guy with olive skin and a neat black beard. I couldn't tell much from the somewhat grainy surveillance video, but it looked like his suit was as expensive as Alexis's, and he carried himself with the confidence of a man used to being in charge. Konstantin, I wondered?

The two of them stopped halfway down the hall, both standing there with expressions of impatience. A few more steps and they would see me, but I guess they figured it was my responsibility to come to them; they weren't about to expend the effort to look for me.

I watched them for another five minutes. Their body language got progressively more impatient as they waited. I didn't see anyone else come in after them—not anyone who acted like they were slipping in on the sly, that is—so I closed my laptop and shoved it back in my backpack. Then I took a deep breath and stepped into the main part of the lobby, where they could see me.

"Oh!" I said in feigned surprise when Alexis caught sight of me. "Have you been standing here the whole time? I was right over there waiting." I jerked a thumb toward the seating area.

Alexis narrowed his eyes at me. I had to resist the urge to glance at the spy camera, which I would have to come back later to collect. It was inconspicuous enough that I doubted Alexis would notice it unless I drew attention to it.

"You must be Ms. Glass," Alexis's companion said, and I took a closer look at him. He wasn't particularly good-looking in a traditional sense, but he fairly reeked of power, and I suspected women fell at his feet in droves. I saw no sign of a glyph on him, but perhaps it was hidden by his clothing, or even by his beard. His Mediterranean dark hair was just starting to gray at the temples, and there were the beginnings of crow's-feet at the corners of his eyes. On another man, they might have looked like laugh lines, but not on him. His smile was warm as he reached out his hand for me to shake, but I couldn't miss the hint of danger in his eyes. This was not a man to mess with, those eyes said, and I was inclined to believe them.

"I am Konstantin," he said as I reluctantly placed my hand in his. Not surprisingly, his handshake was crushing, though I gave back as much as I could before I remembered I'd decided not to mess with him. "It is truly a pleasure to meet you."

He released my hand, and I had to resist the urge to rub my now-sore knuckles. The predatory amusement in his eyes told me he was quite aware of his own strength; the crushing grip had been no accident. I hate bullies with a passion, and it took some serious willpower to keep myself from going on the offensive. I wasn't in a position to fight back, not yet, so for now I was determined to keep my cool and not be any more antagonistic than necessary.

"Alexis was quite insistent I make this meeting," I said, which was far more diplomatic than what I *wanted* to say.

Konstantin's face showed regret, but I had the strong suspicion it was only skin deep. "I apologize for the Draconian tactics, but I understand Anderson has attempted to poison you against us already. I think it only fair that we be able to argue our case, which is difficult to manage if you refuse to meet with us."

Oh, yeah, right. He'd forced me into meeting with him because it was the *fair* thing to do. I'd convinced myself I had to stay as civil as possible, but that didn't mean I had to roll over and show him my belly. "You've done a better job of poisoning me against you than Anderson could ever have done. Hasn't anyone ever told you that threatening someone's family is a sure way to get a relationship off to a bad start?"

Konstantin shot a quick look in Alexis's direction. There was no missing the reproach in that glance. Alexis looked away. "Again, I apologize. Alexis can be rather impetuous at times. He should have cleared it with me before making threats. We have had a long talk, and he's assured me nothing like that will happen again."

Alexis's shoulders tightened at the rebuke, and his gaze remained pinned to the floor. All very convincing, but I had a hard time believing Konstantin really had a problem with what Alexis had done. Maybe he'd have preferred it if Alexis tried a little harder to make contact peacefully before resorting to threats, but the threats would have come eventually, one way or another. And if Konstantin were really sorry about it, he'd have said so right from the start.

"So are you retracting the threat?"

He smiled at me, the expression condescending, though his tone remained completely pleasant. "My friend threatened harm to your sister if you didn't show up today. You're here, so the threat is no longer valid."

I wondered if he thought he was being subtle. Some people are such good liars that they can respond to questions with a complete non sequitur and make you believe they actually answered you. Konstantin wasn't one of them.

"So if I walked out of here right now, we wouldn't have a problem anymore?" I asked, pressing the issue even though I knew the answer.

"Let's not make this meeting a waste of both my time and yours," he said. "We can have a civilized conversation over lunch."

He gestured in the direction I presumed was toward the restaurant, but I didn't budge. I didn't want to spend a moment more than necessary in the company of these men, and I sure as hell couldn't see sitting down to lunch with them.

"I've got a very busy afternoon," I told Konstantin, still trying to be at least relatively diplomatic. "I don't have time for a fancy lunch. Why don't we have a seat over there," I continued, gesturing toward the nook where I'd been sitting, "and we can get right down to business."

Konstantin was clearly taken aback by my refusal.

Guess he was surprised I didn't automatically do what he wanted. He paused for a long moment before he spoke again.

"I can see how you and Alexis would rub each other the wrong way," he said with a wry smile that didn't reach his eyes. He may have been genuinely trying to create some kind of rapport based on shared humor, but the attempt was too forced to be effective. Beneath his urbane veneer, an aura of cruelty clung to him.

"Yeah, I don't think he and I will ever be on each other's Christmas lists," I said.

Alexis said nothing, merely stood to the side and glared at me, his arms crossed over his chest.

"Then perhaps it would be best if you and I spoke alone," Konstantin said. Without waiting for my response, he headed toward the sofa in the corner of the seating area. I guessed I was supposed to follow.

I felt Alexis's glare on the back of my head the moment I turned away from him. He hadn't uttered a sound of protest, but I knew he was majorly pissed off that he was being left out of the conversation. And he hadn't appreciated Konstantin's public rebukes, either, no matter how insincere they might have been. Like he needed another reason to hate me.

I sat gingerly on the edge of the sofa, feeling anything but relaxed around this self-proclaimed king of the *Liberi Deorum,* but he sprawled in the seat at the other end as if he owned the place. For all I knew, he did. I knew nothing about this man, not even his last name. Not that I *wanted* to know anything about him.

"So what was it you were so desperate to talk to me

about?" I asked, trying to release some of the tension in my spine. We were in a very public place. I could hardly expect Konstantin to try to attack me here. Still, I couldn't dismiss the possibility out of hand, which was why I'd done my surveillance before the meeting. There was just too damn much I didn't know, and the only people who could give me information were people I didn't want to talk to. "Alexis suggested you wanted to hire me for something?"

Konstantin nodded. "Yes. As a Descendant of Artemis, your skills would be a great asset to us."

I wondered if his "us" was a royal "we," or if he actually meant the Olympians as a whole. "Go on," I said. I already knew there was no way in hell I was working for him, but I figured it behooved me to hear him out for diplomacy's sake.

"We Olympians function as something of a police force for the *Liberi Deorum*. As such, we often find ourselves needing to track down people who do not wish to be found. Ordinarily, we use private investigators to help us locate these fugitives, but even a skilled private investigator has limitations, especially considering the level of secrecy we require. You, however, would be perfect for the position. Not only a descendant of Artemis, but already an experienced private investigator. You would make it infinitely easier for us to track down our fugitives."

He made it all sound terribly . . . benign. Of course, even if everything Anderson had told me about the Olympians was true, they were no doubt the heroes of their own stories. What I might see as a ruthless slaughter of innocents, they might consider a necessary purge to protect their own people. Even so, I didn't think that was what *Konstantin* believed. He might have started his crusade against Descendants under the pretext of protecting the *Liberi,* but these days it was all about enjoying the power. Maybe I was reading things into his tone and body language, but his words carried no sense of self-righteousness or conviction like they should if he really believed them.

"What would happen to these 'fugitives' once I found them for you?" I asked.

"They would be dealt with in an appropriate manner."

"Would dealing with them in the 'appropriate manner' involve killing them, by any chance?"

"It would depend on the circumstances. However, it would be your job to find them, not to carry out their sentences, whatever those sentences might be."

Maybe that was supposed to allow me to soothe my conscience if I accepted the job. As if the fact that I wasn't personally killing anyone would make me feel better about tracking people down so the Olympians could kill them.

"The rewards you would reap if you chose to work with us are considerable," Konstantin said. "We are richer than many countries, and we are generous with those riches. Your pay would be in seven figures, with bonuses for success. You could live like a queen." He sounded much more passionate about this argument than he had about the "it's for a good cause" thing.

I shrugged. "Money doesn't tempt me."

He laughed, like I'd just made the funniest joke in the world. "Oh, Nikki, money tempts everyone."

And just like that, I'd heard enough. I'd listened to what he had to say, and there was no hint of doubt in my mind that I wanted nothing to do with Konstantin or his Olympians. The time for diplomacy was over. "Let me rephrase that: I don't want your money."

Konstantin's urbane veneer thinned a little more, until it was practically nonexistent. "Perhaps you don't understand. I am the king of the *Liberi Deorum*. I realize you have only been recently introduced to the *Liberi,* but that doesn't exempt you from our laws. You are *Liberi,* and therefore you answer to me."

I snorted softly. "Most of the *Liberi* I've met *don't* answer to you."

He went completely still, shedding the last vestiges of his pseudo-friendly persona. The darkness in his eyes spoke of power and of deadly danger. "I have a treaty with Anderson and his people. That treaty does not extend to *you.*"

He leaned toward me on the sofa, and it was all I could do not to recoil. His anger wasn't as ostentatious as Alexis's, but it was all the more chilling for its calculated control.

"Make no mistake, Nikki," he said, his calm, unruffled voice at odds with the fury that radiated from his every pore. "I have presented you with a choice, but the consequences of making the wrong one are beyond the limits of your imagination."

I swallowed hard, hating that I couldn't hide my fear. "I thought you weren't into making threats."

He shrugged and sat back, banishing all signs of anger in a fraction of a second. The veneer was back, but I'd already gotten a clear view of what lay beneath it. "I prefer to catch my flies with honey, when possible." He gave me a charming smile that scared me almost as much as his glare. "But a good king must sometimes make compromises to ensure the well-being of his people. It is important to our people that we find these fugitives, and therefore I'm not in the position to take no for an answer."

He reached into the inner pocket of his jacket and pulled out a folded piece of paper. "On this paper are three names, those of our most wanted." He tried to hand me the paper, but I refused to take it from him. Then he grabbed my wrist in a crushing grip and forced the paper into my fingers, smiling pleasantly all the while.

"I know they will be difficult to locate," he continued, still holding my wrist so hard I felt like my bones were scraping together. "I'll be generous and give you one week to find your first fugitive. It can be any of the ones on that list, although eventually you must find all three. When you have the location of the first fugitive, you will call Alexis with your information, and he will send a squad to confirm you're telling the truth. When you find that first fugitive, I will pay you one million dollars." He smiled again and let go of my wrist. "In case that isn't incentive enough, I'll have you know that Alexis has taken quite a liking to your sister.

"If you refuse, or if you fail, I will give Alexis

permission to do whatever he wants with her. Let your imagination run wild. He won't kill her, though. He'll let her live so that you can see the wretched ruin he has made of her. If that doesn't motivate you . . . then we will have to get more creative. I have walked this earth for many centuries, my dear. Let me assure you, when it comes to cruelty, I've seen every form imaginable in my day, and there is nothing I would not scruple to do."

His eyes bored into me as I sat there in horrified silence, unable to force a single word from my mouth.

Konstantin reached over and patted my shoulder. I was too frozen to react. Then the lines of his face softened and he gave me what looked like a sad smile. Another veneer, no more convincing than the other.

"It doesn't have to be like this," he said softly. "You can join with us and work in a spirit of cooperation. No one need get hurt. You are *Liberi Deorum,* Nikki Glass, and you will live forever. The choice is yours whether that life will be one of pleasure and privilege, or pain and strife."

I still couldn't speak, didn't know what I could say in the face of such blatant evil. Words of defiance might get Steph hurt, but it was beyond me to in any way suggest I was in agreement with him. About *anything* he had said.

I remained silent as Konstantin rose to his feet, headed toward the front door, and beckoned Alexis to follow.

TEN

I sat in the hotel lobby for a good half hour after Konstantin and Alexis left, trying to pull myself together and think clearly. I didn't have much luck.

What was I going to do now? I couldn't let Alexis hurt Steph. And yet I couldn't live with myself if I tracked down the people on Konstantin's list and thereby got them killed.

Of course, it was still possible Anderson had been lying. Maybe the people on Konstantin's list were all bad guys, fugitives from justice, just as he had described them. I didn't actually believe it—the threats he'd made against Steph told me all I needed to know about the strength of his moral fiber—but I clung to the unlikely possibility.

I finally managed to get myself moving again. I collected my spy camera from under the chair, then left the Sofitel, keeping a careful eye out for any sign that I was being followed. I was pretty sure Konstantin was convinced he had me over a barrel and therefore wouldn't waste his time having me tailed, but you never can be too sure.

I took a very long and roundabout route back to my hotel, then retreated to my room to do a little research. I couldn't see complying with Konstantin's demands—surely I would find some other way out of this mess without endangering Steph—but I figured it couldn't hurt to see what I could dig up on the people he was asking me to find.

He'd given me very little to go on. Just names, and dates and places of birth. Under normal circumstances, I would have refused to try to locate someone with so little information. I'm good, but I'm not *that* good. But these were not normal circumstances. And besides, everyone seemed to think I had some kind of supernatural hunting ability. I'd seen the evidence that I'd become a ridiculously good shot, but so far I had no idea how that could translate into finding someone. Maybe once I tried, I'd unlock a special ability I didn't know I had.

I started with the first name on the list: Joseph Swift. Born March 15, 1955 in Madison, WI. At least that gave me a starting place for my search, although it was obvious Joseph Swift wasn't in Madison anymore, or the Olympians could have found him easily without my help.

I didn't need any fancy new supernatural abilities to find out some basic information about Swift, not when the local papers had a gruesome story to revel in.

Swift had lived a fairly ordinary life as a child. His

parents were working class, but steadily employed. He was a straight A student, and a star of his high school football team. Colleges were recruiting him aggressively, and his future looked almost unbearably bright. Until the spring of his senior year in high school, that is.

Just a few days shy of his eighteenth birthday, there was what was described as a failed burglary attempt at Joseph Swift's home. Several masked men broke into the house around midnight. According to Joseph, everyone in the household had gone to bed, and all the lights in the house were out. He, however, had been having trouble sleeping and had gone downstairs for a glass of water. He was in the kitchen drinking his water when he heard his father's startled cry, and then his mother's scream.

Joseph sprinted to his parents' aid, having no idea what was happening. When he was halfway up the stairs, his eight-year-old sister came running out of her bedroom, pursued by one of the masked intruders. The girl was stabbed to death before Joseph's eyes. When he saw two more masked men with bloody knives emerging from his parents' room, Joseph ran for his life. He managed to escape, but his entire family had been slaughtered.

I read several newspaper accounts of the murders. Everyone seemed to think that the masked men were burglars, and that Joseph's father had surprised them at their work. But the theory made little sense. The "burglars" sounded like a sophisticated crew, but the Swifts hardly seemed wealthy enough to attract them.

Plus, what self-respecting professional burglars would break into a house when they knew there were four people inside? Far less risky to wait until the house was empty.

It was hard to see the murders as anything other than a premeditated slaughter of a family of Descendants perpetrated by the Olympians.

Joseph seemed to drop off the face of the Earth after the murders, which I supposed was why the Olympians wanted my help to find him. I tried locating other members of his extended family, thinking maybe he'd gone to live with them, but not only did I not find any sign of him, I found even more evidence that pointed to a purge. I couldn't find evidence of a single surviving family member on his father's side. There was one maternal aunt who survived until 1963, when she died of natural causes, and a couple of distant cousins—also on his mother's side—who seemed to have lived—or still be living—long and ordinary lives. But the more I delved into his father's family, the more unexplained deaths I discovered. Car accidents. House fires. Mysterious disappearances. Everything led me to the conclusion that Joseph's divine blood had come through his father's side, and that the Olympians had managed to eliminate them all one by one.

I never got around to doing any serious research on Swift's current location, because I'd already learned everything I wanted to know. There was not a single doubt left in my mind: if I located Joseph Swift, he was a dead man. And if he had any children, they, too, would either die or be kidnapped and indoctrinated by the Olympians.

I couldn't do it. Not even to save Steph. And as horrible as Konstantin's threat had been, I knew my sister well enough to be certain she'd agree with my decision. I was just going to have to find some other way to protect her. Reluctant as I was to admit it, that meant I was going to need help. And there was only one person I could go to for said help.

Perhaps I was digging the hole deeper, both for myself and for Steph. Perhaps Anderson was just as cruel and ruthless as Konstantin. But there was only one way to find out.

It was almost five before I found the nerve to pick up the phone and call Anderson. I couldn't help remembering all the hostility he and Blake and Jamaal had shown me on the other night, and the idea of placing myself at their mercy made me want to hide under the bed. But honestly, I could see no other option, aside from giving up my entire life and making myself disappear, which still wouldn't guarantee Steph's safety. It was possible that by calling Anderson, I was handing myself over to the enemy. It was also possible that I'd already soured any potential we'd ever had of working together. But I had to try.

My heart raced and my palms sweated as I waited for Anderson to answer. Was this my gut trying to warn me away? Or was it just a very natural fear reaction, after all I'd gone through in the past forty-eight hours? I couldn't tell.

Anderson finally picked up the phone just when I thought sure my call was about to go to voice mail.

"Nikki," he said by way of greeting. Guess he had caller ID. "What a pleasant surprise." There was a dry humor to his voice, but no hint of irritation. I chose to take that as a good sign. "To what do I owe the pleasure?"

I'd debated how much to tell him about my current situation, but decided that full disclosure might be my best shot at getting the help I needed. "I met Konstantin today."

He grunted softly. "My condolences."

I surprised myself by smiling. "Yeah. I'm not a big fan."

"Neither am I."

"So I gathered."

"Let me guess what he wanted: he's asked you to use your unique abilities to find some people for him."

Not that impressive a guess, considering he'd pretty much predicted it earlier. "There wasn't really any asking involved."

Anderson sighed. "No, of course not. Konstantin considers his desires to be everyone else's commands. Is he still trying to court you, or has he begun making threats yet?"

"I wouldn't even have met with him today if there hadn't been a threat involved." My heart constricted with fear for Steph. "He's threatened to let Alexis . . . hurt my sister if I don't do what he wants."

Anderson hesitated a moment before answering. "I didn't know you had a sister," he said. "If she's still alive, it's only because Konstantin thinks he can use her to control you for the time being. He won't allow another Descendant—even a Descendant of Artemis—to survive when he can harvest her immortality for one of his pets. He won't destroy you as long as you're useful, but your sister . . ."

"Steph and I aren't related by blood," I clarified. "I'm adopted."

"Ah. Good. Otherwise, all your family members would be in danger."

Yeah, I'd already figured that out. But if Konstantin was going to use Steph against me, I had no doubt that he'd be just as happy to threaten my adoptive parents if he thought that might make me more pliable. I could only thank my lucky stars that they were out of the country and out of his reach, at least for now.

"If I do what Konstantin wants, he's going to kill anyone I track down for him. Right?"

"Yes. He always makes his purges of Descendant families as thorough as possible, but sometimes people slip through his fingers. I suspect he's worked up detailed genealogies of all the families he's ever identified and has extensive lists of people he'd like to locate."

"He gave me a list of three."

"Trust me, that's not even the tip of the iceberg. He'd rather present you with a short list and try to lull you into a sense of complacency than let you know that once he's got the leverage he needs, he'll set you to tracking down hundreds of people for him to kill."

I winced. "Hundreds?"

"At least. The Olympians have been around a long time. Konstantin has been their leader since the early fifteenth century."

I felt momentarily dizzy at the concept. I was finally getting around to accepting that the *Liberi* were immortal, but it was still hard to absorb the idea that I'd talked to a man who'd been alive since before Columbus discovered America.

"He was bent on destroying Descendants even then, though of course it was a lot harder before the days of modern transportation and computerized records. But just think—if he missed a family member in one of those Descendant purges back in the fifteenth century, how many Descendants might that person have running around today?"

I saw his point. And I once again saw that I couldn't do what Konstantin ordered, no matter what the risk. I blew out a frustrated breath. "Listen, I need your help."

"Oh, do you now?" he responded, and there was no missing the calculation in his voice.

"You keep trying to convince me you're one of the good guys," I forged on. "If that's the truth, then you won't let Konstantin and Alexis hurt an innocent woman, right?"

He thought about that a long while before he answered. "I hate to sound like a mercenary. But I can't forget you're the woman who killed Emmitt and shot Blake. I'm not a hundred percent sure that *you're* one of the good guys. I'm sure your sister is a lovely woman, and she doesn't deserve whatever Konstantin has threatened. But why should I stick my neck out for her when you've been so terribly . . . disobliging?"

"Because it's the right thing to do." I swallowed the lump of anger that rose in my throat. He had a point, and I knew it. He wasn't even fully convinced I hadn't killed Emmitt on purpose, so there wasn't any particular reason for him to feel kindly toward me. That didn't mean I had to admit it.

"I'm sure that's very clear-cut from where you're standing, but from where I'm standing . . . not so much."

"So that's it? I didn't fall at your feet and adore you after you threatened to torture me, and therefore to hell with me? And to hell with Steph? If that's the way you feel, then why the hell have you called me about a billion times?"

"I didn't say to hell with you," Anderson responded quietly, his calm making me feel like a child throwing a tantrum. "I was explaining why I'm not going to help your sister unless you give me something in return."

I guess it had been foolish of me to hope that Anderson would help me out of the goodness of his heart. It sucked that I wasn't in a position to tell him where to shove it.

"What do you want?" I asked through gritted teeth.

"I want you to find someone for me as well, but I promise it's not for nefarious purposes."

Too bad I didn't have a clue what Anderson's

promises were worth. But I also didn't have a whole lot of options.

"Who?" I asked, trying not to sound as wary as I felt. "And why? And please don't give me the runaround the way Konstantin did."

"I won't. But it's rather a long story. Perhaps you should come to the house so we can talk in person. I'll make dinner, and we can have a civilized conversation."

"We can have a civilized conversation anywhere," I countered, not at all anxious to set foot in the mansion again. The place didn't exactly fill me with warm, fuzzy memories. "If you want to make it a dinner meeting, choose a restaurant."

He hesitated a moment before answering. "If we come to an agreement and I am to protect your sister, then you will have to come live here. My . . . arrangement with Konstantin is that he will not harm those who live under my roof or the families of those who live under my roof. It's not a perfect arrangement, and he wouldn't hesitate to break it if he thought he could get away with it, but it would provide your sister a great deal of protection."

As usual anytime I had a conversation with one of the *Liberi,* I had about a million questions. However, they were all drowned out by my outrage.

"You want me to come *live* with you?" I cried. "Are you crazy?"

"Perhaps so," he said drily. "Offering you my protection won't be my most popular decision ever, but this is my house, and my rules.

"At least come have dinner with me. I promise you'll have safe passage, even if you and I can't agree on a single thing."

I shook my head, though of course he couldn't see. "Why should I believe you won't just shove me back in that basement jail of yours the minute I show my face?"

"You're asking for my help. What good is that if you trust me so little?"

Reality check time. I couldn't protect Steph on my own. Sure, I could warn her that my problem-client had threatened her, and she could hire some security. But I couldn't warn her without having to give her an explanation of the threat. If I told her the truth, she'd never believe me. If I made up an explanation that left out all the supernatural stuff, she'd insist we call the police. And even if I thought of a way to overcome those obstacles, who was to say human security would be able to protect her? I had no idea what Konstantin and the rest of the Olympians were capable of.

But Anderson did.

"All right," I said reluctantly. "I'll come to the house. But you'd better guarantee you won't let Blake or Jamaal near me. I catch sight of either one of them, and all bets are off. Got it?"

It was an empty threat, of course. We'd already established that I needed Anderson's help, which left me very little bargaining power. But Anderson didn't press the issue.

"I'll make sure you don't run into them," he promised.

That didn't make me feel a whole lot better. Anderson might be the leader of his people, but they hadn't so far shown themselves to be the most obedient lot.

"Would seven o'clock work for you?" Anderson asked. "Or do you need more time?"

The sooner we got this over with, the better. "I'll be there at seven."

"I look forward to it."

Too bad I didn't share the sentiment.

ELEVEN

Having been suddenly turned into an immortal caught between two warring factions of the *Liberi Deorum,* I hadn't exactly had time to deal with the mundane challenges presented by having my car totaled. I had a suspicion that wasn't going to be changing anytime soon. My car had been towed, but I had no idea where or by whom, nor did I know how Anderson had explained the accident. He'd have had to offer *some* explanation, right? I mean, there was blood all over the place—both mine and Emmitt's—and I didn't imagine a wrecker service would haul the car away without any questions being asked.

If I thought there were any chance of going through legal channels peacefully, I'd have called my insurance company about the accident. They might even have reimbursed me for car rental. As it was, I decided that at least for now, I would ignore the whole problem. I rented a shiny new silver Taurus, then drove out to Anderson's mansion in Arlington.

Renting the car had taken less time than I'd thought, so I was a little early. The warmer weather of the last couple of days had melted all the ice, but I couldn't help the chill that ran down my spine when I caught sight of the iron gates at the head of the driveway. A big part of me longed to turn the car around and just go home. Pretend none of this had happened. Pretend Steph wasn't in danger, and I was just an ordinary woman.

Shoving down my disquiet, I lowered my window and hit the button on the intercom outside the gates. I wasn't sure what to say, but apparently silence was good enough. Moments after I hit the button, there was a faint buzzing noise, and the gates parted. I dried my sweaty palms on my pants legs as I waited for the opening to be large enough to drive through.

The visibility was a lot better today than it had been the last time I'd navigated the twisting driveway that led to the house. Even so, I drove like a nearsighted granny, my hands clutching the steering wheel way too tightly. My heart rate jacked up as I fought against the memory of driving through the sleet. When I rounded the final curve and hit the straightaway, I slowed to a crawl.

Everything had happened so fast the other night that I couldn't really say where the exact spot was that Emmitt had suddenly appeared in the middle of the road, nor where his body had lain when I'd crawled out of my car. My headlights illuminated gouges in a couple of trees beside the road—the trees that I'd plowed into. My stomach lurched, and for a moment, it as was if I were living at both times simultaneously. I could have sworn I smelled blood and scorched rubber.

I brought the car to a complete stop, then lowered my head to the steering wheel and closed my eyes, forcing myself to take slow, deep breaths. My head was spinning and my skin was clammy with sweat. I wondered if I was having a real live panic attack. Obviously, I had yet to deal with the horror of that night, and I wished I could have told Steph about it. She wouldn't have been able to say magic words to make it all better, but just the act of talking might have eased some of the pressure inside me.

After a while, my heart rate slowed to something just a little faster than normal, and I no longer felt like I might pass out behind the wheel. Cautiously, I raised my head, half-expecting to find sleet clattering against the windshield. But no, the sky was clear. The past was back in the past where it belonged, at least for now.

Blowing out a deep breath, I put the car in drive again and proceeded to the house. I parked in a circular drive that surrounded a decorative fountain, then got out of the car, my legs still a little shaky from my brush with panic.

As I've mentioned, the house was easily big enough to be termed a mansion, and I wouldn't have been surprised if it turned out to be a renovated pre-Civil War plantation. The front door was framed by a series of columns and featured a porch that was bigger than some houses I'd lived in. A cluster of elegant outdoor furniture formed an almost cozy seating area on one half of the porch. The other half featured a whitewashed swing and several dozen potted plants, all of hearty varieties that could survive a Virginia winter outdoors.

Anderson was waiting for me on that swing, one leg curled under him, while his other foot pushed on the porch floor just enough to create a little motion. He was dressed in a pair of faded denim jeans and a navy blue sweatshirt, his feet tucked into sneakers that had seen better days. The casual, comfortable outfit seemed almost out of place with the majestic mansion in the background.

Moving slowly, as if trying not to alarm me, Anderson rose to his feet. I had to admit, I felt extremely wary. If he'd made anything I could have interpreted as a hostile move, I'd have been running for my car in a heartbeat. But he kept his distance, and even stuffed his hands in his pockets for good measure.

"What happened out there?" he asked, jerking his chin toward the driveway.

I felt the blood rush to my face as I realized he'd been sitting here watching while I had my little panic attack. If I wanted Anderson to think of me as a tough chick he didn't want to mess with, I wasn't exactly going about it the best way.

I licked my lips, then regretted the nervous gesture. "I couldn't help . . . remembering," I said, because I had to say something.

Maybe I was just seeing what I wanted to see, but I thought there was a softening in Anderson's expression. "Why don't you come inside," he beckoned, heading toward the door. "It's a little chilly out here."

At that point, I was eager to comply. If I was inside the house, I wouldn't be able to see the spot where I had killed Emmitt, and maybe I'd be able to keep the memory at a more comfortable distance. I forgot to be wary as I hurried to cross the threshold while Anderson held the door open. Luckily, there was no mob of angry *Liberi* waiting to jump me, or I'd have blundered into them blindly without even a hint of a fight.

The foyer was everything you would expect in an enormous mansion. The floor was of intricately patterned green marble, and the walls were decorated by oil paintings that might well have been the work of grand masters—I'm not enough of an art aficionado to tell an imitation from the real thing. There was even a crystal chandelier that looked like something right out of *Phantom of the Opera*.

If Anderson took any particular pride in the grandeur of his home, he didn't show it. He barely seemed to glance at the house, or notice my reaction to it, as he led me through room after elegant room until we came to a huge state-of-the-art kitchen.

The rooms we had passed through on the way to the kitchen had all been pristine and formal, almost like they were more for show than for actual living. The kitchen was a different story. It was as large and well-appointed as any other room I'd seen, but there was no missing the signs of habitation. A couple of dirty cups in the sink. Some crumbs on the counter near the toaster. A walk-in pantry crammed with a disorganized array of boxes and cans and bags.

The air was rich with the smell of spices, and I saw a huge vat of something simmering on the stove. I couldn't be certain, but it smelled a lot like chili. My stomach grumbled its approval, and my mouth started watering. Who'd have thought the leader of a group of such powerful immortals would cook chili for dinner, just like an ordinary single guy? I bet neither Konstantin nor Alexis had ever let such peasant food cross their lips.

At one end of the kitchen, there was a breakfast nook, surrounded on three sides by windows looking out onto the back lawn. A butcher block table occupied the nook; Anderson had laid out a couple of place settings there. An open bottle of wine breathed in the center of the table.

"Please, have a seat," Anderson said.

I was strangely glad he didn't try to pull out my chair for me. Both Konstantin and Alexis were such stuffed shirts I couldn't help appreciating Anderson's more casual manners. I sat down while Anderson gave the pot on the stove a stir.

"I hope you like chili," he said. "It's about the only thing I can cook that anyone other than me would willingly put in their mouths." He shot me a self-deprecating smile over his shoulder.

"Chili's great," I assured him. "Can I help with

something?" I asked, belatedly remembering my manners. Then I was surprised at myself for asking. Ever since I'd first met him, I'd been considering Anderson an enemy, or at the very least an antagonist, but over the course of just a few minutes, I seemed to have dropped my guard entirely.

"No, no," he answered. "One of the advantages of chili is that all I have to do is scoop it into a bowl. Strictly a one-person job."

He got a couple of bowls out of one of the cabinets and generously ladled in the chili. Then he reached into the oven and pulled out a foil-wrapped bundle, which turned out to be cornbread. He put the bowls and cornbread on a couple of plates, then carried them into the nook and set them down. The chili smelled heavenly.

"Don't worry," Anderson said, one side of his mouth curling up in another of his wry smiles. "I didn't cook the cornbread, so it's safe to eat."

The meal was surprisingly pleasant. We didn't talk about the Olympians or Emmitt's death or what either faction wanted from me. Instead, we talked about the kind of trivialities that almost reminded me of the getting-to-know-you part of a first date. We learned we were both Redskins fans, and I was appropriately jealous to discover he had season tickets. He had typically male tastes in movies—action flicks good, anything remotely mushy bad—but showed no hint of the veiled sexism I'd seen in Alexis and Konstantin. He didn't even make a face when I admitted I liked romance novels. And, unlike Jim, the Date from Hell,

Anderson showed interest in what I was saying and didn't try the steer to conversation toward himself.

If it really *had* been a first date, and nothing had come before, I'd have said I had a good time. Too bad it wasn't a first date.

Observing Anderson's "cult" in the days before I'd joined the ranks of the *Liberi,* I'd noted that although he served as their leader, Anderson had a remarkably laid-back manner. That manner was very much in evidence tonight. I kept reminding myself that Anderson was dangerous and not to be trusted. I even forcibly reminded myself of the way he'd hurt Jamaal, and the way he'd threatened to hurt me. But it was hard to reconcile that memory with the man who sat across the table from me, chatting amiably and smiling easily.

I stuffed myself on chili and cornbread, both of which were blazing hot. I was half-expecting it from the chili, but the cornbread took me by surprise, since I didn't see the jalapeños until I'd shoved a big hunk in my mouth. Good thing I like spicy food, though I'd have preferred to wash it down with a cold beer rather than room temperature red wine. I'm pretty sure the wine was good stuff, but my taste buds were burning too much to notice.

When I could eat no more, Anderson made a pot of after-dinner coffee, which he served with a generous splash of Bailey's. When he returned to the table, I could tell by the serious look on his face that social hour was over, and we were about to get down to business. The strength of my regret surprised me.

Being in no hurry to put an end to the festivities, I sipped my coffee in silence, waiting for Anderson to begin. I didn't have to wait long.

"Your sister and anyone else you care about is going to be in some amount of danger, no matter what you do," he started, and the baldness of his statement made me wince. There was sympathy in his voice, but he made no particular attempt to soften the blow. "I figure it does neither of us any good if I make promises I can't keep."

At least he was honest about it. "So if you can't protect Steph, what's the point of me coming here?"

"I'm not saying I can't protect her. I'm just saying that even if I do, there will always be some danger. Konstantin and I have agreed to tolerate each other for the sake of expediency, but if at any time he should decide our truce is more trouble than it's worth, he could break it. That's a reality all of us in this house have to live with. We don't have any Descendants at our beck and call, which means we can't kill Konstantin or any of his people. If he decides to break his truce with us, he'll do it by having his pet Descendants attack us, and even if we win the battle, it's likely some of us will die—and increase the Olympians' strength by doing so."

I frowned as I thought this over. "Then why did he agree to a truce with you in the first place?"

Anderson smiled, and in his eyes I saw a flash of the ruthlessness that was usually well hidden beneath his friendly demeanor. "Consider that a trade secret."

I decided not to press. "Okay. So you have a shaky

truce with the Olympians, but you're not confident enough in it to promise you can keep Steph safe."

"That's it in a nutshell. But I *can* promise to keep her a whole lot safer than she is right now. Even if you agree to hunt the people on the list Konstantin gave you, that won't guarantee her safety. If you ever balk at anything he commands you to do, he'll trot the threat out again. I can't imagine you could have spoken to him for more than five minutes and not know I'm telling the truth about this."

Unfortunately, he was right. Konstantin had tried to make it sound like we could be best buds if only I'd do this one little thing for him. But I knew a bully when I saw one, and I knew Konstantin was the kind of guy who'd enjoy flexing his muscles on a regular basis.

I had to suppress a shudder at the thought of Steph being subjected to Konstantin's malice. There were times I couldn't help being jealous of my sister's relatively easy life. She'd been born beautiful and personable, to a wealthy family who doted on her. Sure, she'd had her share of heartbreaks, just like any normal person, but nothing really *bad* had ever happened to her. She'd never been abandoned by her mother, or been passed from foster home to foster home, or been threatened with juvie.

The downside to this gilded life was that she'd never had to develop the kind of armor I had. There's a difference between knowing that there's ugliness in this world and being subjected to that ugliness yourself. My early life had inoculated me against some of the worst the world had to offer. I was reeling under the stress of what had happened to me the other night, but I was at least *coping* with it. Steph wouldn't have those kinds of coping skills. Even a small dose of violence would be a terrible shock to her system. I feared that if Alexis got his hands on her, he wouldn't have to work very hard to break her.

"The best thing you can do for your sister," Anderson said softly, "is to ally with me. I'm not a tyrant like Konstantin, and my people do what we can to make the world a better place."

I pushed my fears for Steph to the side and met Anderson's eyes. Maybe it was just my imagination, but I thought I saw something warm and wise in those medium brown eyes of his. Eyes I'd once dismissed as ordinary.

But as friendly and non-threatening as he was being now, I'd seen another side of him that first night. I wanted to trust him, if only because it would make my own life so much easier, but I couldn't allow myself to forget how little I knew about him.

"So that Hand of Doom thing you did to Jamaal isn't something you consider tyrannical?" I challenged, watching his face carefully in hopes his expression would reveal more of his hidden depths. No such luck.

"Hand of Doom?" he asked with a little smile. "I've never heard it called that before."

"You think it's funny?"

His smile faded, replaced by an almost sad expression. "No. No, it's not funny at all." He sighed and reached for his cup of coffee, which was almost empty. I think he was just stalling for time as he tipped the last few drops into his mouth.

"I suppose I have my own tyrannical moments," he admitted, staring into his empty cup. He seemed to catch himself doing it, then carefully placed the cup on the table and looked at me once more. "Gentle rebukes don't have much of an effect on most *Liberi,* especially not on someone like Jamaal. I know you've seen no evidence to support this, but he's a good man at heart. He *wants* to control his dark side, but he isn't always able to, especially without Emmitt to help him. When he loses control, there have to be consequences."

"So that was special treatment you reserve just for Jamaal?" Instinct told me the answer was no.

"I don't run around hurting my people on a regular basis, if that's what you're asking. But I am their leader, and I do expect them to obey me when I make a direct order." He leaned forward, his expression intense. "Understand this, Nikki: you're very new to being *Liberi,* but the rest of my people are not. Being immortal and having supernatural powers will change you over time, will corrupt you, if you let it. If I let my people get away with defying me, then I risk losing them. Not right away, but over time, as they find they can do anything they want without suffering any consequences, year after year after year. I've seen it happen too many times, and so have my people. They're with me because they don't want to go down that road, and they believe I can keep it from happening."

"And what's to keep *you* from going down that road? Or do you punish yourself when you've been a bad boy?"

I thought my sarcastic question might piss him off, but Anderson just smiled. "There are some checks and balances in place."

Not the most specific answer in the world, but it was apparently all I was going to get.

"All right. Let's say I accept that you're not a tyrant and that becoming your ally is the best way to protect my family. What would I have to do to join up?"

"First, you would have to move into the house, because those are the terms of my agreement with Konstantin. Any *Liberi* who lives in this house is considered to be one of mine."

I had no intention of moving into the mansion permanently. I loved my condo, and there was no way I was giving it up. I also loved my freedom, and sharing communal quarters with Anderson and his flock of *Liberi* would be like living in a barracks. A luxurious, beautiful barracks, but a barracks all the same.

However, I'd already established that I needed Anderson's help, and if temporarily moving into the mansion was what I had to do to get it, then I was going to have to suck it up, at least for a while. I'd just have to consider it as an indefinite hotel stay.

Unfortunately, Anderson had already let me know there was another condition I had to meet to earn his help.

"And second," I continued for him, "there's

someone you want me to find for you. Who? And why?"

The corners of his eyes tightened with what looked like pain. "Her name is Emma Poindexter," he said. He swallowed hard, then took a deep breath and let it out slowly. "She's been missing for almost ten years. And I want you to find her because she's my wife."

TWELVE

I sat in stunned silence at Anderson's kitchen table. I don't know why I was so surprised. He might not be drop-dead gorgeous, but Anderson was certainly attractive enough, and he obviously had money and power. Why would I assume a man like him was single? Especially when he was most likely centuries old?

"Your wife," I repeated when I could find my voice. I glanced at his left hand, but there was no ring on his finger. At least I hadn't missed so obvious a clue as that.

He nodded. "She's a *Liberi,* descended of Nyx—the Greek goddess of night." He shifted in his seat, no longer meeting my eyes. "Konstantin and I may not be at open war with each other now, but that wasn't always the case. Konstantin hates me more than words can express for challenging his 'rule.' So to punish me for luring some of his Olympians out of the fold, he kidnapped Emma."

Anderson closed his eyes. His fists were clenched in his lap, his shoulders tight with strain. I felt a very feminine urge to comfort him, but I managed to stifle it. I didn't know him well enough to offer comfort.

When he opened his eyes, there was a hint of red around the edges, like he'd been crying, although I saw no evidence of tears. "He claims he interred her. Buried her alive."

I couldn't help the little gasp that escaped me. "But she's *Liberi* . . ." I whispered.

"Yes. She's *Liberi*. If he's telling the truth, if he didn't just have one of his pet Descendants kill her, then she's been in the ground, unable to escape even through death, for almost ten years."

He blinked rapidly, as if trying to stave off tears. His voice was steadier when he resumed, but there was a faint, husky tone to it. "You see, Nikki, I know what it's like to have someone you love used as a weapon against you. I'll do everything in my power to help you protect your family if you will do everything in *your* power to help me find Emma."

In all honesty, it's a case I might well have taken on without any need for threat or ultimatum. How could I not take pity on someone who'd suffered so horribly? Even if Emma was a raving bitch, I'd have felt sorry for her, but since I didn't know her it was even easier to picture her as the innocent victim of an evil, vindictive bastard.

As a P.I., I'd always specialized in locates and skip traces—basically, finding people who didn't want to be found. But this wasn't going to be a typical locate.

None of the tools I used to find missing persons—things like online searches and interviews with people who might have heard from her—was going to help me find someone who was buried, and had been in the ground for almost ten years. Everyone seemed to assume I had some kind of supernatural hunting powers, but other than my sudden improvement in marksmanship, I'd seen no sign of them.

"Will you help me, Nikki?" Anderson asked, and the plea in his voice made something in my chest hurt. I wasn't trusting enough to believe everything he'd said, and I had the distinct impression there were plenty of things he'd left out of the story, but I *did* believe he was hurting. A lot.

"Yes," I said, because what else could I possibly answer? Even if I didn't need his help myself, I doubt I could have resisted that plea. Never mind that I hadn't the faintest idea how I could actually go about helping him. "If you'll help me protect my family, I'll do everything I can to help find Emma."

"Thank you," he said, then heaved a big sigh. "I've been without hope for so long I'd forgotten what it feels like."

The knot in my chest tightened. I hated to get his hopes up when the chances that I could find Emma seemed so slim.

Anderson smiled wanly. "Don't worry. Unlike Konstantin, I am not prone to unrealistic expectations. I know there's a chance he's lying to me and she's been dead all along. I also know there's a chance even *your* skills won't prove equal to finding her, and that even if we find her, she may be irreparably damaged by what she's been through."

Anderson shook off some of his sadness. He sat up straighter in his chair, and his hands finally relaxed in his lap. I wondered if he'd been clenching them hard enough to leave nail marks on his palms.

"You'll need to move in as soon as possible," he said. "If Konstantin finds out you and I have reached an agreement before you're actually under my roof, he'll declare open season on you."

I was in no hurry to install myself in the mansion, and I didn't like the sense that Anderson was trying to rush me. However, the idea of spending another night in the hotel didn't have much appeal, either, and I still wouldn't feel safe going home. I had to stay *somewhere* tonight. Besides, I reminded myself, I was planning to consider this mansion an ultra-luxurious hotel. A stopgap measure until I could figure out a better way to protect Steph.

"I'm ready whenever you are."

He nodded briskly. "Good. I'll open up one of the spare bedrooms for you."

"Thanks. What about Jamaal? And Blake?"

He raised an eyebrow. "What about them?" I would have thought he was playing stupid, except he looked genuinely puzzled by my question.

"You might have noticed they don't like me much. How are they going to feel if I move in under your roof?"

Anderson shrugged. "Their feelings about it don't enter into the equation. This is *my* house, and I can invite whomever I please." He seemed to notice the severity in his voice and flashed me a rueful smile. "There I go being tyrannical again, huh?"

I smiled back. "I wasn't going to say it."

He acknowledged that with a nod. "Blake might not like it, but he'll understand. Jamaal will need some careful handling, but I'll have a long talk with him while you're gone. I'll make it very clear that he's to play nice with you."

"Even though he still thinks I killed Emmitt on purpose?"

Anderson's brow furrowed. "I have to wonder if he really believes that. It would be awfully hard for a Descendant not affiliated with the Olympians to find out we existed at all, much less understand her own heritage and our vulnerability, then arrange to kill one of us."

"Who said she's not affiliated with the Olympians?" a voice asked from the hall just outside the kitchen, and we both jumped a little.

The adrenaline kept pumping as I turned to watch Jamaal walk casually into the kitchen. He was looking much more sane today. There was still an unmistakable spark of anger in his eyes, but he no longer looked crazed by it. That didn't make him any less lethal.

On the scale of male beauty as judged by Nikki Glass, Jamaal was the most gorgeous of all the *Liberi* I'd met. Tall and broad-shouldered, he had the build and the grace of an athlete. He wore his hair in shoulder-length beaded braids, the braids following the contours of his elegantly shaped skull up to about his ears. High cheekbones, luxuriously long eyelashes, and full, sensual lips made his face into a work of art. I'd never seen him smile, but I suspected the effect would be devastating.

Of course, I'd have found him a lot more attractive if he weren't looking at me with such loathing. At least he wasn't charging at me with murder in his eyes.

Anderson pushed his chair back from the table, watching Jamaal carefully although he didn't get up.

"I thought I made it clear that I wasn't to be disturbed," he said, and though his voice was mild, there was a threat implied in his words.

Jamaal didn't come any closer, but he didn't go away, either. "Sounded to me like you were wrapping up."

"Eavesdropping?" Anderson asked with a quirk of his eyebrow. "You've been hanging around Jack too long."

Jamaal grimaced in distaste. "Low blow, boss."

I gathered that Jamaal and Jack weren't great friends, which I supposed made sense. Jack was a trickster, and I'd seen no evidence to date that Jamaal even knew what a sense of humor was.

"I call 'em like I see 'em," was Anderson's unrepentant reply. "How long have you been listening?"

Jamaal hunched his shoulders like a little kid getting scolded by his dad. "Long enough to think it was time to let you know I was here. Sorry." He flicked a glance at me, his expression no warmer than it had ever been when he looked at me. "My question stands: who says she's not working for the Olympians? Wouldn't Konstantin just laugh his ass off if we accepted his murdering little spy into our house with open arms!"

"If I had my choice," I said before Anderson could answer, "I'd have nothing to do with any of you. I want my life back."

"So you say," Jamaal countered. "But talk is cheap."

"Children . . ." Anderson chided, making a long-suffering face. I chose not to respond to Jamaal's jibe, and he subsided. Anderson nodded his approval.

"If it turns out she's a spy working for Konstantin," Anderson said, "we'll deal with it when we have proof." The look he shot me then spoke volumes about just how he would "deal with it." He might be giving me the benefit of the doubt, but he wasn't wholly convinced of my innocence.

I was too stubborn to drop my gaze, though it was hard to look into his eyes when his expression was so forbidding. Apparently satisfied with what he saw, he turned to Jamaal.

"I need you to prove to me that you can keep it together without Emmitt around to balance your temper. Nikki is now under my protection, and I won't have her being threatened or harassed by one of my own people."

Jamaal's chin jutted out stubbornly, and the look in his eyes was downright mutinous, though he didn't argue. At least not out loud. Anderson apparently read his expression the same way I did.

"I don't want to lose you," he said, "but you have no place under this roof if you can't accept my authority."

I squirmed and wished I could be anywhere else but here. The sudden pain on Jamaal's face was too much to bear. He was still grieving for his friend, still furious at me, and Anderson had just delivered a threat that caused a soul-deep hurt.

I didn't like Jamaal, of course. But I *could* empathize with him. I wasn't sure what the relationship had been between him and Emmitt— had they been more than friends?—but the pain of that loss was obviously agonizing. I knew what it was like to act out when in pain. I'd spent years doing it after my mother abandoned me. I suspected Jamaal was feeling abandoned himself right now, and to have Anderson threaten to kick him out for my sake must have been like a dagger to his heart.

"So," Anderson prompted when Jamaal just stood there looking devastated, "are you going to accept Nikki's right to stay in my house? Or are we going to have a problem?"

Jamaal shot me a look of pure loathing. "There's no problem," he replied. "As long as you don't expect me to *like* it, I can accept her presence."

Internally, I groaned. I was supposed to stay in the same house with this guy? That meant I'd probably have to come face to face with him on a regular basis, which seemed like a recipe for disaster.

But I was only going to move in for a little while, I told myself. Just until I could figure out some other way to protect Steph. If putting up with Jamaal and his hostility was the price I had to pay for her safety, then I was ready to pay it.

But I had a sneaking suspicion matters were not settled between Jamaal and me, no matter what Anderson had ordered, or what Jamaal had grudgingly promised.

THIRTEEN

After dinner, I went back to my hotel and packed up my meager belongings. I hadn't brought a whole lot of stuff, but I was reluctant to go home and pack a bigger suitcase. It wouldn't surprise me if Konstantin was having my place watched, and I wasn't foolish enough to ignore Anderson's warnings. I needed to establish myself as being under Anderson's protection before I ran into Konstantin or Alexis again. Anderson had promised to call Konstantin and "register" me as being under his protection as soon as I arrived back at the mansion.

I called Steph before I left and let her know I wasn't going to be at my home number for at least a few days. Naturally, she tried to wring details out of me, but there were none I could give her. I just told her the same thing I'd told her at dinner last night, that a disgruntled wannabe client was giving me trouble. She was far from satisfied, but she let the subject drop, for which I was profoundly grateful.

It was almost eleven o'clock by the time I pulled up in front of the gates of the mansion again. Fate decided to screw with my head and dumped a bunch of unexpected rain on Arlington the moment the gates opened to admit me. My hands squeezed tight on the steering wheel, and I swallowed a lump of dread that formed in my throat. I did *not* want a repeat of the evening's near panic attack. I sucked in a deep breath and hit the gas, concentrating hard to keep any potential flashbacks at bay.

When I parked once again on the circular drive, I was pleasantly surprised to find Maggie waiting for me under the shelter of the porch roof. She was by far the nicest of the *Liberi* I'd met so far, and I couldn't help liking her. The rain pounded down relentlessly as I got out of the car and popped the trunk. It wasn't terribly cold out, but the rain came with a generous dose of wind, and I wished I'd worn a heavier coat.

Maggie could have stayed safely under the porch roof and kept dry, but instead she beat me to the trunk and was lifting my suitcase out before I could get to it. The suitcase wasn't particularly heavy, being a small roll-aboard and only lightly packed, but I was still surprised by how easily Maggie plucked it out of the trunk and scampered up the front steps with it.

I slammed the trunk shut and hurried to follow, eager to be out of the rain. When I caught up with Maggie on the porch, I reached for my bag.

"Let me take that," I said. "You don't have to carry my bag for me."

She grinned at me. "Anderson's got you on the

third floor. Trust me, you don't want to haul your suitcase all the way up there."

I put my hand on the handle of the suitcase and gave a gentle tug, but she didn't let go. I rolled my eyes. "Come on, I'm supposed to be living here now, right? So it's not like I'm a guest and you have to carry my bag."

"You don't understand," Maggie said, still grinning at me, a cheerful twinkle in her eye. She twisted the suitcase's handle out of my grip, then lifted it one-handed over her head like it weighed no more than an empty grocery sack. "I'm descended from Zeus, through Heracles. I don't have any storm magic, but I am seriously strong." Yes, I could see that. "I even carry things for the guys sometimes, though it offends their masculine sensibilities so much it's an argument every time."

She said it lightly, and there was no change in her expression I could put my finger on, but I got the feeling that it bugged her. I guess it had to be kind of tough to be a strong woman in a household full of supernatural alpha males, most, if not all, of whom had been born in times when society accepted it as fact that women were lesser beings.

I followed Maggie up the grand front staircase, which featured a remarkably genuine-looking reproduction of Winged Victory on the landing, making me feel like I had been magically transported to a museum. When we reached the second floor, Maggie gestured with her free hand toward the long hall leading to the right.

"That's the east wing, which is Anderson's. The first door on the left is his study, and you can go in there whenever you want as long as the door is open. If the door is closed, knock first or he'll get cranky. The rest of the wing is off-limits unless you're invited or unless there's an emergency."

This information naturally set my suspicious mind to wondering what Anderson might be hiding in the east wing, but maybe I'd just seen *Beauty and the Beast* too many times. It was, as he had pointed out, his house, and it was only fair that he have his own private space within it, even if he was living with a bunch of other *Liberi*.

"The west wing is where Jamaal, Blake, and Logan's apartments are," Maggie continued, gesturing to the left and then starting up the next set of stairs. "Jack, Leo, and I all have rooms on the third floor."

"I haven't met Leo yet," I said. I was beginning to think he was a bit of a recluse, because even when I'd been in the process of investigating Emmitt's so-called "cult," I'd rarely caught sight of him.

"He's not very sociable," Maggie responded. "He's a descendant of Hermes, who was a god of commerce. If we didn't remind him to eat and sleep every once in a while, he'd spend every second of every day sitting at his computer scrutinizing the market. We tease him about it, but the kind of money he brings in makes it possible for us to do a lot of good. And live well ourselves, while we're at it."

"Who's Anderson descended from?" I asked. "You've told me everyone else's ancestor, but not his."

"That's because I don't know. He's very mysterious about it. No one recognizes his glyph, and he's not saying."

"Any idea why not?"

"Nope," Maggie replied cheerfully. "But if you want to see if you can pry the secret out of him, have at it."

My only response was a soft snort. If Anderson wasn't going to tell his closest friends, I was damn sure he wouldn't tell me, so there was no point in even asking.

We'd finally reached the third floor, and Maggie led me down another long hallway. Even with eight or nine people living in the mansion, there were plenty of rooms to spare. Dust covers draped the furniture in many of the upstairs rooms.

The "guest room" Anderson had assigned me was actually a generous suite, with a huge bedroom, a luxurious bathroom, and a cozy sitting room, complete with a rectangular table against one wall that could serve as either a desk or a dining table. It was a hell of a lot nicer and more comfortable than my hotel had been.

"Do you want to take some time to unpack and freshen up?" Maggie asked. "Or would you rather have the grand tour first?"

I stifled a yawn. I hadn't had a good night's sleep in what felt like forever, and the king-sized four-poster in the bedroom was calling to me. However, I doubted I could sleep comfortably without thoroughly examining my surroundings first.

"Let's do the grand tour," I said. "I'm going to crash if I hold still for too long."

"All right then. Follow me!"

The tour of the house lasted the better part of an hour, and it left me wishing I'd drawn a map as we went along. I'd been right about the house's origins—it had once been a plantation. Which meant that it was huge, with a zillion rooms, and also meant that there were servants' corridors and staircases all over the place. Combine those classic plantation features with a century's worth of additions and renovations, and you had a dizzying maze. Or maybe it was just my own fatigue that made everything so confusing.

By the time I got back to my room, I doubted I could find my way to the front door without help, and I was so tired my eyes ached. I locked both the door to my suite and the door to my bedroom before finally allowing myself to collapse into bed and fall into a deep, untroubled sleep.

It was still pitch dark out when I awoke. A nightlight glowed faintly from the open bathroom door, and there was a little light cast by the digital clock by the bedside, but otherwise the room was oppressively dark. I was used to the lights of the city creeping around the edges of my curtains, and to the sound of cars passing by at all hours of the day and night. Here in Anderson's mansion, I felt cut off from humanity, alone and out of my element.

I didn't know what had awakened me, but the shiver of unease trailing down my spine told me *some-*

thing was wrong. I lay still and peered into the darkness, checking to see if anything was amiss. When nothing immediately tweaked my threat radar, I almost let my eyes slide closed again. I was still dead tired.

But there's something inherently disturbing about sleeping in an unfamiliar room, especially when that room is part of a huge, pre-Civil War mansion inhabited by supernatural beings, and I couldn't just dismiss my nerves. I stifled a yawn and sat up, wishing the room weren't so damn dark.

I started to reach for the bedside lamp, and then froze as my eyes picked out a man-shaped patch of shadow in the darkness. A man-shaped shadow that wasn't looming over me, as I'd half-expected, but that was lying on his side on the bed beside me, his head propped on his hand.

I couldn't make out his features in the dark, and so I had no idea who it was. Until he moved and I heard the telltale clicking of the beads in his hair.

With a yelp of alarm, I tried to throw myself off the bed, reaching for the lamp as I did so. I figured Jamaal knew the layout of this room better than I did, and I'd have a better chance of making it out the door if I could see where I was going. But Jamaal was faster than me, and before I could pull the chain on the lamp, he'd grabbed my arm and yanked me back onto the bed.

I tried to get in an elbow jab, but my movements were hampered by the sheets tangled around my legs. My jab missed, and moments later I found myself pinned face-down with my arm wrenched up behind my back. Jamaal was big and powerful, and my struggles were useless. I considered screaming for help, but then decided against it. I doubted anyone else in the house was close enough to hear, just as I doubted there were a whole lot of them who would be eager to help me against Jamaal, who was one of their own.

"How did you get in here?" I gasped. "I locked the doors."

Okay, it was probably a pretty dumb question under the circumstances. It really didn't matter how he got in my room. But I guess I wasn't eager to face the important question—what was he going to do to me?—so I ignored it in favor of the trivial one.

Jamaal laughed humorlessly, but at least he wasn't actively hurting me. Yet.

"There is no lock strong enough nor wall thick enough to keep Death out," he murmured, his lips close to my ear so that I could feel the puff of his breath against my skin. The ends of a couple of his braids had found their way under the collar of my flannel night-shirt and tickled the base of my neck.

"Are you speaking literally or metaphorically?"

I felt his slight jerk of surprise. I guess he'd expected me to cower in fear at his menacing words, and there was certainly a part of me that was afraid. But there was another part of me that was getting just plain fed up with all the bullying and threatening, and that part was keeping my fear at bay.

Jamaal's hand tightened around my wrist, although his grip had not yet gone from uncomfortable to painful. "You think because I can't kill you that I can't make you suffer?"

I snorted. "I'm not an idiot. But you're going to do whatever you're going to do no matter what I say, so I figure I might as well speak my mind."

I no longer made any attempt to struggle against his hold. What was the point? "Fair enough," he said, still talking into my ear. I noticed his breath smelled faintly of clove cigarettes. I guessed as an immortal, he didn't have to worry about lung cancer. "I'll speak my mind, too. I think you're a lying, murdering spy who works for the Olympians." His grip on my wrist tightened at the words, and I clenched my teeth to suppress a whimper of pain.

"I think you murdered my friend and that you're going to string Anderson along with hopes of finding Emma while you gather information for your boss. And I think Anderson is too desperate to believe in you to think straight."

"Ever considered that *you* might be the one not thinking straight?" I asked, my voice tight enough that he couldn't miss the fact that I was in pain. He surprised me by loosening his grip.

"I'll be watching you," he continued, ignoring my question. "If I see even the slightest hint that you're playing us false, there will be hell to pay."

He rolled off of me and sprang to his feet in one fluid motion. My lizard brain urged me not to move from where he'd left me, fearing any movement might incite him, but I couldn't just lie there on my stomach being Little Miss Submissive.

Swallowing the lump of fear in my throat, I carefully turned over onto my side and pushed up onto my elbow. Jamaal didn't pounce, but he didn't go away, either.

"I was speaking literally," Jamaal said, and for a moment I had no idea what he was talking about. "Locks can't keep me out. If you fuck with us, there's nowhere you can hide that I can't get to you. If you're out of here by the time the sun rises, I'll give you a free pass no matter what you deserve for killing Emmitt. But if you stay in this house and I find out you're working for Konstantin . . ."

Before I could even think what to say, he stalked away from me. I could barely pick out his shadow in the darkness of the room, but I was pretty sure he passed through my bedroom door without even bothering to open it.

FOURTEEN

After Jamaal left, I got up and turned on the light. I'd never be able to get to sleep if I didn't explore every nook and cranny of my room to make sure I was alone. I was not at all comforted to find that the bedroom door and the entrance to my suite were both locked. I wished I could believe I'd dreamed Jamaal's visit, but I knew I hadn't. If he could pass through locked doors, then I supposed he could have escaped from his basement cell on the night of Emmitt's death, despite all the pounding and shouting I'd heard. Of course, if passing through the locked door would have earned him another date with the Hand of Doom, I didn't blame him for choosing a different form of protest.

I made a halfhearted attempt to go back to sleep, but I failed miserably. The dark was too oppressive, and my fears were too overwhelming.

Jamaal had threatened to hurt me only if I double-crossed Anderson, but it was obvious he'd be looking for the slightest excuse to condemn me. What if I couldn't find Emma? After all, I had as yet found no evidence of any supernatural hunting ability, and with Emma I didn't even know how to start. Would Jamaal take my lack of progress as evidence of betrayal?

I shoved the covers away and got out of bed, turning on the light. Sleep was an impossibility, no matter how much I might prefer to escape my situation by slipping into dreamland.

It was almost five in the morning, so at least I'd gotten a few solid hours of sleep before Jamaal had awakened me. I tended to be an early riser anyway, so I tried to tell myself I wasn't really getting up in the middle of the night, even though my body cried out for more rest.

A part of me was beginning to suspect I should cut my losses and run. Earlier, I'd talked myself out of disappearing because of all the things I didn't want to give up. Unfortunately, I seemed to be giving up a lot of those things anyway. I hadn't spent the night in my own home since the accident, and I'd put so little thought into my job that I hadn't even checked phone messages. I put referring my current clients to other investigators on my day's to-do list. It was easier to face than figuring out what to do with the rest of my life.

I decided I needed a serious coffee infusion before I made any life-altering decisions. If I'd really felt like I *lived* in the mansion, I wouldn't have hesitated to go downstairs in my nightshirt. But no matter what my supposed status, I felt more like a reluctant guest at an oversized B&B, which meant I wasn't going anywhere until I was showered and dressed.

I only made two wrong turns before I found my way to the kitchen.

The coffee didn't magically make all my problems go away, but it was warm, delicious, and caffeinated. That was all that mattered.

I spent the remainder of the wee hours of the morning doing some basic Internet research on Emma Poindexter of Arlington, Virginia. I assumed most of what I learned was pure fiction. Depending on how old she was, she could have dozens of different assumed identities. None of which would have much to do with who she really was. Still, it was a start.

At around eight there was a knock on my door. I answered cautiously, hoping it would be Maggie, because so far she was the only one of the *Liberi* I could actually say I liked. Instead, it turned out to be Blake, probably my least favorite of Anderson's *Liberi*. Jamaal was hostility personified, but at least I understood where he was coming from. Blake just seemed slimy.

I probably made a face, but if so, Blake ignored it, holding up a manila envelope.

"Anderson sent me to give you this," he said. "I believe the subtext was 'kiss and make up.'"

This time I was *sure* I made a face. "I'd rather kiss a copperhead." I grabbed the envelope from his hand.

He laughed and held up his hands in surrender. "Don't worry. It was only a figure of speech."

He didn't seem particularly perturbed that I'd shot him yesterday, but I didn't believe he'd gotten over it that easily.

"How's your boo-boo?" I asked. I don't know if I was trying to rile him, or trying to remind him I wasn't someone he wanted to mess with.

He touched his chest, presumably where the bullet had hit him. "Still a little sore, but not too bad. I'm touched by your concern."

He said it with a self-deprecating smile, as if there were no hard feelings, but I still didn't believe it. I'd seen too much malice in him to think he'd let me off the hook that easily. Even so, I couldn't help feeling guilty about what I'd done, and I couldn't force myself to be as indifferent as I wanted to be.

"I really am sorry about that," I found myself saying, though it made me feel like a wuss.

Blake waved off my apology. "As Anderson pointed out, I had it coming. If I'd left my attitude in the car, I probably could have persuaded you to come with me without the strong-arm tactics."

I was momentarily at a loss for words. This was not the reaction I'd expected from him.

"Alexis brings out the worst in me," Blake continued. "When I saw him sitting there with you, I started to wonder if Jamaal was right and you were a plant."

It wasn't quite an apology, but it was close. "And now you've changed your mind about me?"

"I don't know what to make of you," he said with refreshing honesty. "But if there's a chance you're telling the truth and can find Emma, then I'm willing to give you the benefit of the doubt."

"Sounds like you're as anxious to get her back as Anderson is." I belatedly realized that sounded accusatory, like I thought he and Emma were lovers, when all I'd really meant to do was fish for information.

He hesitated a beat, but didn't respond to my unintentional implication. "Anderson hasn't come close to getting over her yet. And the longer she's been gone, the more saintly she's become in his memory."

"Meaning she wasn't that saintly in real life?"

"Let's just say she was a bit high-maintenance. And it had been a long, long time since she and Anderson were happy together. By the end, they weren't even sharing a bed anymore. But you know what they say—absence makes the heart grow fonder."

He pointed at the manila envelope, which I hadn't bothered to open yet. "There's a full dossier on Emma's current identity in there. There's also an outline of Anderson's security plan for your sister. He's hired a private security firm we've worked with in the past, and the rest of us are going to help out as time permits. She'll be as safe as we can possibly make her, and she'll never even know her guardian angels are there."

"Angels, huh?" I asked with a lift of my brow. That wasn't a term I'd associate with any of the *Liberi* I'd met.

Blake just laughed.

Over the next couple of days, I spent countless hours chained to my computer, looking for something that might help. I figured that since my non-supernatural abilities to find people had stemmed largely from my computer skills, maybe my supernatural ones would as well.

I had Anderson compile a list of all the known Olympians and all the Descendants who worked for them. The list was long and intimidating, but I started doing methodical searches on each person. It was true that Konstantin could have buried Emma anywhere, including out in some national park miles from civilization, but instinct told me he'd want to have easier access to her. Which meant wherever she was, it was most likely on property owned by Konstantin or one of his many toadies.

When you watch TV shows featuring private investigators, the job always looks like it's exciting and full of action. The reality is somewhat different. Scouring databases looking for properties that belong to one of about thirty people—many of whom had multiple names as they changed identities over the years—was the antithesis of exciting.

The list of properties grew depressingly long, and though in theory I was making progress, it felt more like I was running in place. Even if I identified the right property, how would I find Emma once I got there? If I was a supernatural tracker, the power was taking its own sweet time to manifest.

On Saturday afternoon, I decided to take a break and get out of the mansion for a while.

Actually, it wasn't so much my decision, as Steph's. Her charity auction was on Wednesday night, and she called to remind me. Then she asked me what I would wear, and when I didn't answer fast enough, she declared we were going shopping.

I could have fought her on it. Although Steph has

a steel backbone, I have a pretty good streak of stubbornness in me, too. But one thing I'd learned over years of working as a P.I. was that it really was possible to work too hard. The brain needs to take a break every once in a while, or you start missing things that are right in front of your face. So I let myself be persuaded.

Steph's favorite store is the Saks out in Chevy Chase, but I didn't make enough money from my P.I. business to buy so much as a single shoe there. Trust me, if I was ever going to be persuaded to tap into my trust fund, it wouldn't be for the sake of designer clothes. In deference to my budget concerns, we hit the shops and boutiques of Georgetown instead.

I enjoy shopping as much as the next girl, and I'd been on countless excursions with Steph over the years, but there was nothing like watching my beautiful sister trying on clothes to make me feel like an ugly duckling.

I know I'm not ugly. But I'm no Steph, either. Usually, I do a pretty good job of shoving my jealousy into a back corner of my mind, where I can ignore it. But the stress of recent events, and my relentless worries about the future, made it impossible to keep the green monster completely under control. Especially when Steph came out of her dressing room wearing a stunning, fire-engine red cocktail dress that clung perfectly to her curves without looking even remotely slutty. I swear, if you'd teleported her to the red carpet before the Oscars, she wouldn't have looked out of place.

I had on a simple black number at the time, and I couldn't help comparing our reflections in the mirror. Steph, tall and blond and sophisticated, wearing a dress that would draw every eye in the room. Me, short and average-looking, in a dress meant to blend in with the inevitable sea of little black dresses. And then, of course, there was the glyph that only I could see. The glyph that meant I had to give up even the semblance of a normal life that I had built.

We went out for coffee afterward. I kept trying to spot Anderson's private security team, but I hadn't caught sight of anyone following us. Maybe they felt Steph was safe enough with me. Or maybe they really were just really good at being inconspicuous. I knew the typical tricks of covert surveillance, but even knowing what to look for, I couldn't spot anyone.

"So," Steph said when we sat down in a cozy corner with our coffees, "what's going on with your stalker-client? I'm guessing since you're still not at home and you're in a crappy mood that he's still giving you trouble."

I grimaced and took a sip of my coffee, burning my tongue. I thought I'd been hiding my state of mind better than that. Probably if it had been anyone but Steph, they would have been fooled.

"Yeah," I admitted, because there was no reason not to. "The situation's still complicated." I gave her a half smile. "And I still can't talk about it."

"You ever consider that talking about it might help?"

My half smile turned to a full one, though I doubted Steph would miss the strain behind it. "No, I never considered that possibility."

She rolled her eyes. "Whoever said 'no man is an island' obviously never met *you*."

I bit back the urge to go defensive, but it was hard. If she'd been through what I'd been through as a kid, she'd understand why I didn't make a habit of blabbing out my problems. You learn to talk about your problems when you have a sympathetic ear available. I hadn't had any truly awful foster parents. No one molested me or beat me, at least not beyond the occasional spanking. But until I'd moved in with the Glasses at age eleven, there'd been no real warmth, either. My fault, entirely. I was one hell of an angry little girl. But by the time I had something like a warm, supportive family environment, I had already settled into the habit of keeping to myself.

Steph reached over and put a hand on my arm, the touch light and brief. "Sorry. I didn't mean that to hurt. I was just teasing."

I did my best to shake off the gloom. "I know. I'm just grumpy and not very good company today."

"Think it might cheer you up if I told you about this new guy I'm seeing?"

I'm sure my eyes lit up at the idea. For all my unworthy jealousy of Steph, I really, truly loved her. I wanted to see her happy, and though so far she hadn't shown the greatest taste in men, I was always hoping she'd meet Mr. Right.

"Ooh yes, do tell!" I urged.

There was a twinkle in her eye as she smiled at me. She was proud of herself for chasing away the little black thundercloud that had been hovering over my head.

"It's all very preliminary," she warned. "Maybe saying I'm 'seeing' him is a bit of an exaggeration. I only met him a couple of days ago, and we've been on exactly one date."

"I have a feeling I've just been conned," I muttered, but I couldn't go back to being as surly as I'd been. I'd much rather talk about Steph's love life than keep evading her questions about my "stalker."

"Where and how did you meet? Details, please."

"You know that little bakery around the corner from my house?"

I nodded. It was the kind of place I didn't dare set foot in for fear of surrendering to I-want-one-of-everything syndrome.

"Well, I've gotten into the habit of going over there every morning. I take my laptop and do a lot of my correspondence. It's got a nice atmosphere, and it smells heavenly."

And unlike me, Steph could smell the various pies, cakes, breads, and assorted goodies and resist gorging herself. Just one more reason to hate her.

"Well, Blake came in to pick up a cake he'd ordered, and we got to talking, and . . ." Steph frowned as she watched my face go white. "What's wrong?"

"Please tell me his name isn't Blake Porter."

"You know him?" she asked, looking both confused and worried. "Oh, God, is he someone *you're* interested in?"

"Blake?" I cried with a comical squeak. "Hell no!" The blood that had drained from my face when Steph said Blake's name came back in a rush, my cheeks heating with rage I did my best to tamp down. "I am going to kill him," I muttered under my breath, though of course I wasn't physically capable of killing him. But shooting him a couple more times might turn out to be therapeutic. No wonder he'd taken to playing friendly with me lately—he must have found it really amusing to hold out an olive branch while secretly stabbing me in the back.

"What's going on?" Steph asked, shaking her head. "This isn't the stalker guy, is it? Please tell me my taste in men isn't *that* bad."

For a split second, I was tempted to lie, tempted to tell Steph that yes, indeed, Blake was the wannabe client who was making my life miserable and who had indirectly threatened her. I resisted the temptation, but it wasn't due to any goodwill toward Blake. I just didn't want Steph to let her guard down because she thought she knew who the bad guy was.

"No, he's not the guy," I said through gritted teeth. "But he's bad news anyway. He's messed up in this whole business."

"You've got to give me more to go on than that."

"I can't," I told her for the millionth time. She was getting sick of hearing it, and I was getting sick of saying it.

"Fine," Steph retorted, thumping her coffee cup

back down on the table. "If you're not going to tell me why you think he's bad news, then there's no reason for me not to see him again."

"Please just trust me on this."

She folded her arms. "I've had enough, Nikki. I like Blake a lot, and it's going to take more than your cryptic warnings to make me give up on him before we even have a chance."

I wanted to kick the table in frustration. I almost wished Steph really *were* my biological sister. Then I'd have a good reason to tell her everything I'd learned about Descendants and the *Liberi*. But that was self-ish of me. If I could go back to the days when I'd been blissfully ignorant, I'd have done so in an instant, immortality be damned. I wasn't going to shatter Steph's perfect world, even if I thought there was any chance she'd believe me.

"He's not what he seems, Steph," I said, know-ing I was still being too vague to convince her of any-thing. "Just like Alexis called me on your phone to get to me, Blake is trying to seduce you to get even with me for . . . something I did." I was slipping a bit—I'd almost said "for shooting him," which would have left me majorly screwed.

Steph pushed back her chair with a loud scrape. "You know, Nikki, the world doesn't actually revolve around you, no matter what you might think."

I gaped at her, shocked into silence by her accu-sation. I didn't think the world revolved around me. What the hell was she talking about?

"You don't get to order me around and expect me

to do whatever you say just because. I'm an adult, and capable of making my own decisions. You won't tell me what you think is wrong with Blake? Then I'll just have to find out for myself."

"Steph, it's not—"

"Stop it, okay? I don't know what kind of power trip you're on with all these mysterious secrets and threats, but I'm not playing that game anymore. I'm sick to death of being treated like some ditzy blond who can't handle the truth. You have two choices: tell me the truth, or butt out."

There was nothing I could say that was going to fix this. I couldn't explain what Blake was, what he could do, or why he might want to do it. And if I couldn't explain, Steph was going to ignore any warning I tried to give her.

"I'm just trying to look out for you, Steph," I told her, though her closed-off expression said she didn't want to hear anything I had to say just then.

Steph shook her head and picked up her shopping bags. "I know you think I've led this easy, charmed life and I need someone stronger and more worldly, like you, to take care of me. I'm sorry you had such a sucky childhood before you became part of our family, but just because I haven't been through that kind of hell doesn't make me the weakling you've always thought. I don't need your protection, and I don't want it, either."

With one last angry look, Steph headed for the door, leaving me sitting at the table feeling utterly wretched.

FIFTEEN

I drove back to the mansion in something of a daze. I had never seen Steph so angry before. And the things she'd said . . .

I knew I was carrying around a load of baggage everywhere I went. How could I not have baggage after everything I'd been through as a kid? But I'd never realized how it had affected Steph. I could freely admit to myself that I was jealous of her at times, but I thought I kept those unworthy emotions well hidden. It had never occurred to me that *she* might have any ill feelings toward *me*.

Steph had been the ideal older sister from the moment I'd moved into the Glasses' house. I was a sullen handful of bad behavior during that first year, when I was sure the Glasses would be as temporary as any of my other foster families. Not that we hadn't ever fought—she was ideal, but she wasn't perfect, and a saint couldn't have put up with all the crap I pulled when I first moved in. But she'd never seemed to harbor any real resentment.

Had her words today meant I'd been seeing her through rose-colored glasses this whole time? Deep inside, did she hate me for having usurped a portion of her parents' love? Surely she didn't really think I was self-centered. Did she? I mean, I was self-*sufficient,* but that wasn't the same thing. I was almost sure of it.

I brooded and wallowed right up until I reached the gates of the mansion. Then, as I waited for the gates to open, I swallowed my hurt feelings and summoned up my righteous indignation. I might not have been able to convince Steph that Blake was bad news, but I could sure as hell make him rue the day he decided to mess with my sister.

I entered the house like a guided missile.

I climbed the stairs two at a time, practically sprinting to my room to get my gun. I hadn't liked leaving it behind, but I'd worried what Steph would say if she saw it. A physical sensation of relief flowed though me when my hand closed around the butt of the gun, and I cocked it with vicious glee.

I pounded down the stairs to the second floor, angrier than I'd ever been in my life. Angrier even than I'd been when Alexis threatened Steph. It was one thing to have the bad guy make threats; it was another when the supposed good guys did it.

When Maggie had taken me on the tour of the house, we'd only gone through the public rooms, so I didn't know which of the rooms in the west wing belonged to Blake. Come to think of it, I had no way of knowing if he was even home. That didn't stop me from marching up to the second door on the left and pounding on it. Don't ask me why I chose that particular door—it just kinda happened that way.

"Blake, you son of a bitch!" I yelled. "Open this door!" I was going to feel like an idiot if this wasn't his room, but I was running on adrenaline and instinct and ignored all logical concerns.

The door cracked open and I lunged forward, holding it open with my body so Blake couldn't slam it on me. He took a startled step back, and by the time he recovered, my gun was aimed squarely at his forehead. His eyes widened, and he held his hands up as if to show he wasn't armed. I was fully prepared to shoot if I felt the slightest hint he was about to use his aura against me, but he wasn't an idiot. We'd already established that I could pull the trigger faster than he could put me under.

"You stay the hell away from my sister," I ordered, and though my hands were shaking with fury, I didn't for a moment doubt my aim.

"Take it easy, Nikki," he said. "I was just—"

"You were just *what?*" I interrupted. "Taking a page out of Alexis's book and threatening Steph to keep me under control?"

"I didn't threaten her!" he snapped, putting his hands down. "I was helping keep an eye on her, and she happened to notice me. Women do, you know, and it's not something I can control."

"You took her out on a date." I kept the gun pointed steadily at his forehead.

"I didn't sleep with her, if that's what you're freaking out about. I asked her out because I'd already blown my cover, and I figured that way I could help protect her without having to try to hide."

He sounded perfectly sincere, but how could I believe him? I'd seen how ruthlessly he'd used that aura before, and the idea of him turning it on Steph made me sick to my stomach.

"I don't believe you," I said, moving my aim from his forehead to his crotch. His eyes went a little wider, and he swallowed hard. I was glad to know he was less scared of me blowing his brains out than shooting him somewhere *really* important.

"I'm telling the truth," he said, a little desperately. "If I were the kind of guy who preyed on innocent bystanders like that, I'd be with the Olympians, not with Anderson."

For some reason, his words had a ring of truth to them, and I took a baby step back from the edge. I still kept the gun pointed at his family jewels, but I didn't feel like I was moments away from pulling the trigger.

"I don't want you anywhere near her."

"I'm one of the few people Alexis is actually afraid of. You saw how he reacted to me in the diner. He's not getting within a hundred yards of her as long as I'm around."

I shook my head. "And I'm supposed to think that letting you seduce her is okay as long as you keep Alexis away?"

Blake rolled his eyes. "I'm not going to seduce her. I won't let things go further than a little flirtation."

"Why not? Don't you like women?" I couldn't imagine there were a whole lot of straight men who wouldn't leap at the chance of getting Steph into bed.

To my surprise, Blake blushed. "Yeah, I like women. Look, any chance we can continue this conversation without you threatening to shoot me? Because you're almost as berserk as Jamaal, and it's getting old."

Crap. I *was* acting a bit like Jamaal, come to think of it. Assuming the worst and threatening violence. That wasn't the kind of person I wanted to be, but I'd already really stuck my foot in it. "What's to stop you from doing something nasty with your aura if I put the gun away?"

"The fact that Anderson would 'lay hands' on me if I did. He takes a pretty dim view of infighting."

Again, there was that ring of truth. Plus, there was the fact that I couldn't keep him at gunpoint forever. Reluctantly, I uncocked the gun and lowered my arm.

Blake let out a sigh of relief. "Just to clarify something: I made some threats to you at the diner, but I wouldn't have followed through on them. I'd have used my aura to lower your inhibitions and get you to go with me, but I wouldn't have taken advantage of it. I could do it to Alexis without my conscience uttering a peep, but that's because I know exactly what he's capable of. Rampant abuse of power is an Olympian thing."

I wasn't sure whether I believed him or not, but at least he wasn't on the attack at the moment.

"So, if you like women, then why aren't you interested in Steph?"

Once again, he blushed. It was almost cute. Emphasis on "almost."

"I never said I wasn't interested. It's just . . ." He cleared his throat and looked at the floor. "As a descendant of Eros, I have certain . . . skills. If a woman has too much exposure to those skills, she'll have a hard time being satisfied with normal men."

I gaped at him. "I've heard men brag about their sexual prowess before, but you take the cake."

"It's not a boast, and I'd turn it off if I could. If I were an Olympian, it wouldn't bother me to make a woman unable to achieve satisfaction with another man for the rest of her life, as long as I enjoyed myself. But I'm not an Olympian, and it *would* bother me. As far as sex is concerned, I will always have to be a one-night-stand kind of guy. That's nothing to boast about."

I'd never thought learning the guy who was dating Steph was into one night stands would be a relief. "If you decide to make Steph one of those one night stands, we'll be having this conversation again. And I might find myself pulling the trigger by accident. Got it?"

Blake gave me a wide-eyed innocent look. "I got it. Now how about you and your gun do an about-face and get out of my apartment?"

By that point, I was happy to oblige.

SIXTEEN

I spent the next couple of days splitting my time between Internet research, locating every piece of Olympian property within driving distance, and doing some preliminary reconnaissance. Good old Google Maps let me get satellite views, and I weeded out the properties that didn't look like they had convenient burial spots. Of course, for all I knew, Emma was buried under someone's basement, but I figured I'd try the places with significant amounts of land first.

I did a series of drive-bys, hoping for some kind of supernatural X-Marks-the-Spot, but no such luck. I tried not to worry about what would happen to me—and to Steph—if I didn't make any demonstrable progress soon. Jamaal wasn't the most sociable of Anderson's *Liberi,* so I didn't run in to him often. But each time I did, his expression seemed darker, more full of accusation. And a little less sane.

One day, when I returned to the mansion after

another round of fruitless drive-bys, I noticed that the potted plants on the porch were looking ragged and overgrown. Hoping that manual labor would shut down the gerbil wheel in my brain and help me Zen out enough to think straight, I decided to do a little impromptu gardening. Anything to escape the feeling of futility that kept trying to creep up on me.

I started off by plucking dead leaves, of which there were many. Shortly afterward, Maggie came out to join me. Without a word, she set to plucking leaves by my side. When I looked over at her, I saw a sheen of tears in her eyes.

"Maggie? Are you all right?"

She sniffed and nodded, a faint smile on her face. "Yeah. It's just that these plants were Emmitt's babies. Big, macho death-god Descendant that he was, he'd talk to them like he thought they'd talk back."

I guessed that explained why they were starting to look ragged now that Emmitt was dead. "Should I keep my hands off them?" I asked, worried that someone would be offended at the idea of Emmitt's killer touching his beloved plants.

"Emmitt would want them taken care of," was her response, so we continued plucking.

There were several plants that needed pruning, and a couple that needed repotting. Possibly, I should have been using my time more productively, but I was enjoying the peace of playing in the dirt too much to quit. When Maggie dabbed at her eyes, I pretended to ignore it.

In the back corner, there was one plant that looked

completely dead. I pulled the pot out of the corner, then looked up at Maggie's gasp of dismay.

"Oh!" she said. "We should have brought that inside before the sleet storm the other night. I guess Emmitt was too busy killing himself to take care of it." Her eyes looked all wet and shiny again.

I poked at the dead foliage, not recognizing the plant. "Maybe it's just dormant and will come back in the spring." I grabbed a pair of shears and started snipping, hoping to find something green and alive at the core. We'd only had one really cold night so far, so there was always a chance . . .

Maggie shook her head. "It's a night blooming jasmine. They aren't cut out for Virginia winters. It was Emma's. And Anderson is going to be very unhappy if he sees it's dead."

I wasn't finding any signs of life, but I kept snipping compulsively anyway, until I'd removed enough dead leaves to see the soil. There was something shiny in the dirt, and for reasons unknown, I found myself poking at it.

Probably a piece of mica in the dirt, I told myself, but my fingernail caught on something, and it wasn't mica. I dug my finger into the soil and pulled out a silver band, dotted with moonstones and what looked like diamonds.

"Look what I found," I said, scraping some of the dirt away as I laid the ring on my palm to show it to Maggie.

"Where did you get that?" Maggie asked, and there was something off about her voice.

"It was in the pot. Why? Do you recognize it?"

She nodded. I didn't like the way she was looking at me, like she suddenly thought I was scum. "It's Emma's wedding ring."

I shivered, though I wasn't cold. Finding Emma's ring while I was searching for Emma had to be some weird sort of coincidence, right? I just happened to be in the mood to prune plants, and I just happened to pick up the dead jasmine, and I just happened to keep snipping at it even when I knew it was dead. It could happen.

But what if it wasn't coincidence? What if it was a sign that my supposed supernatural powers were coming out?

Maggie was still looking at me strangely. Her usually friendly face was closed off, and there was suspicion in her eyes.

"Anderson and Emma had marital problems," she said, and there was a caution in her voice that hadn't been there before. "But Emma *never* took off that ring. She was wearing it on the day she disappeared."

I swallowed hard, realizing that my finding the ring like this could look bad, especially to people who didn't entirely trust me in the first place.

"You can't possibly have that ring," Maggie continued. "Not unless you have access to Emma."

"Come on, Maggie," I said. "You've been with me the whole time. You *saw* me find it."

"I saw you poking around at the pot. That's not the same thing."

"If I'm working for the Olympians, then why

would I pretend to find the ring when I knew Emma was wearing it when she was taken?"

"You were going to use it as a sign of progress. 'Hey, I haven't found Emma, but I've found her ring.'"

"Do you really think I'm that stupid?"

She bit her lip and shook her head, though I could tell she wasn't entirely convinced. If someone like Maggie, who'd given me the benefit of the doubt since day one, thought finding the ring made me look guilty, I didn't want to imagine how someone like Jamaal would take it.

"Maggie, I swear to you, I just found it in the pot. You said this was Emma's plant. Maybe she repotted it and lost her ring in the dirt on the day she disappeared." According to Anderson, no one was sure exactly when Emma was captured. She'd apparently been prone to storming out in a huff when she and Anderson argued, and it had been hours before anyone had realized she wasn't anywhere in the house or on the grounds. "Maybe she was pissed at Anderson and hid the ring there so she could pretend she tossed it or pawned it—without having to actually toss it or pawn it."

"That does sound like something Emma would do," Maggie agreed. "Maybe it happened exactly that way. But maybe it didn't."

"I'm not one of the Olympians."

Her look of polite skepticism hurt. She'd been the closest thing I had to a friend in this house, and it sucked to lose her over something like this.

"Are you going to tell Anderson about this?" I

asked. "I haven't done anything wrong, but my job's going to be a lot harder if he starts being all suspicious again."

She crossed her arms over her chest. "I really *should* tell him. He has a right to know. And I'm sure he'd want the ring back."

"I'm not asking you to keep him in the dark forever," I assured her. "I just need a little more time to locate Emma, and I won't be able to do that if Anderson decides I'm a spy after all."

"How much time?"

That was the million-dollar question, wasn't it? Should I take the finding of the ring as some kind of good sign? I had no way of knowing.

What I *did* know was that Maggie wasn't going to keep her mouth shut forever.

"Give me one week," I said, wondering if the ticking clock was going to make the job even harder. "If I haven't found her in a week, I'll talk to Anderson myself."

Maggie thought about it a minute, then nodded. "All right. You have one week. Make it count."

Tick tock, tick tock, tick tock.

Despite the looming deadline, Wednesday night rolled around, and I reluctantly got ready for Steph's charity auction. I'd held out a faint hope that our fight would get me out of it, but no. Steph called and informed me in no uncertain terms that I was going. She seemed content to pretend our fight had never happened, and I was happy to go along with it.

I wore the admittedly nondescript little black dress I'd bought on our shopping trip and a pair of stiletto-heeled pumps that would have my feet hurting in fifteen minutes flat. Remembering Steph's gorgeous red dress, I knew I was going to spend most of the night feeling like one of the ugly stepsisters from a fairy tale. I'd have to try to keep to myself as much as possible, because I wasn't exactly feeling like Little Miss Sunshine.

I left the house around six thirty to get to the pre-dinner cocktail party. That would be the most painful part of the evening—I wasn't a big fan of mingling with the rich and snooty. But I knew Steph would want me there the whole time, and I'd have done just about anything to smooth the waters. Even stand around in high heels drinking cocktails and talking to people with whom I had nothing in common.

The country club that was hosting Steph's auction reminded me a bit of Anderson's mansion, if only in its attempt to hide from the sight of passers-by. There was even a set of gates—though these were usually kept open and were more ornamental—and an artificial forest lining the driveway. The "forest" was as well-manicured as the one at the mansion, devoid of the weeds and underbrush that would accompany natural growth. The driveway, however, was a lot straighter, and there were actually streetlamps to guide the way.

The patch of woods didn't last long, giving way to the inevitable golf course. This being the height of winter, it was already too dark for even the most fanatical of golfers, so at least I didn't have to dodge golf carts on my way in. There was convenient valet parking if I drove right up to the clubhouse, but I chose to park myself in one of the outer lots. It meant an uncomfortable walk in my high heels, but by the time the night was over, the last thing I would want to do was wait for someone to retrieve my car for me.

The glittering crowd was just starting to trickle in as I headed into the bar and lounge area. My eyes were immediately drawn to Steph in her fire-engine-red dress. She looked even more fabulous than usual, with her blond hair swept into an elegant up-do and her long neck adorned by a pearl and diamond necklace.

Standing right beside Steph, with a proprietary hand resting on her lower back, was Blake. I had to admit, he looked good enough to eat in his conservative black tux, the perfect Ken to Steph's Barbie. I didn't like the way he was touching her, though, not one bit. Despite Blake's promise that he would behave like a gentleman, I was all too aware of the malice that lurked beneath his cultured exterior. He was a dangerous man who used sex as a weapon. Was it any shock I didn't want him around my sister?

Steph caught sight of me while I was giving Blake the evil eye. I tried to blank my expression as she made her way across the room toward me, Blake following in her wake. She stopped right in front of me and smiled brilliantly, and I wondered if she'd thought I was going to stand her up. Sad to say if I had, it wouldn't have been the first time. Have I mentioned how much I hate these affairs?

"You look gorgeous!" Steph said, giving me a

warm hug. She was busy enough hugging me not to see the way Blake rolled his eyes at her words.

Steph released me from the hug, then looked back and forth between me and Blake. His expression was one of polite disinterest. I have no idea what my own face looked like. I hoped my flush of embarrassment had faded. Bad enough to be pathetically insecure about my looks, but to have others know it was almost unbearable.

"I take it you two know each other," Steph said with a raise of her eyebrows. I could tell by the sparkle of curiosity in her eyes that Blake hadn't made up a story about how we'd met. Which was a good thing, since I'd have had no idea what the cover story was and would probably have blown it the moment I opened my mouth.

"We've met," Blake said drily, but he held out his hand for me to shake.

It felt like a challenge, so I didn't hesitate. Of course, he then lifted my hand to his mouth and kissed my knuckles. It was all I could do not to jerk my hand out of his grip and make a scene.

"Charming," I muttered under my breath, and he laughed softly at this evidence that he'd gotten to me.

Steph kept looking back and forth between us, no doubt hoping one of us would cave and tell her how we knew each other. She knew, of course, that I didn't like Blake, but Blake wasn't giving any overt signs of how he felt about me. Not signs that *Steph* could read, that is.

Blake held on to my hand a little longer than necessary, and Steph looped her arm through his, forcing him to let go. Her action might have been subtle, but I knew beyond doubt she'd done it because I looked uncomfortable.

"We still have some serious mingling to do," she said, and I was just as happy to let her and Blake go.

I hoped the look in my eyes gave Blake the message that I would feed him his balls if he hurt my sister. There was no way of telling from the little smirk on his face as he and Steph stepped away into the burgeoning crowd.

I worked my way to the bar and ordered a glass of white wine, then found myself a convenient corner shadowed by a large potted plant where I could mingle by myself without drawing too much attention. Yes, I was playing the part of wallflower and wasn't particularly bothered by the fact.

For the record, standing in a corner by yourself in a snooty country club watching the filthy rich strut around in their one-of-a-kind designer gowns and ostentatious jewelry is not my idea of a good time. The wine helped a bit, taking the edge off, but after I'd finished my first glass, I didn't dare get another. I'm a bit of a lightweight when it comes to drinking, and I did have to drive home when the evening's fun and games were done.

Steph and Blake, young and good-looking, were quite a striking pair in the midst of the decidedly older crowd. Steph flitted around like an anxious humming-bird, making sure she talked to everyone, smiling and vivacious. Blake stuck close to her and I was pleased to see that, while he made social when necessary, he spent most of his time scanning the crowd, alert for any threats. I'd checked the guest list against the list of known Olympians Anderson had given me, but just because I hadn't identified any Olympians on the list didn't necessarily mean none would show up. After all, Konstantin had made it abundantly clear that the Olympians had money to burn. Someone with that kind of money could probably find a way to get themselves on the guest list at the last minute. So, much as I didn't like Blake, I had to reluctantly admit I was glad he was there.

The cocktail party was only an hour long, but it felt like an eternity. My feet were killing me, and I was bored out of my skull. I wasn't exactly looking forward to the dinner and auction parts of the evening, but at least then I would be able to sit down.

When eight o'clock finally rolled around, I followed the herd into the sumptuously appointed dining room. Annoyingly, there were assigned seats, so I had to either wander around the tables looking for the place card with my name on it, or stand in line to ask the nice man by the doorway to check his alphabetized list. I chose to wander.

Steph knew how much I enjoyed these affairs. She also knew I didn't like mingling with the sort of people who attended them. I made an educated guess that she would have been her usual considerate self and seated me at her table. I scanned the room, figuring that red dress of hers would stand out like a beacon, but I didn't see her.

At first, I wasn't even remotely concerned. She was, after all, in charge of this event, not a guest. I figured she was taking care of administrative details, or just talking to the stragglers who hadn't come into the dining room yet. But as the seats at the tables filled up and I still saw no sign of her, a niggle of alarm ran through me.

I located the table that Steph and Blake were going to be sitting at—right at the front, of course—and I found my own place card directly opposite hers. But still no Steph. No Blake, either. Maybe that meant they'd slipped away for a quick make-out session, but I didn't think so. Steph wasn't what I would call a control freak, but she did put a lot of time and energy into these events, and she wouldn't just wander away for a little me-time. Unless Blake used his nasty power on her, but that was a thought I could hardly bear to contemplate.

Telling myself I was being paranoid and overprotective, I slipped out of the dining room toward the bar and lounge. There were still a few people out there, ignoring the signals that dinner was nigh. But no Steph. I was going to start questioning the staff to see if they could tell me her last known location, but my cell rang, sending a shiver down my spine. True, the call could be completely innocuous, from anyone. But in my heart, I knew it was bad news.

My instinct was confirmed when I pulled out my cell phone and saw the caller ID: Alexis. What were the chances I would mysteriously lose sight of Steph, Alexis would call me moments later, and the two were not related? I prayed for a miracle as I reluctantly answered.

"What do you want?" I asked, my voice harsh with a fear I couldn't hide.

Alexis laughed. "What's the matter, Nikki? You sound tense."

"I'm not in the mood to banter with you. What do you want?"

"Do exactly as I tell you, and I promise no harm will come to dear Stephanie."

I swallowed a cry of anguish as he confirmed my worst fears. "You can't hurt Steph!" I said. "My family and I are under Anderson's protection."

Alexis laughed again. "Is that how he told you it would work? Or just wishful thinking on your part?"

"He and Konstantin have a deal!" Oh, please, God, let that be true, let me not have been a complete dupe.

"A deal that doesn't include Stephanie. She isn't *really* your family, after all."

"She's my sister!"

"But adopted. Not related by blood. A technicality, perhaps, but one we mean to exploit. Because you chose to seek asylum with Anderson, we cannot touch you. But Stephanie is fair game."

"Let her go, you bastard! She has nothing to do with this."

"I'll be happy to let her go. No one has to get hurt in this scenario. Come to me, renounce Anderson's protection, and she'll go her own merry way, none the worse for wear."

What were the chances I could trust Alexis's word? Slim and none. The problem was, I didn't see that I had any alternative. Alexis had Steph, and that left me with precious few options.

"How do I know you really have Steph?" I asked. I knew deep down in my gut that he was telling the truth, at least about that. But stalling for time seemed like a better alternative than rolling over.

There was a little scuffling noise on the other end of the line. Then I heard Alexis's voice in the background, saying "Let your sister know you're all right."

My entire body went tense as I braced myself for the impact of my sister's terrified voice. But Steph is made of sterner stuff than that, and she was every bit as protective of me as I was of her.

I knew she was there, knew Alexis wasn't lying, but she didn't make a sound. My throat tightened as I understood what she was doing: keeping her mouth shut in hopes that by not giving Alexis proof that he had her, she would keep me from coming after her. My eyes teared up.

"I'm not going to let him hurt you," I said, the words feeling hollow. Even *I* didn't believe I could protect her from Alexis. Why should I expect *her* to be convinced?

Alexis didn't like her show of defiance. I heard a harsh slap, and Steph's involuntary gasp of shock and pain.

"You'd best learn to do as you're told," Alexis growled in the background.

Steph still didn't say anything, though her gasp had already given her away. I cursed myself for asking Alexis for proof when I had believed him all along.

"I believe you!" I shouted into the phone, hoping my voice was loud enough for Alexis to hear.

There was a little more shuffling around, and his voice came back on the line. "You have thirty minutes to get to 28 Hillsboro Road in D.C. The door will be unlocked, so you just come right in. You come in, your sister goes out. If you don't get here in thirty minutes, the party will start without you."

I recognized the address from my list of Olympian properties. It was in Woodley Park and, if memory served, it was up for sale. I mentally calculated the distance and fought another jolt of terror. "That's not enough time," I told him. Maybe if I drove like a maniac and hit every light green, but . . .

"You'll have to *make* it enough."

"Please," I said, hating to beg, but willing to do it for Steph's sake. "It'll take me ten minutes just to get my car. Give me forty minutes to get there." I was already hurrying toward the exit. "I'm on my way now. Please don't hurt her."

"All right," he answered in an almost sensual purr, "I'm feeling generous tonight. You have your forty minutes. I look forward to seeing you again."

I turned my phone off before I was tempted to answer him with too much honesty.

SEVENTEEN

Forty minutes gave me a fighting chance of making it to the rendezvous on time, but I was still going to be cutting it damn close. Despite the wintry temperature, I slipped my heels off as I burst through the front door and ran toward the parking lot. I'd run faster carrying them than wearing them, even if I ended up with a collection of pebbles buried in the balls of my feet. I stayed on the grass instead of the sidewalks whenever possible.

It was a long sprint to the parking lot, made longer, no doubt, by my fear. The cold air burned my lungs and stung the skin of my bare arms. I hadn't even considered stopping to pick up my coat on the way out, and little black dresses with spaghetti straps aren't great cold-weather gear.

Where the hell was Blake? I wondered belatedly. He'd been sticking to Steph like glue the whole evening. How had he let Alexis snatch her out from under his nose?

My gut cramped with fear again. Had Blake sold her out? Had he come with her tonight so he could more easily separate her from the crowd and hand her over to Alexis?

I shoved that thought out of the way. For the moment, it didn't matter. What mattered was getting to that damn house before Alexis went to work on Steph, and it was going to be a close call. Gravel tore the bottoms of my feet, and my breath formed frosty clouds in the night air as I continued to sprint. I was so focused on my ultimate goal that I didn't immediately notice that all four streetlights in the lot were out, not until the waxing moon slid behind a bank of clouds and made me suddenly aware of the darkness.

I stumbled to a halt just as my feet hit the asphalt. This was a country club, not some neglected inner city parking lot. If even *one* streetlight had burned out, they'd have fixed it within the hour. For all four to be burned out at the same time seemed so unlikely as to be impossible.

The little hairs at the back of my neck prickled, but I decided I didn't have time to be cautious. My silver rental was parked in the rear corner of the lot, and I started forward again at a brisk jog, too winded to manage another sprint.

I made it about halfway across the lot before I ran into something like an invisible wall. I hit it full force, rebounding wildly. My arms flailed for balance, and the shoes I'd been carrying in my left hand went flying. The impact had knocked what little wind I had left in my lungs out of me, and my legs were too quivery from the long run to hold me.

I sprawled inelegantly on the asphalt, my dress making an alarming ripping sound as the skirt hiked up my thighs. I broke the fall with my hands, scraping the skin off the heels and grinding dirt and pebbles into the wounds.

When I looked up to see what I'd hit, Jamaal's body seemed to coalesce out of thin air. I belatedly recognized the uniquely yielding properties of flesh and bone that had characterized my invisible wall.

Jamaal grinned down at me, the expression fierce as any snarl. "Going somewhere?"

I tried to draw some air into my lungs, but I hadn't recovered from the impact yet and could only stare up at him, imploring him with my eyes to get out of my way.

"You shouldn't have fucked with us, Nikki," he said, the grin/snarl growing wider.

I had no idea what he was talking about, of course. I also didn't give a damn, not now, not when Steph was in danger.

I finally filled my lungs enough to get some words out. "We can do this later," I gasped. "My sister's in trouble."

He snorted, the cold air making his breath a soft white cloud like the puff of smoke from the fire-breathing dragon's nostrils. "You don't get to decide when we do this."

He reached for me, and I rolled violently to my left, scraping more skin off my bare arms as I avoided his grasp. I'd torn my dress enough when I'd fallen to give me some freedom of movement, and I managed to lurch to my feet.

"Alexis has my sister!" I tried again, though I didn't have high hopes of getting through to Jamaal. Maybe he and Blake were in this thing together, Blake to hand Steph over to Alexis, Jamaal to delay my rescue attempt and give Alexis time to . . .

I didn't want to think about what he might do to Steph if I didn't make it there in time. "Please, Jamaal!" It came out a sob, but he didn't strike me as the kind to be moved by feminine tears. "Let me go!"

"You think I believe a single word that comes out of that lying mouth of yours?" he asked. "You'd say anything to get out of taking your medicine."

Because of my profession, I'd taken pains to learn a fair amount of self-defense. However, I knew I couldn't defend against Jamaal, at least not for very long. If he were an ordinary person in an ordinary situation, maybe I'd be able to fight him off long enough to make a run for it, but I couldn't *afford* to run for it. I *had* to get to my car, and he was in my way.

"I don't have time for this," I muttered under my breath as my heart kicked frantically behind my ribs. I had no hope that I could fight Jamaal off in hand-to-hand combat. That meant I had to try to reason with him. But how could I reason with a half-crazed death-god descendant who was convinced I was the enemy?

I held up my hands in a gesture that was supposed to indicate surrender, hoping Jamaal would take a step back from the edge. "Look, I don't know what you think I've done this time, but—"

"I heard you talking to Maggie," he replied, stalking toward me, muscles bunched to pounce, eyes practically glowing with his hatred.

It took me a minute to figure out what he was referring to. When I did, my eyes widened. He was talking about the day I'd found Emma's ring. I suppose he'd been eavesdropping. I'd speculated at the time that Jamaal would jump to the worst possible conclusion if he found out, and it looked like I was right. I backed away from his approach but forced myself not to run, despite the dangerous intensity of his expression.

His lips pulled back from his teeth in a snarl. "I'm *glad* Maggie didn't tell Anderson. Glad she left you to me."

"I know you don't want to believe it, but I found that ring in the pot, just like I said."

He shook his head hard enough to rattle his beads. "The truth is your boss Konstantin sent you to kill Emmitt, then ordered you to spy on us. You've been leading Anderson on, telling him you would find his Emma, but you never had any intention of finding anyone, did you?"

Sweat dewed my skin, despite the cold. Every moment I stood here talking to Jamaal was a moment I lost in my race against time. If only I'd thought to bring my gun.

"If it's within my power, I swear I will find Emma," I said. "But right now, I have to help my sister. She's an innocent bystander, Jamaal, whatever you might think about me. Please let me go to her, before Alexis hurts her."

Jamaal turned his head to the side and spat like there was a bad taste in his mouth. "Don't try to sell me that crock of shit! Blake is with her, so Alexis wouldn't get within a hundred yards of her. You think you can lie to us, kill one of our own, and I'm just going to let you run away? True, I'd catch up with you eventually. But I'm tired of waiting for my pound of flesh."

I wanted to scream with my overwhelming frustration. In the distance, a car engine gunned, and headlights headed down the main driveway toward the gates. This lot was too far away from the clubhouse for anyone there to hear me if I screamed, but maybe when the car got close enough, I'd be able to get the driver's attention.

I sucked air into my lungs, preparing to let loose the longest, loudest, most blood-curdling scream in the history of the universe. Tires squealed as the car I'd spotted gunned the engine again, hurtling forward at a speed that would do a NASCAR driver proud.

Before I managed to get any sound past my lips, Jamaal's fist connected with my jaw.

He'd been well out of arm's reach when I'd allowed my attention to stray to the approaching car for that brief fraction of a second, but that moment of distraction was all he'd needed. His punch lifted me off my feet and threw me backward. Pain exploded through my head, my vision dancing with fireworks as my legs turned into jelly.

My back slammed into one of the parked cars, foiling my second attempt to force out a scream as the impact knocked the air from my lungs. The scream probably wouldn't have done me much good anyway, I decided as I sat on my butt and tried to blink the fireworks away. The car I'd been hoping to flag down was going so fast I expected a sonic boom to follow in its wake. It was well past us by the time I staggered to my feet to avoid Jamaal's next attack.

My head was swimming from that first punch, but my desperation helped me hold on to consciousness. If I blacked out, Jamaal would be on me in a heartbeat, and I'd never make it to Steph in time.

Something trickled over my upper lip. I brushed at it with the back of my hand. Blood. For the moment, I was glad it was dark, or I might have gone even more lightheaded with the sight.

Jamaal was grinning like a madman—which is pretty much what he was at that moment. As he closed the distance between us, both his hands clenched into heavy, dangerous fists. He swung at me again, his right fist aiming for my nose. This time, I managed to duck. Unfortunately, I wasn't prepared for the follow-up from his left, which caught me right in the gut.

Gagging, desperate for air, I collapsed to the ground once again. I retained just enough brain power to roll, this time avoiding a vicious kick from Jamaal's booted foot.

I pushed myself up to my hands and knees, scanning the parking lot to regain my bearings. My car was only a few yards away. I lurched to my feet and flung myself toward the car, but Jamaal caught me in a flying tackle before I took more than two steps.

Despite my breathlessness, I did manage a rough imitation of a scream of frustration as I went down once again. I kicked out blindly and got lucky, hitting Jamaal in the nose by the crunchy sound of it. He absorbed the pain with no more than a stoic grunt, but at least it distracted him enough to let me get to my feet again.

I had closed the remaining distance between myself and my car before I realized the fatal flaw in my plan. My evening bag, which had been draped bandolier-style across my chest while I ran, had come off sometime during the struggle. My car keys were in that bag.

Blood continued to trickle from my nose as I turned to face Jamaal once more. His nosebleed looked even worse than mine, but I saw no sign that it bothered him. He had drawn a knife from somewhere—his boot, maybe?—and was brandishing it in the occasional glimmers of moonlight that escaped the clouds.

I swallowed hard, tasting blood in the back of my throat. I hurt everywhere, from the punches, from the barefoot run, and from scraping off skin as I rolled around on the rough asphalt. My dress was in tatters, most likely indecent. Jamaal stood between me and the evening bag, and I was so hurt and exhausted already I didn't know how I could hold him off a moment longer. But I had to. Somehow.

Jamaal wasn't going to let me go. He'd long ago closed his mind to me, decided I was a traitor and that I was lying about Steph. Which meant that if I wanted to get into my car and drive away, I had to take him out.

It occurred to me that I'd been handling my fight with Jamaal as if I were no more than human. Perhaps I was shrugging off my injuries better than I might have before, not worrying that they would cause permanent damage, but I had abilities now that I hadn't had when I was mortal. And maybe those abilities would help me now.

If Jamaal closed with me, I was a goner, and probably would have been even if he didn't have the knife. So I didn't dare let him close.

I started darting glances left and right, quick glances that were meant to suggest to Jamaal that I was picking out an escape route. Only I knew better than to think I could escape. I edged around the car at my back, giving myself room to move. Then, I feinted to the left.

Jamaal had been thinking of me as little more than a puny human female himself. A not-too-bright one at that. When I feinted, he fell for it, lunging forward on what would have been an intercept course if I'd really been making a run for it.

Instead, I took advantage of his distraction and threw myself forward, heedless of the pain that seared my already tender skin as I slid face-first across the asphalt. My hand closed around the discarded shoe I'd caught sight of when I'd been pretending to look for an escape route. I rolled over onto my back.

The feint hadn't bought me much time. I hadn't expected it to. Jamaal had checked his charge and now whirled to face me.

I hesitated for a fraction of a second, a part of me horrified by what I was about to do. But it was for Steph, and it was necessary. Wincing in anticipation, I took aim and hurled the shoe at Jamaal's face with as much force as I could muster.

I had gambled that my throwing would be as accurate as my shooting had been. The gamble paid off.

Not surprisingly, Jamaal didn't immediately think of a thrown shoe as a dangerous weapon, and he made only a halfhearted attempt to avoid it. But my supernatural aim could make a dangerous weapon out of a lot of ordinary objects, and those heels were fashionably pointy.

The spiky, three-inch heel slammed into Jamaal's eye and lodged there. He screamed, a sound full of pain and rage. Even a tough guy like him wasn't able to retain his calm after having his eye put out. He fell, wrenching the shoe out of the bloody socket and hurling it away. His hands clasped the wound and he bent over until his forehead almost touched the asphalt, unable to suppress his agonized moans.

Sobbing in pain, in terror, and in horror, I limped to my evening bag to get the car key. Jamaal was still down when I collapsed into the driver's seat and started the engine. My stomach wanted to take a minute to empty itself out, but I'd run out of spare minutes about ten minutes ago, and I swallowed to keep my gorge down.

Trying not to look at Jamaal and what I had done to him, I slammed the pedal to the floor and pulled out of the parking lot at top speed.

EIGHTEEN

My hands shook and my teeth chattered as I drove, fear chewing a hole in my gut. How much time had Jamaal cost me? It seemed like forever, but my sense of time was completely out of whack.

My entire body throbbed from the beating I'd taken, and my stomach was still attempting to stage a rebellion. I'd fully intended to take out Jamaal's eye when I threw that shoe at him, but even in my fear for Steph, I couldn't help shuddering at the memory.

"He's *Liberi,* Nikki," I told myself, clenching my teeth, hoping that would make them stop chattering. "He'll heal."

At least, I hoped he would. For all I knew, the wound would heal and leave an empty socket. My gorge rose, and I swallowed fiercely. I'd done what I had to do. Besides, who knew what Jamaal would have done to me if I'd given him the chance? I suspected he had more than a beating in mind, a suspicion made stronger by the knife he'd brandished at me. He couldn't have killed me, but I knew I'd have been in for a world of hurt.

I've said before I'm a bleeding heart. No matter how much I told myself Jamaal had deserved what I'd done to him, I couldn't help feeling awful about it. Which is why I called Anderson while I was barreling down the street, trying to keep my speed to something that wouldn't inspire the cops to pull me over. If the way my own wound had healed after the car accident was any indication, Jamaal would be in pain and without an eye for at least a couple of hours, and I didn't want to leave him alone in that parking lot. Aside from any pity I might feel for his pain, I also didn't want any innocent bystanders to stumble on him. I didn't imagine having his eye taken out had improved his mental health.

Anderson answered on the first ring. "Nikki! Where are you?"

I blinked in surprise at the alarm in his voice. "On the road," I said. "Alexis—"

"Has your sister. I know. I just got off the phone with Blake."

Anger overwhelmed my fear, turning everything red. "Where the fuck was he?" I yelled. "He was supposed to be *protecting* her." I couldn't restrain a sob, and I had to blink away the tears that obscured my vision. I couldn't afford tears, not now.

"Explanations later," Anderson said curtly. "Do you know where he's taken her?"

I blurted out the address. If one of Anderson's people was closer than I was, then maybe they could get there in time to help Steph.

"And where are *you*?" he asked.

"Still in Chevy Chase, but going as fast as I can."

There was a hesitation on the other end of the line, as though Anderson was surprised by my answer. But then, if he'd already talked to Blake, he knew when Steph was taken, and he had to wonder why I wasn't already halfway to the rendezvous.

"Jamaal delayed me," I said, no longer caring if that made me a tattletale. "You might want to send someone to the country club to pick him up. He's not in very good shape at the moment."

"I'll call you back," Anderson said, then hung up abruptly.

I frowned at the phone. Why had he hung up on me like that? Even in those few words, I'd been able to hear the rage in his voice, but it was *Jamaal* he was angry at, not me. Right?

I closed the phone and tossed it onto the passenger seat. It didn't matter who Anderson was angry at or why he'd hung up. He was at the mansion, too far away to help. I'd deal with the fallout from my fight with Jamaal later.

The phone rang a couple of times as I sped through the streets of the city, cursing every red light I couldn't afford to run for fear of police intervention. I ignored it, because at the speed I was driving, it was safer to keep all my attention on the road. I wouldn't do Steph much more good if

I wrecked the car than if I got stopped by the cops.

The minutes ticked away, and though I tried not to, I couldn't help checking the clock on the dashboard every time I could spare the attention. I let out a sob when Alexis's deadline came and went, although I'd known from the moment I'd run into Jamaal that I wouldn't make it in time. I prayed Alexis would hold off for just a little while, give me a little grace period, since he knew just how unreasonable his deadline had been.

I turned the final corner a good ten minutes past the deadline. The street was quiet and secluded—which, of course, suited Alexis's purpose. There weren't any legal parking spaces available, but I wasn't about to sweat legalities at this point.

As I pulled into a "space" blocking a narrow alley, the door to the house across the street—the one where Alexis had instructed me to meet him—flew open. I blinked in surprise when Alexis charged out at a dead run, vaulting the ornamental railing that lined the stoop and taking off down the street like the hounds of hell were after him.

Maybe I'd watched too many movies, but my immediate thought was that he'd planted a bomb in the house and was running to avoid the explosion. I slammed the car into park and decided I didn't care why Alexis was running. I only cared about Steph.

The wounds on the bottoms of my feet had been superficial enough that they had already healed, but it wouldn't have mattered if they'd been raw and bleeding. I still would have leapt out of the car and dashed up the steps. Alexis had left the door open when he fled, so I burst right in, not pausing for even a moment to consider the possibility of ambush.

"Steph!" I screamed, desperate to hear her voice, to know that she was alive and okay.

"In here!" answered a voice that most definitely was not Steph's.

Dread making me shiver, I followed the sound of Blake's voice.

I found them on the floor in a room toward the back. The house was up for sale and completely empty, but I suspected the room was meant to be an office, based on the desk-and-shelf combo built in to the wall.

Blake was kneeling on the floor, leaning protectively over Steph, her head on his lap. Her elegantly coiffed hair was a bedraggled mess and draped her face like a veil. She was naked, though Blake was doing his best to tuck her torn dress around her body to restore her modesty. Her shoulders were shaking with silent sobs.

I stopped in the doorway, clapping my hand over my mouth to stifle my cry. *She's alive,* I told myself over and over, though the nudity and the tears reminded me of the difference between *alive* and *well*.

"Oh, Steph," I whispered, my heart breaking.

Blake pulled her gently into his arms, rocking her as he cradled her head against his chest. His own eyes when he looked at me were rimmed with red, the evidence of his sincere distress giving me another shock. He did a double-take when he caught sight of me. I'm sure I looked like I'd been dragged behind a pickup truck on a gravel road, and I felt drafts in places I shouldn't feel drafts while fully clothed, but I didn't give a damn about my appearance.

"I'm going to kill him," I growled, not sure if I meant Alexis or Jamaal at the moment. Maybe both.

I remembered seeing Alexis fleeing the scene, and my anger rose another notch. "You let Alexis get away. And where the hell were you, anyway? You were supposed to keep her safe!"

He flinched at the virulence of my tone, but rebounded quickly. "Somebody spilled a whole glass of red wine on me," he said. "I went to the men's room to clean up. She was right outside . . ." His voice trailed off and he gathered Steph even closer. "He locked me in, and he took her," he said. "I wasn't delayed for long, but I had to hurry after him. I couldn't stop to look for you, didn't have time."

The expression in his eyes hardened. "As for why I let the bastard get away, would you really rather I left Steph alone and chased after him?"

I let out a harsh breath, wishing I could hit rewind on my life. "No. Of course not."

I forced myself farther into the room, though seeing Steph's pain was almost unbearable. Blake stroked her hair away from her face, and the hollow ache inside me went from bad to worse. I staggered and almost fell.

He'd beaten her. Badly. Both of her eyes were

blackened, and her lip was split and swollen. A ring of bruises circled her neck, where Alexis must have choked her.

All at once, it was too much. The beating I had taken. The horror of putting out Jamaal's eye. The constant pump of adrenaline through my system as I ran my losing race against time. And the awful, sickening revelation of what that sadistic bastard had done to my sister.

The room spun and bucked around me, and my brain shut down. My legs crumpled and I fell to my knees on the carpeted floor. I didn't quite pass out, but it was a near thing.

"Nikki," Steph rasped.

I fought to push back the gray fog that surrounded my mind. Falling to pieces would be the easy way out, and I was never one to do things the easy way. I swallowed the huge, aching lump in my throat and blinked to hold back tears.

Steph was holding her hand out to me, and I shuffled toward her on my knees until I was close enough to take it. Her fingers curled around mine in a surprisingly firm grip.

"Are you okay?" she asked. Her voice was rough and hoarse, either from screaming, from crying, or from being choked nearly to death.

My jaw dropped as I looked at her battered face, at the tears that stained her cheeks. "Am *I* okay?" I fought a hysterical laugh. After everything Steph had been through, she was worried about *me*?

She sniffled and blinked away some tears. "You look

like someone shoved you through a paper shredder."

For a moment, I'd actually forgotten what a wreck I must look. But I would be healed in a few hours, and Steph . . .

"I'm fine," I assured her, the sound breaking in my throat as I struggled not to cry.

"You are not. And you have a lot of explaining to do."

Even in her obvious distress and with her ravaged voice, Steph managed to imbue those words with a tone of command. I wondered if Alexis had revealed his supernatural nature to Steph while he . . .

I stopped myself from going there, although the question remained in my mind. If his threats were anything to go by, he'd never intended to kill her, figuring that leaving her alive and suffering would hurt me more. But he was an arrogant bastard, and he might have figured she'd be too terrified and traumatized to say anything about any supernatural powers he might reveal.

"Let's get you taken care of first," Blake said gently when I took too long to answer. "We can do explanations later."

"Have you called an ambulance?" I asked Blake.

"No!" he and Steph answered at the same time.

I understood why Blake would object—he was worried about the potential of police getting involved in *Liberi* business—but if he thought I was going to let him stand in the way of Steph getting the medical care she needed, he was sorely mistaken. I squeezed her hand a little harder.

"You need help, hon," I said, but Steph shook her head.

"No doctors," she said firmly. She forced her swollen eyes open enough to meet my gaze squarely. "He didn't do anything to me that won't heal on its own in time. And I suspect siccing the police on him would probably get them killed. I don't know what he was, except that it's not human."

Crap. That meant Alexis had spilled at least some of the beans. I wanted to pretend I had no idea what she was talking about, to keep her sheltered from the knowledge of how formidable a foe Alexis was. I wanted to urge her to go to the hospital, to talk to the police, to do all the normal things that a rape victim should do. But I was too run-down to manage it. I might be able to say the words, but I wouldn't be able to make them convincing.

"We'll bring her back to the house," Blake told me. "She'll be safe there."

I was too depressed and guilt-stricken to argue. We helped Steph get back into what was left of her dress, and then Blake gave her his tuxedo jacket to cover up in. I retrieved my car from its illegal parking space and pulled up right in front of the door as Blake carried Steph out and bundled her into the backseat.

"I could have walked," I heard her grumble as Blake climbed in after her. I supposed he'd come back to get his own car some other time.

"But carrying you made me feel less useless," he said.

I glanced at his face in the rearview mirror, then had to look away from his raw expression. He couldn't know Steph very well, but despite my earlier suspicions, it seemed obvious he genuinely cared about her. And that he felt almost as guilty as I did about failing her.

NINETEEN

I drove back to the mansion in a daze. Steph lay curled in the backseat, her head once again on Blake's lap as he soothed and petted her. Her tears had dried up long ago, but I knew there would be more to come. The wounds Alexis had inflicted on her psyche were far worse than the physical pain, and I wished like hell I were still a mortal so I could have the pleasure of killing him.

Blake called Anderson while we were en route, giving him an update. I couldn't hear anything Anderson said over the phone, of course, but I swear I could *sense* his anger. I wasn't sure who he was angry with, and I wasn't sure I cared. I did my best to retreat into a numb sense of unreality, not ready to deal with the emotions that roiled within me.

When we got to the house, Blake once again insisted on carrying Steph, despite her protests that she could walk. Maybe it made him feel better to be gallant, though I couldn't help noticing how she curled into him, her arm slung around his neck, her head resting just below his chin. Protests aside, it seemed she needed the comfort, too. Maybe he was doing it for her sake after all. I raced ahead to hold the front door for him, then followed him into the entryway and came to a dead stop.

Anderson was waiting there for us, and he wasn't alone. Jamaal stood beside him, his eye thoroughly bandaged. I expected him to be in a towering rage after what I'd done to him. Instead, he took one look at Steph's battered form as she cuddled against Blake's chest, and lowered his head in what looked a hell of a lot like shame.

The rage I'd been fighting since the moment I'd seen what Alexis had done to my sister came boiling up through my chest. It was all I could do not to hurl myself at Jamaal and try to scratch his other eye out.

"Take her upstairs," Anderson ordered Blake, who nodded and headed toward the grand staircase. "Not you," Anderson continued when I made to follow Blake.

"But—" The look in Anderson's eyes made me swallow my protest. I didn't want to let Steph out of my sight, but a part of me knew my own emotional turmoil might do her more harm than good. The last thing she needed was to worry herself over my well-being after what she'd been through, and she was enough of a mother hen to do it. Curling my hands into fists, I stayed where I was and watched as Blake carried her upstairs.

Slowly, I turned back to Anderson and Jamaal. Jamaal still stood with his head bowed, his shoulders hunched like he was trying to make himself smaller. Maybe he sensed me looking at him, because he raised his head and met my gaze for a moment. The expression in his unbandaged eye was bleak. He opened his mouth to say something, then shook his head and returned his gaze to the floor.

"There are no words," I thought I heard him say under his breath.

One thing I can say for Jamaal, he's no actor. I doubted he could fake remorse if his life depended on it, and I knew what I was seeing was genuine. He had convinced himself every word out of my mouth was a lie, and therefore he had never believed holding me up would actually hurt anyone but me. Now that he was faced with the truth, his malice had drained away.

He might be genuinely sorry for what he'd done, but that didn't do Steph any good, and therefore I didn't give a damn.

"Tomorrow morning at nine," Anderson said to Jamaal, his voice cold steel, "we will hold a tribunal in my study to determine your punishment." Jamaal nodded his acceptance without looking up. "You'll spend the night downstairs." In one of the cells, I presumed. "Go. Now."

Jamaal bowed from the waist and, still keeping his gaze fixed on the floor, backed out of the room and away. It was as submissive a gesture as I'd ever seen, and it made me wonder just what kind of punishment this tribunal might sentence him to. For all that I was nominally a part of Anderson's merry band, I didn't know all that much about them.

Anderson turned to me when Jamaal was gone, his expression somber. Had Jamaal told him about the ring? Was I going to be having a tribunal of my own? At the moment, I wasn't sure I cared.

Anderson looked me up and down, inspecting the damage. The cuts and scrapes I'd suffered from rolling around on the asphalt were all well on their way to healing, but from the feel of it, several of the deeper bruises still had a ways to go. My head ached fiercely, but I suspected much of that was the aftermath of the stress rather than real physical injury.

Anderson shook his head. "I never would have guessed he'd do that," he said. "I knew he still suspected you, and I knew he was unstable, but . . ." He let his voice trail off, and for the first time since I'd met him, a look of true uncertainty crossed his face.

I heaved out a sigh. "It's not your fault," I told him, and despite my anger at the *Liberi* in general, I realized I meant it. Maybe if I had told him about Jamaal's nocturnal visit, he'd have been able to head off tonight's disaster. Keeping quiet had seemed like the honorable thing to do, but I'd had even more evidence than Anderson that Jamaal was out of control. I should have done something about it, and Steph had suffered because I hadn't.

"What are you going to do to him?" I asked, crossing my arms and shivering in a phantom chill. Despite his mild-mannered affect, I'd seen hints that Anderson had a ruthless side. No matter how angry

I was at Jamaal, I wasn't sure I wanted to see that ruthless side unleashed.

"We'll decide that tomorrow." There was no give in his tone, and I knew the subject was closed.

"And his eye . . ." I swallowed hard, sickened once again at the memory of what I had done. "Will it heal?"

Anderson looked at me in surprise. "Don't tell me you're feeling sorry for him!"

Logic said I shouldn't. I never wanted to be so bloodthirsty that I reveled in another's pain, no matter what that other had done, but that didn't mean I should feel sorry for him. And yet still I couldn't help being aware of the deep river of pain that ran beneath Jamaal's hostility. He needed someone to blame for Emmitt's death, and I was the obvious candidate. I knew too well what it was like to try to offload pain onto someone else. Just ask some of the unfortunate foster families who got stuck with me before the Glasses tamed me.

I glanced at the doorway through which Jamaal had disappeared. "What was he like before Emmitt died?" I asked instead of answering Anderson's question.

Anderson sighed and ran a hand through his already disheveled hair. "Not like this," he muttered, confirming what I'd already guessed. "He was always strung pretty tight, but Emmitt helped balance him. Emmitt had centuries of experience dealing with the effects of his death magic, and Jamaal's only had a couple of decades. It isn't an easy adjustment."

Despite the situation, I couldn't help being curious.
I'd seen firsthand what Maggie and Blake could do,
and I was pretty sure I'd seen Jamaal walk through a
closed door, but other than that, I had very little grasp
of the powers of my fellow *Liberi*. "Death magic?"

Anderson nodded. "It's a very . . . dark power,
particularly in Jamaal. He can kill people without
even touching them, and the power practically has a
mind of its own. It *wants* to be used, and it's always
a struggle to keep it contained. Emmitt had some of
the same power, and he'd learned to master it. He was
teaching Jamaal his techniques, and Jamaal was stabi-
lizing." His jaw clenched. "Then the bastard decided
to shuffle off this mortal coil with the job unfinished."

I hadn't known Emmitt very well, and most
of what I'd known had been a fiction anyway. He'd
seemed like a pretty nice guy, at least on the surface.
But truly nice guys didn't walk out on people who
needed them.

"Too bad we can't bring him back from the dead
and give *him* a tribunal," I said, and Anderson cracked
a small smile.

"Indeed." The smile faded before it had a chance
to take hold. "You should get cleaned up and tend
your wounds. We'll have an early day tomorrow."

"Look, I don't know if Jamaal told you—"

"That you found Emma's ring?"

Well, that answered that. "Um, yeah."

Anderson met my eyes. "If you tell me you found
that ring in the pot, then I'll take you at your word.
For now."

I wasn't sure if saying he believed me was legitimate when it was paired with "for now," but at least he wasn't threatening me with the Hand of Doom. "I found the ring in the pot," I said, looking him straight in the eye. "I swear it."

He stared at me a long while, but I didn't look away. Finally, he nodded. "All right then. We'll say no more."

I knew a dismissal when I heard one. I didn't much want to be alone with my thoughts, but I headed upstairs anyway. I took a shower and changed, avoiding taking too close a look at myself in the mirror, then went looking for Steph.

Not surprisingly, she was in Blake's suite. He was in his sitting room, sipping from a tumbler of amber liquid and pacing. The door to his bedroom was ajar, but the lights inside were out.

He stopped pacing when he saw me, putting his finger to his lips in a shushing motion. "She's sleeping," he whispered.

I wanted to go to her, to look her over and assure myself that she was all right. But of course, she *wasn't* all right, and if she'd temporarily escaped her misery in sleep, I wasn't about to wake her.

"You should get some sleep, too," Blake continued, still in that soft whisper. "You look like you're about to keel over."

I felt like it. Healing definitely seemed to take a lot out of my body, and I felt like I hadn't slept in three days. "Take good care of her," I urged, surprised to find I felt perfectly comfortable leaving Steph in his care. Just a few short hours earlier, I'd have said I didn't trust Blake as far as I could throw him. He'd failed to protect Steph, but he'd done more for her than *I* had. Who knew how much worse it would have been if Blake hadn't shown up at the scene when he did?

Hoping that I could find oblivion in sleep, at least for a little while, I headed back to my own room and collapsed on the bed fully clothed.

I've had more than my fair share of bad nights throughout my life, but that night was among the worst. As exhausted as I was, I couldn't sleep. I could barely even keep my eyes closed. Instead, I lay there on my back in the dark, cataloging the sins of my past and wondering how Steph had had the bad luck to get stuck with such a crappy adoptive sister. As I lay there wallowing in guilt, I realized that this wasn't the first time someone had gotten hurt because of my misguided desire not to be a tattletale. Considering how horribly wrong things had gone the last time I'd made the fateful decision to keep my mouth shut, you'd think I'd have known better by now.

I was eight years old, and was already on my eighth foster family, the Garcias. They had a twelve-year-old son, Dave, who had been every bit as much of a problem child as I was, so they were sure they could "fix" me. The thing was, they hadn't "fixed" Dave as much as they'd thought.

Mr. Garcia was a gun enthusiast, but a very responsible one. He kept his guns safely locked away, with the ammo in a different safe and both keys hidden. Dave was fascinated with those damn guns, and one summer day when Mr. Garcia was off at work, Dave figured out where the keys were hidden. He was very proud of himself and excited about being able to handle the guns with impunity. He showed off for me and even let me hold one myself.

Playing with guns had appealed to my wild nature, and of course I thought of Dave as older and wiser. To tell the truth, I never even considered telling on him.

About a month later, Dave had some of his friends from school over. I was out shopping with Mrs. Garcia. Mr. Garcia was supposed to be keeping an eye on the boys, but they were old enough not to need constant supervision. He was comfortable sitting down in the living room and watching a baseball game while the boys played video games in Dave's room.

Dave was now making a habit of sneaking into the gun safe. Wanting to impress his friends, he'd stuck a gun into his dresser drawer. I'm pretty sure he thought it wasn't loaded, or that he'd fired all the bullets the last time he'd snuck it out for some target practice in the woods. One of his friends found out the hard way that there was one bullet left. The gun went off in Dave's hand, and he'd have his friend's death on his conscience for the rest of his life.

Dave told all in the aftermath, and when the Garcias found out I'd known about the gun, they couldn't wait to get rid of me. They couldn't find it in their hearts to be mad at Dave, their flesh and blood. So instead, they heaped all the blame on me. It was blame I'd never accepted, and my bitterness and anger when they packed me off was monumental.

I should have learned my lesson. No, the death hadn't been my fault, and yes, it had been wrong of the Garcias to blame me. Even so, there'd been a life lesson I could have learned if only I'd opened my eyes to it. I wasn't to blame for the death, but I could have prevented it.

Now that it was too late, I'd finally figured it out: I should have told Anderson the truth about Jamaal's threats. But even the best hindsight couldn't change the past.

TWENTY

I managed to doze fitfully through the darkest hours of the night, but was up and out of bed as soon as the sun peeked up over the horizon. I was tired, dejected, and on the verge of a headache, but I knew I wasn't getting any more sleep. I ventured down to the kitchen and made a pot of coffee, then fixed myself two hearty mugs full and took them back upstairs to my suite. With the tribunal at nine, I knew the rest of Anderson's clan would be getting up earlier than usual, and I didn't want to run in to anyone.

If I'd thought I could avoid the tribunal, I'd have done it in a heartbeat. Pissed off as I was at Jamaal, I thought that having his eye put out and then having to live with the guilt of leaving Steph to Alexis's tender mercies was punishment enough. He might still think I was a spy—Steph getting hurt proved that Konstantin was a bastard, but not that I wasn't in league with him—but I seriously doubted Jamaal would make another unsanctioned attack against me.

I wasn't really one of Anderson's people, no matter what he claimed to Konstantin. And moving into the house hadn't even saved Steph. There was no good reason for me to follow Anderson's orders and attend the tribunal. Maybe I should have just packed my bags and gone home. But Jamaal was being punished on my behalf, so when nine o'clock rolled around, I headed for Anderson's study.

Anderson had pulled in additional chairs from somewhere and pushed his usual furniture to the walls. Jamaal sat with his back to the wall on a metal folding chair, and the rest of the chairs were set up in a semicircle around him. In the center, directly facing Jamaal, was Anderson, his chair larger and more comfortable-looking than all the rest, looking almost like a throne. The others were all ranged around him, and there was only one empty seat, between Maggie and Blake. Apparently, I was the last to arrive.

Dragging my feet a bit, I made my way over to the empty seat. No one was talking, the tension in the room so thick I could almost feel it sliding against my skin.

Jamaal sat with his head bowed and his hands clasped in his lap, the picture of penitence. His eye was no longer bandaged, but it wasn't finished healing yet, either. The flesh all around the socket was swollen and bruised, but the eye itself seemed to have regenerated. I breathed a little sigh of relief at that. Like I said, a bleeding heart.

"Where's Steph?" I whispered to Blake as I took my seat. I didn't like the idea of leaving her alone, although I supposed having her sit in on the tribunal wouldn't be such a hot idea.

"Still sleeping," he answered, his voice equally soft. "She took a Valium, so she'll be out for a while."

I wanted to ask where Steph had gotten a Valium—it didn't seem like something the *Liberi* would have around—but just then Anderson called the tribunal to order. He asked me to tell everyone exactly what had happened last night, and I squirmed. Silly, perhaps, seeing as it was after the fact and everyone already knew, but I didn't want to sit there and publicly rat Jamaal out. Guess I *still* wasn't over my fear of being seen as a tattletale.

"Is that really necessary?" I asked. "We all know what happened."

"It's necessary," Anderson said in a clipped voice that told me he didn't appreciate his orders being questioned. Gone entirely was his usual, easygoing manner. This morning, he was all alpha-male leader, grim and intimidating.

I struggled to come up with a tactful way to explain the situation, but to my surprise, Jamaal put me out of my misery.

"I fucked up," he said quietly. He raised his head and looked us squarely in the eye, one by one. It wasn't a gesture of defiance, but one of accountability.

"I convinced myself Nikki was working for Konstantin, and I decided to teach her a lesson," he continued. There was misery in his eyes, but his voice was flat as he recounted the facts. "I thought if I ambushed her at the auction, I'd have the time to do what I wanted without fear of being interrupted. I waited by her car, and when she came running into the parking lot, I jumped her. She tried to tell me Alexis had her sister, but I wouldn't listen. I told myself she was lying again, and I wouldn't let her leave. She managed to fight me off." Was there a hint of approval in his voice when he said that? Hard to believe he'd approve of me taking out his eye.

"But my attack delayed her, and she was unable to get to her sister in time. Because of me, Alexis brutalized an innocent woman." His voice wasn't so flat anymore, and the words rasped out of his throat. "I have no excuse for anything I've done, and I'll willingly take whatever punishment you think I deserve."

A long, tense silence followed Jamaal's speech. I glanced at the other *Liberi,* trying to be subtle as I read their faces. There were a couple of people—specifically, Maggie and Jack—who regarded Jamaal with expressions of sympathy. Logan and Leo looked neutral, like they didn't care what happened to Jamaal one way or another. Blake was giving him a death glare, and Anderson looked cold and deadly.

"You've broken our trust," Anderson said, and he sounded about as warm as an iceberg. "You disobeyed my direct orders, and you hurt someone who was under my protection. Pack your bags. I want you out by noon."

Jamaal's jaw dropped, and his face turned ashen

gray. "No," he whispered, not in refusal but in dismay. "Please." He gripped the seat of his chair until his knuckles turned white, as if he were holding onto it for dear life. "Anything but that."

My throat tightened in sympathy. Damn it, it was too easy for me to empathize with him! I'd been kicked out of too many homes in my life not to know the sickening lurch of it. And most of the homes I'd been kicked out of hadn't really felt so much like homes to me as way stations. Jamaal might not have an easy rapport with the rest of Anderson's people, and he definitely held himself a bit aloof, but this was truly his home.

What would he do if he were no longer part of Anderson's crew? His divine ancestor wasn't Greek, so he couldn't become an Olympian even if he wanted to. And if being separated from Emmitt had worsened the effects the death magic had on him, I couldn't imagine what being separated from all his friends and his home would do to him.

"Maybe he deserves another chance," Jack said into the silence.

That surprised me—and everyone else, too, by the look of it. Jack seemed to have embraced his trickster heritage with gusto, and I'd never seen him be serious about anything. Of course, Jamaal, with his nonexistent sense of humor, was Jack's favorite target. The jokes sometimes had some pretty sharp teeth, but he wouldn't have teased Jamaal so much if he didn't like him.

"He's had enough chances," Blake countered with

a snarl. "He's proven he can't control himself—or *won't*—and there's no place for him here."

"Surely he's learned his lesson," Maggie put in softly, and I was glad I wasn't the only bleeding heart in the room.

"Too late!" Blake snapped.

The tribunal was about to devolve into a free-for-all, but Anderson nipped that in the bud.

"Show of hands. How many of you think we should give Jamaal another chance?"

Maggie, Jack, and I all raised our hands. I got a couple of startled looks—and a sneer from Blake—but I was sure giving Jamaal another chance was the right thing to do. I didn't think he would fall over himself in gratitude because I supported him, nor did I think he would suddenly be convinced I didn't work for Konstantin. Maybe I'd end up regretting the decision later, but I couldn't vote to throw him to the wolves. Steph might have been hurt because of him, but that certainly wasn't what he'd *meant* to happen. And there was no guarantee Steph wouldn't have been hurt if I'd made the rendezvous in time.

Blake, Logan, and Leo didn't raise their hands, despite the sad look in Leo's eyes. That left us deadlocked, though in truth I wasn't sure how much our opinions really counted. Anderson had made it very clear: his house, his rules.

Anderson thought about it for a long moment, then nodded. "Since Nikki, as the injured party, is willing to give you another chance, I'll let you choose your punishment. You can either pack your bags and leave. Or you can submit to an execution once a day for the next three days."

There were gasps and winces all around the semi-circle of *Liberi,* and I saw the flicker of fear in Jamaal's eyes. Nevertheless, he didn't hesitate in his answer.

"I'll submit to whatever I have to if you'll let me stay."

I wasn't sure exactly what it all meant. Obviously, the *Liberi* couldn't die, so this wasn't a real execution we were talking about. (Not to mention that a real execution is a one-time deal.) But something about it sure gave the rest of the *Liberi* the shivers.

Anderson nodded regally. "Logan will perform the executions," he continued. "I'll leave it to him to decide the methods." He looked at his watch. "We'll convene at sunset at the clearing. Attendance is mandatory." He shot a look at me, as if knowing how little I'd want to watch whatever was going to happen. "Jamaal, you will remain downstairs until the sentence has been fully carried out. No passing through the door, or you're out. Clear?"

Jamaal held his chin high. "Clear."

Anderson stood from his chair, still running arctic cold. "Everyone out," he said as he turned his back on all of us and headed toward his desk to pull it out of the corner it had been shoved into. I think more than one of us considered offering to help him put the room back to rights, but we all thought better of it.

I gave Maggie a significant look as we left the room, and she got the message, following me up to my own suite.

"I don't want to go into this thing tonight uninformed," I told her as soon as I'd closed the sitting room door. "Jamaal can't die, so what's with the execution thing? And why did everyone look so sick about it?"

Maggie shuddered as she dropped onto the sofa, wrapping her arms about herself like she was cold. "It's not true that we can't die," she said. "We just don't stay dead."

I joined her on the sofa, feeling a similar chill. "Huh?"

"If we're dealt a serious enough wound, we die. Our bodies will heal the damage eventually, and we'll revive, so it's not permanent. But it is dead.

"I've never had a fatal wound myself, but from what I've heard, it's horrible. It has nothing to do with the pain of the wound or of the healing—though that can be considerable in itself, depending on the cause of death—but dying itself is a massively unpleasant experience. Even as an immortal, you want to avoid dying at all costs."

I salted this information away for later. I probably wasn't cruel enough to kill Alexis over and over again if I ever got my hands on him. But at least for now, it made a comforting, if gruesome, fantasy.

TWENTY-ONE

I checked on Steph every couple of hours until the Valium had worn off and she was awake and alert. I had to admit, Blake seemed to be taking good care of her. Her face and throat were still darkly bruised, but judicious applications of ice had reduced the swelling. There was also a bottle of Advil on the bedside table, beside a cheerful flower arrangement exactly like the kind you might send someone in the hospital.

He'd given her an oversized T-shirt to wear, along with a pair of drawstring running shorts that would probably fall off if she tried to walk around in them. She was propped up in his bed, surrounded by mounds of pillows as she sipped from a mug of hot chocolate, when I came in.

Blake, still in guardian angel mode, was sitting on the side of the bed, his hand stroking idly up and down the covers over her legs as he kept her silent company. They both looked up when I knocked on the bedroom door, but Blake spared me only a brief glance before he turned his attention back to his patient.

Steph cupped her hands around her mug as if they were cold, then looked me up and down, her head cocked to the side. There was no way she could miss how my injuries had disappeared overnight. She didn't look completely shocked, so I suspected Blake had told her all the secrets I'd been unwilling to share. Just one more thing to feel guilty about, though truthfully, if I could have gone back in time I'd probably have made the same decision.

"How are you feeling?" I asked, though it felt like a dumb question.

She raised one shoulder in a halfhearted shrug. "To tell you the truth, right now I'm kind of numb. I don't suppose it'll last, but I'll take what I can get."

The flatness of her voice made her sound as numb as she said she felt, and I wished to God I'd been able to save her. It took about a thousand wrong decisions on my part to put her in this situation, and I couldn't stop myself from mentally recalling and regretting each one.

"How about you?" Steph asked. "You looked pretty rough last night."

"I'm fine now," I answered, which was true as long as we were talking only about my physical injuries. The emotional wounds left me in a state that was very far from fine.

Steph set her mug down on the bedside table, then lightly touched the back of Blake's hand. "Could you give us a few minutes alone?"

I could tell by the look on his face that Blake was

reluctant to leave her side, but he sighed and nodded. "I'll be right outside if you need anything," he said. "Just give me a holler."

She managed a small smile. "I will."

He leaned over and kissed her forehead, like a father comforting a little girl, before he left the room, but I didn't think his affection for her was exactly paternal. Was it just his guilt over having failed her last night that made him act so devoted, or had he really formed such a quick, strong attachment?

"Come and sit down, Nikki," Steph beckoned.

I hadn't realized until that moment that I was hovering near the door as if ready to make a quick escape. It was almost impossibly hard to face my sister and be forced to see what had been done to her because of me. But she needed every ounce of support she could get, so I manned up and took Blake's place at the side of the bed. She reached out and took my hand, giving it a firm, comforting squeeze.

"I'll survive," she told me softly even as she squeezed my hand harder. "You know that, right?"

My throat ached so much I couldn't answer, and if I wasn't careful I was going to start bawling. Steph shouldn't need to comfort me after what she'd been through. I should be strong enough to hide my own pain and guilt, deal with it on my own rather than burdening her with it.

"I'm not as fragile as you think I am, Nikki," she said when I still couldn't force myself to speak. "It's going to be rough for a while, but I swear to you, I'm going to get over it."

I sucked in a breath, and it loosened my throat enough to let me speak. "I'm so sorry . . ."

Steph shook her head. "There was nothing you could have done. This Alexis creep was never going to just let me go. You know that, don't you?"

Actually, I hadn't thought about it, about what he would have done if I'd gotten there on time. I had a suspicion Steph was right. Alexis wasn't what you'd call the honorable type, so expecting him to keep his word was wishful thinking. But having not made the rendezvous, I couldn't be sure. I guess I didn't look convinced, because Steph continued.

"Blake says Alexis wants you to track down a bunch of innocent people so he can slaughter them. Do you think for a moment that's what I'd have wanted you to do?"

I scrubbed at my eyes, wiping away the hint of tears that had gathered in them, wishing I could wipe away the aching exhaustion as easily. Obviously, Blake had done a lot of talking. And been very convincing. "No, of course not."

"I'd like to take you and Blake and knock both your heads together. The self-flagellation the two of you are doing is getting on my last nerve. Bad things happen to people, and unless you've got an infallible crystal ball, you aren't always going to be able to stop them. Just deal with it and move on, because let me tell you, knowing you're miserable about it doesn't help me one iota."

I flinched from the anger in her voice. The numbness appeared to be gone for now. "What do you want me to do? Smile and act like nothing's wrong? I'm not a good enough actress to pull that off."

"No," she replied with exaggerated patience, "I want you to stop wasting your time and energy feeling guilty about it and start figuring out how you're going to get the *son of a bitch who did this to me!*"

There was nothing I wanted to do more. The problem was, how do you "get" someone who's immortal? Unlike the Olympians, Anderson didn't have a bunch of indoctrinated Descendants sitting around waiting for the opportunity to kill a *Liberi*.

An idea struck me before I even managed to finish the thought. "The list," I murmured, not meaning to say it aloud.

"Huh?"

"Konstantin gave me a list of Descendants he wanted me to find. Maybe if I could find one of them, we can use him to kill Alexis." What a sweet irony it would be if the very list the Olympians gave me turned out to be the key to destroying Alexis! I'd enjoy rubbing his smug face in it, right before—

"Wait a minute," Steph interrupted before my thoughts could gallop too far ahead. "Your plan is to hunt down some random civilian who probably has no idea that the *Liberi* even exist, then . . . what, exactly? Hope he's a homicidal maniac who'll be happy to kill Alexis at your command? Or were you thinking of kidnapping him and forcing him to kill Alexis? Or maybe doing to him what this Emmitt character did to you, somehow *tricking* him into killing Alexis?"

Damn. Steph had a few too many good questions

for my taste. I frowned. "I only came up with this idea like five seconds ago. Give me some time to work out the kinks. Besides, how else are we supposed to make Alexis pay for what he did? There's no other way to kill him."

"Who says you have to kill him? Blake told me you've been searching for a woman the Olympians have had interred for ten years. Why not give them a taste of their own medicine?"

There was a sense of poetic justice to the idea, except—

"If we bury him, somebody could dig him up someday just like we plan to dig up Emma." Assuming I could ever find her, which wasn't looking too likely. "I never thought of myself as bloodthirsty before, but I want that man dead."

"And the world would probably be a better place without him." Her voice softened. "But Nikki, you aren't a killer. I want Alexis to pay for what he did, but not at the price of putting a black mark on your soul."

I'd always suspected Steph was so damn nice because she'd had such an easy life. It's easy to be magnanimous toward others when everything is going your way, or at least that's what I'd thought. But here she was, being nice, worrying about the state of my soul after having been through a trauma worse than any I'd experienced. Maybe her niceness had nothing to do with her charmed life after all. Maybe it was just *her*.

"You can't possibly believe you're the only woman

he's hurt," I said instead of voicing any of my true thoughts. "There's not a question in my mind that he deserves to die." *And killing him would make me feel so much better.* Thought the woman who felt guilty about taking Jamaal's eye out. Maybe Steph had a point, but damned if I was going to admit it.

"So you're going to turn vigilante? Use your superpowers to hunt down the baddies one by one?"

She meant for me to respond to the vigilante comment—I guess it was supposed to shame me into seeing things her way—but I didn't want to argue with her, not now of all times. So I deflected the question.

"You're presuming I even have superpowers. I do seem to have acquired really good aim, but the hunting/tracking thing has been a total bust." Unless I counted finding the ring as part of my "superpowers," but that hadn't exactly turned out so well.

Despite her misery, there was a spark of interest in Steph's eyes. I suppose learning about the secret world that existed just beneath the surface of the ordinary one was a good way to distract herself from her present situation.

"How is the power supposed to work?" she asked.

"Beats me," I answered with a shrug. "I didn't get an instruction manual."

She gave me an exasperated look. "No kidding? What have you tried?"

I resisted the urge to give her another flippant answer. I couldn't do near as much as I wanted to help her, but I could at least talk to her and keep her mind occupied. "To tell you the truth, I'm not really sure *what* to try," I admitted. "I've approached the search just like I would if I were using my ordinary everyday skills and hoped I'd figure something out. So far, it hasn't worked. It's not like I've suddenly developed a hound's sense of smell or can tell which way someone went by a blade of broken grass."

Her brow furrowed in thought. "But you've always been good at finding things, even when you weren't *Liberi*. How did you do it?"

I waved her point off. "Yeah, I was good at it, but there was nothing supernatural about it. Like you said, I wasn't *Liberi*."

"But it seems unlikely it's a coincidence that you're descended from a goddess of the hunt and you've always been good at . . . well, hunting."

"I suppose," I said doubtfully.

"Remember that time back in high school when I lost my wallet?"

I frowned at the unexpected question. "Um, yeah. I guess." When we were kids, Steph had always been pretty bad about losing things, though it was a habit she'd outgrown. In fact, she'd lost enough stuff that I wasn't immediately sure which incident she was talking about.

"I was walking back from school and stopped at a coffee shop because a couple of my friends were in there."

I nodded, the memory sparking in my mind. "You got home and realized you didn't have your wallet. We retraced your steps back to the shop, assuming you must have left it there when you paid for your coffee."

"Right. Only it wasn't there."

We'd searched the place thoroughly, even asking the manager if we could look in the trash cans in case someone had found the wallet, taken all the good stuff, and thrown it away. We'd had no luck, and Steph had been in tears because she'd just gotten her first credit card. She was afraid her mom wouldn't let her replace it if she lost it so fast.

Steph was sure someone had stolen the wallet and it would never be seen again. That seemed like a pretty logical conclusion, but I suggested that maybe she'd dropped it somewhere between the coffee shop and home.

We started walking back home, scanning the pavement and the gutters, although Steph wasn't exactly holding out much hope. When we still didn't find it, Steph gave up and went to her room, miserably waiting for her mom to get home and scold her for being so careless with her belongings.

On a hunch, I headed back out. I remember it was in the early spring, the kind of day where you need a coat in the morning but it's too hot to wear by afternoon. Steph had a habit of absently stuffing things in pockets—it seemed like half the things she lost turned up eventually in a pocket somewhere—and I thought it was possible she'd stuffed the wallet in her coat pocket after paying for her coffee. Because it was too hot to wear the coat, she'd have been carrying it over her arm, and it was possible the wallet had dropped out.

We'd checked the sidewalk carefully when we'd

retraced her steps, but what if a Good Samaritan had found the wallet? This was D.C., not the kind of place you could leave a wallet lying around on the sidewalk for very long before someone helped themselves to it. That Good Samaritan would have either taken it with them in hopes of finding the owner—which might be hard, since the only identification in there was the credit card, and that gave nothing but a name—or handed it in to the closest shop.

It seemed like a long shot, but I didn't think it would hurt to check. Figuring the wallet would have fallen out pretty close to the coffee shop, I went into the tiny little shoe store a couple of doors down and asked if anyone had turned in a wallet—and wouldn't you know it, they had.

"How did you find that wallet?" Steph asked me.

"You know the story as well as I do."

"Not really. I wasn't inside your head, you know. Why did you decide to go into a shoe store that you knew I hadn't been in myself to look for the wallet I'd supposedly lost at the coffee shop?"

"Well, uh, it just seemed logical is all." But I had to admit, as sound as my logic had been, the shoe store hadn't exactly been a *likely* place to look.

"It was more logical to assume someone had walked off with it than to assume I'd put it in my coat pocket, that it had fallen out close to the coffee shop, that a Good Samaritan had found it, and that that Good Samaritan would turn it in at the shoe store. I'd given up, so why didn't you?"

I shrugged. "It was just a hunch is all," I said,

unable to explain it better than that. I cracked a smile that felt fragile and tenuous. "Besides, I was trying to impress my big sister, and I wasn't going to do that by assuming the wallet was gone for good."

She returned the smile. "And do you have those same kind of hunches when you're searching for people that other investigators have been unable to find?"

"Well, yeah. But it's really just thinking a little outside the box. I figure everyone's tried the most likely places already, so I try to come up with someplace less immediately obvious."

"So have you had any hunches about where Emma is buried?"

I sighed. "Not really."

"Do you think she's buried at one of the properties you checked out?"

"Yeah, probably, but I have no idea which one."

She nodded sagely. "There are a million other places she could be. What makes you think she's at one of those properties?"

I saw what she was getting at, but I was far from convinced. "It's either a hunch, or it's wishful thinking because if she's somewhere else, I've got nothing. And even if it is a hunch, and even if my hunches are supernaturally fueled somehow, I don't have it narrowed down enough to matter."

"Yet."

I appreciated her faith in me, but honestly, I didn't exactly feel hopeful. Would Anderson still have his people protect Steph if I turned out not to be able to find Emma? The warm, easygoing Anderson might, but I had my doubts about the cold, implacable leader who'd presided over this morning's tribunal. I told myself not to worry about that, but I didn't listen.

"I hope you're right," I told Steph. I had no idea if Blake had told her that she was under Anderson's protection only because I'd agreed to search for Emma. Even if *I* couldn't stop worrying about what would happen if I failed, there was no reason why *Steph* should worry, so I didn't elaborate.

"Big sisters are always right," she said with a grin.

I snorted. "You've been trying to convince me of that for years."

"Can't blame a girl for trying. Now I think it's time for you to stop coddling me and get back to work."

If she weren't so beat up already, I'd have given her a good smack on the arm for that. "I'm not coddling you!"

"You're hovering. I'm going to be fine. If I feel like I'm going to break down and need a shoulder to cry on other than Blake's, I'll come find you, okay?"

I knew I wasn't doing Steph any particular good by being at her bedside. Though I hid it fairly well— at least I thought I did—every time I caught sight of the bruises on her face, I suffered a hammer-strike of guilt. So I let her talk me into leaving her bedside no matter how convinced I was that I should have stayed.

I spent the rest of my afternoon at the desk in my suite, eyes glued to the computer screen as I tried not to think too much. I looked over all the information I had on the Olympian properties, searching for something I'd missed, something that might point me toward one choice over all the others. I also looked for some subconscious hint that one was more likely to be Emma's gravesite, but discovered it was really hard to *look* for a subconscious hint. My conscious mind kept yammering away at me, arguing logic and casting doubt, until I had to give up or go mad.

Hoping to clear my mind, I decided to take a different tack and did some research on Artemis. Maybe if I learned more about the goddess who was my ancestor—a concept I still had trouble wrapping my brain around—I'd be able to figure out how to use the powers I supposedly had.

I read through a lot of Greek and Roman mythology that afternoon, scouring the stories for something that might hint at a secret power I was missing. The only thing that rang anything like a bell with me was the fact that Artemis, aside from being a huntress, was also a goddess of the moon. It made me wonder if any of her descendants' powers were moon-based. If that were the case, then perhaps I'd been making a mistake by doing all of my investigating during the daylight hours.

I felt like I was grasping at straws. It seemed more likely that my newly enhanced aim was my only supernatural power. Then again, it had seemed more likely Steph's wallet had been stolen, but I'd gone with my gut all those years ago and my gut had been right.

I can't say I exactly got my hopes up. But I at

least tried to keep something resembling a positive attitude as I gathered the paperwork for some of the most likely properties and mapped out a route I would travel tonight, after the moon had risen. A faint hope was better than no hope. Whether Anderson would kick me out if I failed or not, my position here would still be stronger if I somehow managed to find Emma. I would do anything in my power to strengthen my position and protect myself—and Steph—from the Olympians.

TWENTY-TWO

Sunset officially came around five that night, but it took half an hour more before most of us were gathered in the kitchen, which was near the back door that would lead us to the clearing where Jamaal's first execution would take place. Everyone was in a grim, nervous mood. Maybe I was being paranoid, but I felt like everyone except Maggie was giving me a mild version of the cold shoulder. They might not have been all one happy family before I came along, but they'd been a lot happier than they were now. I couldn't blame them for holding me at least partially responsible.

Someone had left a bunch of lanterns on the kitchen table—actual oil-fueled lanterns, not the Coleman variety. I picked one up because everyone else did, lighting it with the long-barreled lighter that was being passed around.

We were milling about, no one talking, when Logan stepped into the room.

"Head on out to the clearing," he told us. "We'll meet you there."

"We" apparently referred to Logan, Jamaal, and Anderson, because the rest of us were all present and accounted for. If anyone objected to being ordered around by Logan, they kept their mouths shut. Still tense and unnaturally quiet, we filed out the back door.

When I'd first arrived at the mansion, Maggie had given me a thorough tour of the house, but I'd never been out on the grounds. I had no idea where we were going. I glanced up at the sky as we walked, but though it was a clear night, the moon hadn't yet risen.

We walked past the nicely manicured garden that dominated the view from the kitchen windows, plunging into the woods behind it. The woods were as meticulously pruned as those that surrounded the driveway. Although we weren't following a path, it was a simple matter to slip between the trees without tripping on undergrowth.

It was an eerie sight, this silent procession of grim-faced *Liberi*. The lanterns barely penetrated the dark, and it was easy for the mind to imagine terrors that lay just beyond the reach of the lanterns' glow. Or maybe that was just me and my nerves. Except for that terrible night when I'd killed Emmitt, I'd never seen anyone die before, and though I knew Jamaal would not stay dead, I desperately wanted to run back to the house and hide in my room. But Anderson had been very clear this morning, and I knew I had to bear witness, just as the rest of the *Liberi* did. I might not feel like I was truly one of them, but just as I'd had to in my many foster homes, I had to go through the motions and pretend I belonged.

We walked what I estimated was about one hundred yards before the trees gave way to a perfectly circular clearing. Someone—probably Logan—had already set the stage. A double row of torches flickered just far enough from the edge of the trees to avoid being a fire hazard.

My heart leapt into my throat when I saw what was in the center of the clearing: a low wooden block with a semicircular notch carved into the top. I might have been able to convince myself it was a stool or something else innocuous, if it weren't for the huge sword, held upright in a black iron stand just to the left of it.

I swallowed hard and sweat trickled down my back despite the brisk temperature. Maggie had walked beside me the entire way, offering her silent moral support. I didn't think she'd completely gotten over the suspicions that awakened when I'd found Emma's ring, but she was still friendly, even if not as warm. I reached out to clutch her arm.

"Tell me that's not what I think it is," I hissed, too freaked out to speak above a whisper.

She spared me a sympathetic glance. "Sorry, no can do."

"They're going to cut his head off?" This time, my voice came out in something more like a squeal. Nausea roiled in my stomach at the thought of it.

Maggie patted my back in a gesture that might

have been comforting if I'd been capable of being comforted. "It's a mercy," she said. "It'll be over too quickly for Jamaal to suffer any pain."

I swallowed again, hoping to keep my gorge down. Maybe it was a mercy for Jamaal, but it sure as hell wasn't one for me. I looked around at the other *Liberi*. Although everyone still looked grim, I seemed to be the only one close to passing out or hurling. Even Leo, with his mild-mannered accountant look, didn't seem particularly disturbed by what was about to happen.

"We are none of us young, nor have we led sheltered lives," Maggie said, correctly reading the expression on my face as usual. "We've seen horrors you wouldn't believe, especially those of us who were Olympians for a time."

I took a deep breath, wishing it would settle my nerves. "How the hell can he survive being beheaded?"

"He can't. That's the point."

"You know what I mean!" I snapped, nerves making my temper brittle.

Luckily, Maggie wasn't put off by my snappishness. "It's magic, Nikki. I don't know exactly *how* he'll come back. All I know is that he will."

I was saved from further embarrassing myself when Anderson entered the clearing, closely followed by Blake and Jamaal. Jamaal held his head up proudly, no flicker of emotion on his face when he caught sight of the block and the sword. If he was afraid, he was hiding it well.

I expected speeches and ceremony, but Anderson merely joined our silent ranks while Logan gestured

Jamaal to the block. Jamaal scanned the assembled *Liberi* and caught my eyes. I wanted to look away, too squeamish to deal with what I was about to witness— and too afraid of his continued anger. I managed to hold onto my courage and meet his gaze.

"I'm sorry," he said, so softly that I only understood him by reading his lips. I suspected that apology was harder for him than his actual punishment.

I doubted I'd completely won him over, but I believed the apology was sincere, so I nodded at him in acceptance. He held my gaze a moment longer, then knelt before the block without having to be prompted. Holding on to the block with both hands, he laid his neck in the notch. Logan bent over and brushed Jamaal's braids to the side, baring his neck. Then he grabbed the sword.

Maggie reached over and took my sweaty hand, giving it a reassuring squeeze, for which I was absurdly grateful.

"When you're ready," Logan said to Jamaal, "let go of the block and put your hands to your sides."

Logan held the sword in both hands, poised to strike, while Jamaal took a deep breath. The moment Jamaal's hands moved, I shut my eyes tightly. Anderson had insisted I be present for this, but he couldn't force me to actually *watch*.

I heard the whistle of the blade as it sliced through the air, then the wet thunk as it made contact, then the soft, sympathetic gasps of the onlookers. They might not be as squeamish as me about it, and they might have seen worse horrors during their long lives, but they weren't completely hardened. That made me feel better even as the wind carried the scent of blood to my nose.

"It's over," Maggie whispered to me. She was still holding my hand, a very welcome anchor.

"Good," I said, but I didn't open my eyes. I knew without a doubt that I would hurl if I did.

The light behind my closed eyelids grew dimmer, and at first I was afraid I was about to pass out. Then I realized someone was dousing the torches.

"I'll stay with him until he revives," Logan was saying, and I heard the gathered *Liberi* starting to stir.

I was tempted to let Maggie lead me out of the clearing without ever opening my eyes, but at the last moment, morbid curiosity got the better of me. Still sure the sight was going to make me hurl, I opened my eyes.

There was a lot of blood, though with the torches doused that blood was black enough I could pretend it was just pools of shadow. Logan had laid Jamaal out on his back, placing the head right up against the neck so that I could almost believe the two were attached.

"He'll heal," Maggie reminded me yet again, giving my arm a little pull.

I turned away and followed her back to the house, my stomach unsettled, but so far under control. Despite everything I knew about the *Liberi,* I would have to see Jamaal up and walking around before I could fully believe he could survive beheading.

The moon was just beginning to rise as Maggie and I headed toward the kitchen. If I were following the plan I'd made during the afternoon, I'd immediately get in my car and go visit a couple of properties. Instead, I made a cup of coffee and parked myself in the kitchen. Logan and Jamaal would almost certainly come back this way when Jamaal was healed. Then, once I'd seen with my own two eyes that he was still alive, I'd be able to concentrate on my hunt enough to have a hope of success.

I sat in that kitchen, drinking coffee and waiting, for more than three hours. I don't know how many times I halfway convinced myself to go back out to the clearing and see what was going on, but every time I made it to the back door, I changed my mind. If something had gone wrong, if Jamaal was truly dead against all expectations, I didn't want to know about it until I absolutely had to. There comes a point when you just can't deal with any more shocks, and I had passed that point a long time ago.

I was so wired on caffeine that I jumped and spilled my coffee when I heard the back door open. Lucky for me, the coffee had gone cold as I held it and stared off into space, so I didn't burn myself. I put the mug down on the table, then dried my wet hand on the leg of my jeans as I stood up and listened to the approaching footsteps.

Logan went by first, the sword belted to his side, though I'd seen no sign of the scabbard earlier. He gave me an unfathomable look as he passed by, not stopping for a friendly conversation. He'd voted to expel Jamaal, but I got the feeling he resented me for putting him in the role of executioner—though maybe that was just my own guilt speaking.

Jamaal did not look good, though he looked far better than he had the last time I'd seen him. A bloody, bruised scar circled his neck where his head had somehow reattached itself to his body, and there was dried blood caked in his hair and on his shirt. More dried blood mixed with dirt speckled his face, and behind that blood his skin was unnaturally pale.

He came to a stop when he saw me, swaying on his feet and grabbing onto the doorjamb to steady himself. I took a couple of steps forward. Maybe I was a fool to dismiss him as a threat because of his current condition, but it was obvious from the tightness at the corners of his eyes that he was still in pain, and I knew from personal experience how weak the supernatural healing made you.

"Do you need a hand?" I asked him, because even if I didn't feel threatened at the moment, I didn't think touching him without his permission was the best idea in the world.

His eyes widened at the suggestion, and he swayed a little more. I hoped he wasn't about to fall down, because I knew for a fact I wasn't strong enough to get him back up if he did.

"Thanks," he said, and he didn't even sound sarcastic. "I think I need a rest before I tackle the stairs."

Why Logan wasn't helping him was anyone's guess, since it was clear he was still in bad shape. Maybe he was in Logan's doghouse, though why

Logan should get mad on my account or even on Steph's, I didn't know. I'd had only the briefest interactions with him since we'd met, and as far as I knew, he'd never even set eyes on Steph.

Doing my best to ignore the blood, I draped Jamaal's arm over my shoulders and supported him to the nearest chair. He was built of solid muscle, and the operation would have been a heck of a lot easier if I were bigger and stronger—like, say, Logan. However, I managed to get him into the chair without either of us going down in a heap. He closed his eyes and breathed hard from the exertion. He'd probably have been better off lying out in the clearing for a little longer, though I supposed that would have been cold and unpleasant.

"Would you like a cup of coffee?" I asked. "I made way more than I should drink."

He opened his eyes, frowning in puzzlement. "Why are you trying to help me? You of all people . . ."

What could I say? To properly explain, I'd have to lay out my life's history, and I wasn't about to do that. Instead, I shrugged in what I hoped looked like a casual manner.

"I'm not the type to hold a grudge. If you'd intended Steph harm, that would be one thing, but I know you didn't believe me."

"I intended *you* harm." His expression was almost challenging, although I heard no hint of threat in his voice. It occurred to me that he wasn't very used to people being nice to him or forgiving him and that he was looking for some hidden motive.

"Well I took out your eye, and you just got your head chopped off, so I think that makes us even. Now do you want some coffee or not?"

He opened his mouth to say something, then shook his head like he'd changed his mind. "Yes. Thanks. Black."

I poured him a mug of the now rather stale coffee, then set it on the table in front of him. That should have been the end of our conversation. After all, I had a plan for the evening, and through the kitchen window I could see the moon, almost full, gleaming in the clear night sky. It was a perfect night for me to go hunting if the moon would indeed help me in some way. Yet I couldn't just walk out and leave Jamaal sitting here by himself. Not in the condition he was in. I wasn't sure how he would make it downstairs without falling and breaking his neck— again. So I pulled out a chair and joined him at the table.

Jamaal raised an eyebrow at me, and despite the dried blood and the unnatural pallor of his face, I noticed again how amazingly attractive he was when he wasn't scowling or frothing at the mouth. He'd be devastating if he ever smiled, which I suspected he hadn't done often even before Emmitt's death.

"I'm going to ask Anderson to . . . give you a stay of execution, for lack of a better term." The words came out of my mouth without any conscious thought behind them, so that I was almost as startled by them as Jamaal was. I avoided his gaze, staring instead at the coffee I had no intention of drinking. "You've been through enough already." I wasn't just thinking about tonight's ordeal, either.

"Don't bother."

I looked up again, unable to interpret the tone of his voice. The words sounded brusque, but he wasn't giving me the evil eye.

"It wouldn't do any good," he continued. "He's not going to reverse his decision. He can't without looking weak."

I snorted. "No one who's known him for more than five seconds would think he's weak."

I might have been imagining things, but I think one corner of Jamaal's mouth twitched a bit, as if he'd been considering the possibility of trying on a small smile for size.

"All right, weak was the wrong word. But he's already given me a second chance by not banishing me. If he went any easier on me, it would set a bad precedent. I'll take my medicine, and I won't complain about it. I might not have known your sister would get hurt, but I *did* know Anderson had forbidden me to hurt you, and I did it anyway. I'm not a victim."

He had a point, but considering how many times I'd lashed out at people in my life, I wasn't in any position to throw stones. "I'm so sorry about Emmitt," I blurted, then tensed for Jamaal's inevitable hostility.

There was a glint of anger in his eyes, and the muscles of his jaw worked, but he didn't leap across the table at me. That was an impressive amount of progress, as far as I was concerned.

"I know you still don't really believe me," I said, figuring I might as well spit out the whole apology while Jamaal was weakened enough not to attack me, "but I swear to you, it was an accident. I'm not a killer." The idea was so ridiculous it was all I could do not to laugh. Then I remembered my earlier insistence that Alexis had to die, and it wasn't so funny anymore. "Did you know that when I shot Blake, I actually apologized to him before I ran?"

This time, the twitch in Jamaal's lips was more obvious. Not quite enough to be a real smile, but a hint that he did know how. "He did mention that."

"Well, does that sound like the act of a cold-blooded killer to you?"

He sipped his coffee, thinking about it. "If you're actually one of Konstantin's pets, then it would all be part of your act. Even talking to me now, trying to disarm me—it's all the role you've taken on for the mission."

Gone was the fury and malice he'd shown me time and time again, but somehow his words stung more delivered calmly and at a reasonable volume. Stupid to have hurt feelings over it, I know. What he said was completely true, and he had no reason not to believe I was Konstantin's spy.

"I'm going to find Emma," I told him. My resolve strengthened, and I glanced out the kitchen window at the moon. I wasn't sure how much time I had before it disappeared from view, but the more time I spent here sitting around, the less time I'd have to look for Emma while its light lasted.

"I hope you do, but that won't really prove any-thing—except that Konstantin's desperate enough to get a spy inside that he's willing to give up Emma."

My shoulders slumped. "So what you're saying is there's no way you're ever going to believe me, no matter what I do." It shouldn't matter so much. *I* knew I hadn't killed Emmitt on purpose. What did it matter if Jamaal thought the worst of me? And yet, it *did* matter to me. His suspicions had never bothered me when he was acting like a raving lunatic, but they were a lot harder to take now, when for the first time he seemed completely rational. Either I'm pathetically needy and desperate for approval, or I was just making the logical assumption that my life would be a lot simpler and more pleasant if Jamaal weren't seeing everything I did from behind a veil of suspicion. I tried to convince myself it was the latter.

"Only time will tell," he answered. "But I promise I won't act against you again without proof."

I had the uncomfortable suspicion that his definition of proof and my own weren't quite the same. However, he was making what was for him a big concession, and that had to be a step in the right direction.

I sighed. "Finish up your coffee. Then I'll help you get downstairs."

"I don't need your help."

I pushed back my chair with a huff of exasperation. "Fine. Be that way. Just try not to crack your skull open when your legs give out and you fall down the stairs."

"I'll do my best," he promised gravely. If I didn't know better, I'd have sworn he was teasing me.

Leaving him to his overblown sense of male pride, I headed up to my room to grab the list of properties I planned to explore tonight.

TWENTY-THREE

The moon was one night short of being full, but it was large and bright enough that I could see pretty well even without the aid of streetlights. The first property on my list was a gated monstrosity at least as large as Anderson's mansion. It belonged to Konstantin, and he'd obviously modeled the thing on a palace. I'd have stopped to take a closer look, but even this late at night, the place was brightly lit and well-guarded. When I'd been by during the daytime, there'd been just enough traffic on the street that I could drive past multiple times without fearing I'd be noticed, but the same could not be said now.

I drove by without slowing down, though I kept my eye out for any neon signs saying "Emma is here" that the moon's light might reveal. There were none. I was pretty sure my gut instinct said this was not where Emma was buried. But it was hard to know if that was really my gut speaking, or if it was influenced by my rational mind, which said there was no way in hell I was going to be able to sneak in there and find the grave even if it was the right place.

My next likely candidate was another mansion in Chevy Chase, this one belonging to Alexis. It wasn't quite on the scale of Anderson's or Konstantin's homes, but it was still huge, the grounds vast enough to hold an entire graveyard's worth of bodies. The place even had a large man-made—I assumed—pond in the backyard.

An ornate gate blocked the driveway, but unlike Konstantin's place, there was no wall or fence to keep out people on foot. That didn't mean the grounds were unprotected. The security cameras were well hidden, but I had too much experience with surveillance not to spot them. Again, I drove by without stopping. The cameras might be set up on motion sensors, only photographing people who tried to pass across the borders of the property, but if any faced the road recording a continuous feed, I didn't want to be captured on them acting in any way suspicious.

It was as I was driving away that I felt my first gut-level hunch, one that told me Emma was on that property somewhere. The sensation was so strong, it took some willpower not to slam on the brakes. My pulse sped up, and my palms started to sweat.

Was this a real hunch? Or did some part of me want Emma to be on Alexis's property so I could really stick it to him by sneaking her out from under his nose?

I let out a little growl of frustration. I had no way of knowing for sure.

I checked out the next three properties on my list, trying my best to listen to my instincts without consciously influencing them. Although all of the other properties would have been considerably easier to explore than Alexis's, I didn't feel any sudden piques of interest. My pulse remained steady, and if I'd had to venture a guess, I'd have said Emma wasn't at any of them.

The moon had disappeared behind a bank of clouds by the time I drove by Alexis's mansion the second time. I still had the vague feeling that it was the right place, but there was no quickening of my pulse this time, and I felt no instinctive reluctance to drive by without stopping. Either my reaction the first time had been a fluke, or it had been strengthened by the light of the moon.

Unsure whether or not I'd made any progress, I headed back to Anderson's and vowed to check it out again tomorrow night.

The next day, I spent many hours digging up every scrap of information I could find on Alexis's home: survey maps, floor plans, work permits, going as far back as I could find. I was even able to find out some details about the security setup, having identified the security company involved. They wouldn't tell me anything about the specific setup at Alexis's home, of course—I didn't even ask, or I would have immediately flagged myself as a suspicious character. Instead, I described a fictional property that bore a non-coincidental resemblance to Alexis's and asked for suggestions on how they would help me set up security.

Based on what I learned, and on the information I was able to dig up—illegally, I must admit—on Alexis's financial transactions, I made an educated guess as to which security measures he had in place. It seemed likely that the cameras I'd spotted in the trees were indeed motion-activated. There was probably a security center somewhere in the house, complete with a guard who monitored the cameras. However, it was unlikely that triggering the cameras would trip any kind of alarm. The area around Alexis's home was heavily wooded, and thus full of deer. If an alarm sounded every time a deer passed a camera, it would get old fast.

So, there was definitely security on the grounds, but it wasn't exactly impenetrable. The house itself was likely another story, but if I needed to get in *there* to dig Emma up, I'd have a whole new set of problems.

That evening, Jamaal was executed again. It was a hanging this time, much less gory than the beheading. I'd been relieved when I first saw the noose, thinking that this would be an easier death to witness, but I'd been wrong. It was less gruesome—but it took Jamaal longer to die, and I found his suffering bothered me more than the gore.

Once again, Logan stayed out in the clearing, waiting for Jamaal to revive. And once again, I found myself unable to leave the house on my quest until I'd confirmed that Jamaal was alive.

The one bright spot was that it took Jamaal less

time to heal the damage from being hanged, and he and Logan returned to the house less than an hour after the execution. Jamaal was just as exhausted, however, and when I offered him a cup of coffee, he gladly accepted. His eyes were sunken, his cheeks hollow, as he wrapped his hands around the mug and sipped. Physically, he was healing, but I feared the ordeal was putting scars on his soul. That is to say, *more* scars—I knew without having to be told that he had plenty of them already.

"If I didn't know any better," he said, "I'd think you were worried about me."

I forced something approximating a wry grin. "I've been told I'm a bleeding heart. There's some truth in the accusation."

He cocked his head, the movement causing the beads to rattle and click. "You know I still suspect you."

"Yeah, I know. I also know that it wouldn't take much to 'prove' to you that I'm Konstantin's bitch. I still think you've suffered more than enough already."

For the first time, he smiled. It wasn't a big smile, but he didn't try to fight the expression off, either. And I was right. Despite the haunted eyes and hollow cheeks, the smile was devastating. My hormones woke from their long sleep and danced a jig at the sight, and I suppressed a groan. Jamaal was *not* a man I should be attracted to, no matter how tasty he looked. He thought I was a spy, a traitor who had murdered his friend. He'd threatened me and attacked me, and because of him my sister had been brutalized. Not to mention that he was a descendant of a death goddess and borderline crazy. No smile, no matter how devastating, could erase any of that.

"You really are a bleeding heart, aren't you?" he asked.

"Either that, or I play one on T.V."

The smile made another cameo appearance, but faded even more quickly. "You might want to skip tomorrow night's . . . festivities, then. If you can."

"Why?" I held my breath, already knowing I wouldn't like the answer.

"Logan's going to choose something heinous for the grand finale."

As far as I was concerned, what I'd seen so far was more than heinous enough. Then again, I wasn't descended from some Germanic war god, like Logan was.

"Why?" I asked again. "This whole punishment is barbaric enough as it is. Why would he want to make it worse?"

"Because it's not just about punishing me for disobeying Anderson's orders. It's about giving me a way to prove that I'm committed in spite of what I've done. The more I have to go through to win the privilege of staying, the more Anderson—and all the rest—will believe I'm determined to control myself, which I've done a shitty job of doing since Emmitt . . ." His voice faded as grief clouded his eyes.

Impulsively, I reached out and laid my hand over his, wishing I could bring Emmitt back.

During the last couple of days, Jamaal and I

seemed to have reached a truce, but that truce only went so far. Jamaal glared and I jerked my hand away, my cheeks heating with a blush.

"Sorry," I mumbled, wishing the floor would swallow me. What had come over me? Just because we weren't currently at war with each other didn't mean we were friends. I pushed my chair away from the table, suddenly desperate to flee the room.

"Do you need any help getting downstairs?" I asked without looking at him.

"No."

It was the answer I'd expected, and I left the kitchen at a pace just short of a run.

For tonight's excursion, I dressed all in black, because I'd be getting out of my car and skulking around, not just driving by. The more inconspicuous I could make myself, the better.

The full moon rode the sky like a beacon, only the occasional thin cloud dimming its light. If my powers were moon-based at all, tonight they would be at their peak, and I had to take advantage of them as best I could. I drove straight to Alexis's home, the instinct to search there too strong to deny.

Of course, I couldn't just pull up in front and leave my car in full view while I went exploring on foot, so I drove around until I found a church with a convenient parking lot. My car looked uncomfortably conspicuous in the otherwise empty lot, and I had to walk the better part of a mile to get back to Alexis's house, but it was the best I could do.

I'd packed a bunch of odds and ends that might be useful—including my gun and my cell phone—in a light black backpack, which I slung over my shoulders as I began the trek that I still worried was a waste of time. The temperature was on its way down to freezing. I wished I'd worn something warmer than lightweight black fleece, and I walked at a pace just short of a jog to keep my teeth from chattering.

It was a long, tense, freezing walk. On foot in a ritzy neighborhood, dressed all in black and carrying a gun in my backpack, I didn't dare let anyone see me, so any time I caught sight of headlights in the distance, I took cover.

By the time I reached the fringes of Alexis's property, I was sweaty beneath my fleece, although my cheeks stung and burned from the cold wind and I shivered with chills. I was struck again by the certainty that Emma was here somewhere, the feeling stronger than ever. Unfortunately, "somewhere" wasn't going to do me much good. We couldn't dig up the whole place searching for her, so I was going to have to narrow it down.

Crouching in the darkness, I opened my backpack and pulled out a smooth black rock, small enough to fit in the palm of my hand, but heavy enough to be an effective weapon. Despite the clear sky, the wind whistled briskly through the trees, taking the wind chill down to arctic levels—and giving me a little cover. I waited for a particularly energetic gust of wind, then slung my stone at the nearest security camera.

My aim was, of course, dead-on, though I'd packed extra rocks in my backpack just in case. The blow from the rock didn't break the camera—that was likely to bring someone out to investigate—but it bent the mounting enough to point the camera away from my intended path, creating a blind spot. If someone had been watching at the moment my stone hit, they might still come to investigate—but they would more likely think the wind was responsible and not want to venture out into the cold.

Taking a deep breath for courage, I slipped past the camera and onto Alexis's property.

TWENTY-FOUR

My instincts were still insisting that Emma was nearby. Unfortunately, I wasn't having much luck convincing those instincts to tell me *where*.

At first, I stuck to the woods that bounded Alexis's property, not because I felt it likely Emma was buried there, where roots would have made digging difficult, but because it was easier to stay hidden. I traipsed through those woods for at least forty-five minutes, having no idea what I was looking for but hoping to God I'd recognize it when I saw it.

No luck. If Emma was buried in the woods, I lacked the power to find her.

I turned my attention to the gardens and lawns that surrounded the house on all sides. There weren't any lights on in the house, so it was likely no one would see me if I ventured out from the cover of the trees. Still, I hesitated to do it. I'd seen what Alexis had done to Steph, and he'd been interrupted before he could finish. If he caught me trespassing on his property . . . He might still technically have an agreement with Anderson, but I doubted that would protect me.

I squatted behind a bush at the very edge of the tree line, trying to work up the courage to break cover. The cloud cover was growing thicker as the temperature continued to drop. There were moments when the moon disappeared from view, and I worried that soon the patchy clouds would turn into a heavy overcast. If I had any moon-driven powers, and if those powers depended on actually being able to see the moonlight, they'd better hurry up and make themselves known to me.

I was gnawing my lip indecisively when a flicker of movement off to my right made me jump and gasp. I was frantically trying to unzip my backpack before I'd even finished turning toward the sound, cursing myself for not having the gun in my hand already. Then I saw the doe picking her way through the underbrush and almost laughed myself silly.

My heart was racing, my breath coming short and steaming in the frosty air. I sat down on the cold ground, putting a hand to my heart, waiting for the flood of adrenaline to fade.

Braver than I, the doe ventured out of the woods and onto the outskirts of the manicured lawn. She paused briefly to look at the house, as if assuring herself that the coast was clear, then set off toward the man-made pond at a brisk, elegant trot. Still waiting for my heart rate to return to something resembling normal, I watched her progress and felt reassured by the lack of alarms, blaring lights, or barking dogs. My fear of venturing out from the woods was just a side effect of stretched-taut nerves.

The doe reached the shore of the pond, and stood poised there for a long moment. Her head turned in my direction, until I could have sworn she was looking me straight in the eye. The light of the moon limned her with silver, giving her an ethereal look. I shivered as I remembered that Artemis was often depicted with a deer by her side. Was the animal even real?

The doe quit staring at me and bent her head to drink from the pond. And suddenly, for no reason I could point a finger at, I knew. Emma was in the pond. Not buried, as Konstantin had claimed, but drowned. Tossing her into the water, weighted down with chains, required a lot less effort than digging a grave and burying her. I wondered if the magic of the *Liberi* caused her to revive on a regular basis, and then drown again. I shuddered away from the thought, which was too horrible to contemplate.

All right—I finally had a strong hunch where Emma was. It was based on absolutely zero empirical evidence, and no matter how strong my hunch, I wouldn't be shocked to find out it was wrong. However, the only way to confirm I was right was to take a dip in the pond. The prospect was far from inviting. The water would be freezing, and while the pond was relatively small and probably not very deep, it would take a significant amount of swimming to check the whole thing. All the while out in the open and defenseless against attack.

Slowly, carefully, I edged back into the full cover of the woods. If Emma really was in that pond, I would need help getting her out. I was less certain of her location than I'd have liked to be, but I figured now was a good time to call Anderson and share my theory. Obviously, he knew more about the *Liberi* and their powers than I did. If my evidence was enough to convince him that Emma was in the pond, then I'd feel a lot more confident that I wasn't just imagining things. And if I wasn't just imagining things, then it was time to call in the cavalry and get Emma out of here.

About forty minutes later, I was so numb from cold I felt like I might have frozen in place. That's when Anderson appeared suddenly and without warning at my side. I about had a heart attack, and a strangled scream escaped my throat as I backed hastily away and tripped over an exposed tree root, landing on my butt.

Like me, he was dressed all in black, with a black knit hat pulled low over his forehead. Hard to spot in the dark, for sure, but I should have seen *something*.

He grinned down at me, apparently enjoying the spectacle I'd made of myself. "It's just me."

I closed my eyes and sucked in a deep breath, searching for calm. How had he just appeared out of thin air like that? Emmitt and Jamaal had both pulled similar stunts, and I'd assumed it was an ability unique to *Liberi* who had death magic. Then again, no one seemed to know who Anderson's divine ancestor was, so perhaps he was himself a descendant of a death god, though apparently an obscure one if no one recognized his glyph.

I opened my eyes and glared up at him. "You're lucky I managed to swallow that scream," I told him. "This expedition could have been over before it started, all because you felt like being a comedian." Probably no one would have heard me if I'd screamed—I'd told Anderson to meet me in the woods at the property line, right near the realigned camera—but it was the principle of the thing.

Still grinning, he reached out a hand to help me up. "I didn't mean to startle you. I kind of forgot I was in stealth mode until it was too late."

I brushed dead leaves and pine needles from the seat of my pants. I wasn't sure I believed him, but I didn't suppose it much mattered. I glanced into the woods behind him, but saw no other lurking *Liberi*.

"You didn't bring any backup?" I asked incredulously. When he'd put enough faith in my hunch to agree to come himself, I'd assumed he'd bring at least a couple of his other people in case this turned into a fight.

"It's easier to be sneaky with just two of us," he responded, and I knew at once he was lying, maybe just because it was such a lame explanation.

I gave him a hard look. "What aren't you telling me?"

The look Anderson gave me in return was just as hard. "Things you don't need to know," he said, and took a step forward as if he thought the conversation was over.

I grabbed his arm. "Hey, if I'm putting my butt on the line for you, I deserve full disclosure before I go charging in there." The sneaking about I'd been doing so far had no doubt been dangerous, but not half so dangerous as an actual attempt to extract Emma from the water. Assuming she was even there.

Anderson twitched his arm out of my grip. "Come help me, or go back to the house. It's your choice." He plunged forward again without a backward glance.

Common sense told me to get the heck out of there. I couldn't begin to guess what Anderson was hiding, but chances were it was going to come back and bite me in the butt. That's just the way my life works.

But common sense and I haven't been on speaking terms for a while now, so instead of trekking back to the car and heading for safety, I followed Anderson deeper into the woods. When I caught up to him, I adjusted our course so we'd come out as close to the pond as possible.

We paused for a while when we came to the edge of the woods, both peering into the heavy darkness left by the moon's disappearance. Still no lights on in the house. It would be pretty funny, in a sick sort of way, if after all this fearful skulking around, it turned out that Alexis wasn't even home.

"Any idea where to start looking?" Anderson asked me as he sat on the ground and started unlacing his boots.

"What are you doing?"

"I don't plan to swim in my hiking boots." He

pulled off one boot, along with the sock, then started working on the other one.

"That water has got to be freezing!" I protested, and I meant it literally. Even in the darkness, I could see the thin crust of ice that was forming along the shore.

"You think I can get her out of the water without getting wet?" Off came the second boot, followed by his utilitarian black jacket. "The clothes won't keep me warm if they're wet, and I'd rather have something dry to put on when I get out."

The thought of setting even a toe in that water made my teeth chatter, but of course he was right. And unlike a normal human being, he wouldn't die of hypothermia.

"Of course, I'm not exactly looking forward to it," he continued, pulling his sweatshirt off over his head, "so if you can give me a general idea where to look, I'd appreciate it."

I know I've said before that Anderson is rather unprepossessing, but seeing his nicely muscled chest and sculpted shoulders made me rethink the assessment. Then he slipped out of his jeans, leaving himself naked except for a pair of black briefs that clung very attractively in all the right places. I decided I hadn't just been wrong, I'd been *dead* wrong. Without the camouflage of his scruffy, unflattering wardrobe, he was very nice to look at indeed.

Which was *so* not what I needed to be noticing right now.

The surprising view had momentarily distracted

me, and I all but smacked myself in the head to get my brain working again and remember what he'd asked me. I glanced at the pond, trying to listen to my gut in case it had a message for me, but there was nothing. The clouds had thickened enough to hide the moon, and even the certainty that Emma was in there had faded with its light. I was going to be completely mortified if I made Anderson swim around in that frigid water for nothing.

"Maybe if you go in where I saw the deer?" I suggested doubtfully. The second thoughts were pounding at me now, telling me this was the stupidest idea I'd ever had. I only came looking for Emma on Alexis's property because I wanted him to be the one who had her, and I was making an awful lot out of the fact that I saw a deer take a drink from the pond. It was probably a popular watering hole for the local herds, and what I'd seen had been nothing remotely supernatural.

"As good a guess as any," Anderson said, already beginning to shiver in the cold. "Show me where."

What confidence I'd had was now completely shot, and I wanted to tell Anderson to forget it, that I'd been wrong and we should just get out of here and go somewhere warm and safe. But I knew he wouldn't listen to me even if I said it. If there was a chance he would find his Emma in that pond, then he'd take it, no matter how slim the chance might be, or how unreliable the source.

I visualized watching the deer cross the lawn to the pond, homing in on the spot she'd paused to take her drink, then hesitantly stepped out from the cover of the woods. My entire body was tense, expecting against all reason that Alexis was going to jump out from behind a bush somewhere and attack. I did my best to fight the feeling off as I led Anderson to the spot where I'd seen the deer.

I'd have felt a lot surer of myself if there were some nice, clear hoofprints in the mud, but of course there were none to be seen. Had I imagined the deer? Or had it been a supernatural creature, one that didn't leave prints?

I gestured at the general area, giving Anderson a helpless shrug, feeling like a fool.

"All right," he said, stepping to the edge of the pond. I felt a little better about the possibly imaginary deer when I saw that Anderson wasn't leaving footprints in the mud, either. As he eased his way into the water, wincing at the cold, I reached out and touched the ground, finding it frozen solid. I should have guessed as much. The film of ice around the water's edge had visibly spread since we'd first peeked out of the woods.

Anderson took a series of quick, deep breaths, preparing himself for the shock of cold. Then he dove forward into the icy water and disappeared beneath its surface.

TWENTY-FIVE

I stood on the shore of the pond, chilled down to my bones in sympathy for Anderson as I watched the ripples from his dive glide over the glassy-smooth surface. With the full moon hidden, the only light came from the ambient glow of the nearby city. It was enough that I didn't feel completely blind, but I was uncomfortably aware of the blackness of the shadows—shadows that could hide anything.

Figuring a little paranoia might be healthy under the circumstances, I put my backpack down and rooted through it until I found my gun. I pointed the gun at the ground and kept my finger off the trigger, remembering how badly I'd been startled earlier by the deer. It wouldn't do for me to fire blindly out of startled reflex if another deer made an appearance.

Anderson's head broke the water at the center of the pond. Immediately, steam rose from his skin. The shadows hid his expression, and I didn't dare call out to him. He dove again after a few quick breaths, his feet flashing up into the air as he went straight down.

Did that mean he'd found her? If he was still looking, he should be swimming forward, not straight down. Right? I held my breath in anticipation. It was all I could do not to cross my fingers like a superstitious child.

He stayed down a long time, long enough for me to worry that something had gone wrong. For all I knew, the Olympians had pet monsters that lived in the bottoms of ponds. I had yet to fully embrace the magic I'd already witnessed, and I'd been slow to ponder what my newfound knowledge of the supernatural meant to the rest of my narrow view of the world. I shifted uneasily from foot to foot, hoping like hell he would hurry up and surface before I felt obligated to go in after him.

Moments later, he bobbed to the surface once more, sucking in a great gasp of air. I opened my mouth to call out to him, too curious now to worry about who else might hear me, but before a sound left my throat, I was blinded by a bolt of lightning, traveling horizontally across the lawn.

The lightning hit the surface of the pond, and I heard Anderson's strangled cry of pain. The residual energy of the bolt lifted me off my feet and tossed me onto my back. The gun fell from my fingers as I hit the ground, and a clap of thunder resonated so loud it sent a spike of pain through my head.

Woozy, blind, and deaf, I retained just enough

brain cells to know holding still was a bad idea. I rolled over until I got my feet under me, then broke into a stumbling run, having no idea where I was going. I could have run straight into the icy water, but, for once, luck was on my side, and I managed to stay on the smooth, grassy lawn.

My hair rose on end, and I instinctively dove forward just in time. The next lightning bolt struck the ground just a few yards away. I clapped my hands over my ears to dull the roar of the thunder as I squeezed my eyes tightly shut. I was close enough to the point of impact that the electricity in the air made my heart beat erratically, but at least it *was* beating.

Once again, I forced myself to my feet. Even through my closed lids, the flash had been hell on my night vision. However, I could see just well enough to point myself toward the trees before I started running again.

A third bolt incinerated a tree seconds after I made it into the cover of the woods. The concussion knocked me down to my hands and knees, but I was up and running again in a fraction of a second. There were no further bolts as I zigzagged through the trees, slowing my pace just enough to keep from tripping over roots and sprawling on my face.

My ears popped and my vision started to clear— not that I could see much in the darkness. But the return of my physical senses signaled the return of my higher reasoning as well. If *I* couldn't see in this darkness, then probably my enemies couldn't, either. However, they *could* hear me crashing headlong through the underbrush. My flight was making me more conspicuous rather than less so.

I forced myself to slow down, sucking in one calming breath after another. I hadn't caught even a glimpse of our attacker, but since Alexis was a descendant of Zeus, it seemed a logical conclusion that he was the one who'd thrown the lightning bolts. And, while the bolt in the water wouldn't have killed Anderson—at least, not permanently—it would certainly have disabled him for a while.

Anderson's "treaty" with the Olympians obviously wasn't anything close to bulletproof. Perhaps Alexis had only been taking advantage of a perceived loophole when he attacked Steph, and the treaty itself was still nominally in place. Maybe that treaty meant Alexis would fish Anderson out of the water, then let him go. But though I'd been forced to retreat, there was no way I was going to abandon Anderson and hope for the best.

Of course, I wasn't sure what use I was to Anderson in the current situation. My gun lay abandoned on the lawn somewhere, and though I'd have loved to call for help—for the backup Anderson had failed to bring with him, the idiot!—my cell phone was in the backpack at the edge of the pond.

I stopped for a moment to think, listening intently for any sounds of pursuit. The only sound I heard was the wind whistling through the branches above. No doubt Alexis thought I'd done the sensible thing and run for my life.

It was hard to get my bearings in the depths of

the darkened woods, but I'd always had a pretty good sense of direction. I relied on that sense of direction now as I attempted to steer myself back toward the security camera I'd knocked out of position earlier. I managed to find it, then groped around on the ground until I found the rock I'd thrown at it. As weapons went, it wasn't much, but it was heavy enough to do some damage if I threw it just right.

Heading back through the trees toward the pond, I hoped I wasn't making the world's biggest mistake.

The situation was pretty damn grim. Alexis, looking smug and superior, stood by the side of the pond. Beside him stood another man—unfamiliar to me, but with a haughty bearing that immediately pegged him as another Olympian. They watched the water as a third man towed an unconscious—or maybe temporarily dead—Anderson toward the shore.

Three men, one rock. I didn't like the odds. I tried to spot my gun in the grass, but either the shadows hid it, or one of the bad guys had picked it up.

The third man labored out of the water, visibly shivering as he dragged Anderson's limp body through the shallows and then up onto dry land. Neither of the *Liberi* looked inclined to help, and I guessed that the third man was a mortal Descendant—a lesser being from the Olympians' point of view.

"Bind him," Alexis commanded.

Panting with exertion, Alexis's flunky turned Anderson over onto his stomach, then dragged his hands behind his back and secured them with a pair of handcuffs he drew from his sopping pants. Unlike Anderson, he'd gone into the water fully clothed. I suspected he was regretting it now as the wind gusted over his wet skin.

"M-may I t-take him now, my lord?" the Descendant stammered, hunching his shoulders and crossing his arms over his chest as if that would keep him warm.

My lord? Talk about delusions of grandeur. Unfortunately, the question made me realize the treaty was truly out the window. I had no doubt the Descendant was asking for Alexis's permission to kill Anderson and steal his immortality.

"Not yet, Peter," Alexis said in a tone of almost affectionate condescension. "I'd like to have a few words with him first. Why don't you run back to the house and put on some dry clothes? He'll still be here when you get back."

Peter got to his feet and actually *bowed* to Alexis. I rolled my eyes, amazed at Alexis's arrogance even as I tried to figure out how to take advantage of the slightly improved odds. I wondered if Konstantin, the self-proclaimed king, knew Alexis was having people bow to him and call him "my lord." I would have thought Konstantin the type to reserve such accolades for himself alone.

Peter trotted off to the house, leaving Anderson lying on his stomach in the grass. I couldn't tell whether he was breathing or not. I'd like the odds a whole lot better if he were conscious. I didn't know what his capabilities were—other than that Hand of

Doom thing, which I didn't figure he could pull off while in handcuffs—but as long as he was just lying there, any heroics I tried would be useless. Even if I managed to take out both *Liberi* with my one stone, I wasn't Maggie, and I wouldn't be able to carry Anderson to safety.

I wished like hell I could figure out a way to take advantage of Peter's absence, but with Anderson out cold, there was nothing I could do.

"You really mean to do it?" the second *Liberi* asked as soon as Peter was out of earshot.

Alexis nodded. "I was happy to bide my time, but if the fool is going to deliver himself to me with a pretty bow tied around him, I'm not going to refuse the gift."

The other guy looked uncomfortable, shifting from foot to foot. "What about Konstantin? He won't be happy."

Alexis dismissed Konstantin with a negligent wave. "He can hardly complain about me eliminating his greatest enemy."

"If he wanted Anderson dead, he would be dead by now. There must be a reason he hasn't killed him yet—"

"Enough! If you're feeling squeamish, you can tuck your tail between your legs and go running back to your master. I won't hold it against you, as long as you keep your mouth shut. And you will keep your mouth shut, won't you, Dean?" This last was said in a menacing croon designed to turn blood to ice.

"O-of course," Dean stammered. "I mean, I'm not going anywhere. I'm on your side, always."

On Alexis's side of *what,* I wondered? Was there dissension within the ranks of the Olympians? I *had* sensed some undercurrents between Konstantin and Alexis when I'd met them at the Sofitel, but I'd assumed much of that was playacting, meant to emphasize how big and powerful Konstantin was.

Anderson coughed loudly, and everyone jumped—including me—though we'd all been expecting it. He turned over onto his side and coughed some more, painful, racking spasms that brought up gouts of water and made him gag. But at least he was alive, and awake. I hefted my stone, but until Anderson had quit coughing, I doubted he would be in any shape to take out whichever Olympian I didn't hit.

I decided that as soon as Anderson was able to breathe without retching, I'd take out Alexis. I had no idea which divine ancestor Dean was descended from, or what powers he might have, but I *did* know Alexis could throw lightning bolts, and those were a dangerous long-distance weapon. I had to hope that whatever Dean's powers were, they weren't much use in a fight.

"It never occurred to you that there would be extra security on your lady wife once you took a Descendant of Artemis into your household?" Alexis mocked, though I wasn't sure Anderson could hear him over all the coughing. "I never took you for a fool, but then women do tend to have a negative influence on masculine intelligence."

Still coughing, though not quite as desperately,

Anderson managed to push himself up to his knees. I still didn't think he was capable of doing anything really useful like fighting or running.

A flash of movement in the distance caught my eye, and I realized I was running out of time: Peter was coming back. When he got here, he would kill Anderson, and that would be that.

Of course, Peter was only human for the time being. I hefted the rock, wondering if I could put enough oomph into my throw to kill.

The thought shocked me, but only for a moment. I wasn't a killer, but I wasn't some helpless damsel in distress who would stand horrified and useless on the sidelines, either. I knew next to nothing about Peter, but if he was in cahoots with Alexis, then he was a bad guy, period. I wouldn't feel bad about killing him.

At least, that's what I told myself.

"Stay out of this, Nikki!" Anderson suddenly shouted, his voice loud and clear despite all the coughing.

I was so startled I almost dropped my rock. Dean jumped, and Peter started running faster, but Alexis just laughed.

"You think she hung around to try to save your pathetic hide?" Alexis asked through his laughter. "Or is that supposed to make me paranoid?" He looked straight at Anderson, not glancing away for a moment—proving how unthreatened he felt. Of course, his cronies were doing enough looking around; he didn't have to. I huddled down lower behind the bush I was using for cover.

Did Anderson know I was here somehow? Had that been an actual order? Or was Alexis right, and he'd just been trying to distract the opposition?

The moment of indecision cost me, and by the time I made up my mind to ignore Anderson's command—if it even *was* a command—it was too late. Peter had drawn a gun—*my* gun, I suspected—and was pointing it at Anderson. If I managed to clock him with my rock, the impact might cause him to pull the trigger. I didn't dare risk it.

Feeling a little like that useless damsel in distress after all, I remained crouched behind the bush, hoping Anderson had some kind of a miracle plan up his sleeve, because I was plum out of ideas.

T<small>WENTY-SIX</small>

Anderson spat a couple of times, then shook his head in an effort to get his wet hair out of his eyes. He should have looked like a helpless victim, kneeling there on the ground in his underwear with his hands cuffed behind his back and a gun pointed at his head. Instead, he looked poised and unruffled.

"Have you ever wondered why Konstantin made a deal with me?" he asked Alexis, and despite the dire situation, a small grin tugged at the corner of his mouth.

Alexis looked nonplused, both at the question and the casual tone, but he answered quickly enough. "Because it was not worth our effort to squash you and your little friends like you deserve." He sounded very sure of himself, but both of his accomplices were visibly worried.

Anderson's grin broadened. "Really? Why don't you give your boss a call right now? You've got me helpless, after all, and if you have your pet kill me and steal my immortality, my followers would most likely disperse. So call Konstantin and ask him if he wants you to kill me."

Alexis snorted. "You trespassed on my property. I'm within my rights to kill you, and I don't need to ask anyone's permission."

Anderson shrugged. "Fine. Don't ask him. If ignorance is bliss, you must be in heaven right now."

Alexis landed a crushing punch on Anderson's nose, though he had to bend over a bit to do it. I winced at the crunching sound of cartilage giving way. Blood spurted from Anderson's nose, and he crumpled to the ground. His muscles remained tense, however, so I knew he wasn't unconscious.

Alexis bent and wiped the back of his hand on the grass, cleaning off the blood I supposed. Then he stood up straight and resumed his arrogant, cross-armed pose, towering over his fallen foe.

"You and your people have been a thorn in my side for some time now," Alexis said. "A quick death would be too easy for you." He pulled back his foot and delivered a brutal kick to Anderson's belly. Anderson grunted and curled himself around the pain.

Just how slow a death did Alexis have in mind? Enough that I had time to run for help?

I dismissed the thought with only the briefest consideration. With my car all the way back at the church, and the mansion at least a half-hour's drive away, I couldn't risk it. But the slow death comment gave me hope. Whatever torture Alexis planned, it would probably mean some relaxing of Peter's guard. The Descendant still had the gun pointed and ready, but I didn't think he was quite as poised to shoot as he had been when he'd first arrived on the scene. Maybe if Alexis was going to deliver a beating, he'd get a little careless and place himself between his flunky and Anderson. And wouldn't it be a terrible shame if I hit Peter with the rock and he ended up shooting the wrong guy?

"I'm sure you're not enjoying this," Alexis said. He was panting with eagerness, getting his rocks off on the pain he was inflicting. He delivered another kick before continuing. Unfortunately, Peter still had a clear line of fire. "But I suspect it will hurt you more to hear about all the fun I've had with your dear wife since she's been my guest here."

Anderson froze, his sudden stillness overcoming even the reflexive writhing. I closed my eyes for a moment in an attempt to stave off my sympathetic horror. Behind my closed eyelids, I couldn't help seeing the image of Steph, the damage she'd taken, and the pain she'd endured after less than an hour in Alexis's clutches.

Emma had been Alexis's prisoner for the better part of ten years, and he might not have kept her in the water all that time.

Alexis laughed, enjoying the pain and horror Anderson couldn't hide. "Once a year, on the anniversary of her capture, we fish her out, and Konstantin and I share her. Even after all this time, she still cries for you when we—"

Anderson let out a roar, like nothing I'd ever heard before. So loud my bones and my teeth rattled with it, and so savage it froze Alexis and his cronies in their tracks. Three sets of eyes widened to almost comic proportions, stunned by the fury of that roar.

And then Anderson moved, his pain forgotten as he lurched to his knees.

The sudden movement broke all of us out of our stupor. I knew from the terror on Peter's face that he was totally unnerved and that he was going to shoot. I also knew that my thrown rock would be too late to stop him. I leapt to my feet and hurled it anyway, putting all my strength behind it and aiming for his head.

The gun fired. I watched in horror as Anderson's head snapped back, blood spurting from the back as the bullet passed all the way through. His eyes glazed over, and his body started listing just as my rock caved in the side of Peter's skull.

There was another moment of disordered shock as everyone looked around, trying to make sense of what had happened. Anderson and Peter lay on the grass, both staring sightlessly into the night.

I cursed myself for waiting as long as I had to throw the damned rock. Sure, I'd been worried hitting him with the rock would make Peter reflexively fire the gun; however, I'd known for a fact he was going to fire it on purpose eventually, so the smart thing would have been to take a chance that the blow wouldn't make him pull the trigger or that his shot would miss. I'd wanted a better opportunity, hoped for a sure thing.

And because of that hesitation, Anderson was dead, and the Olympians now had a new *Liberi* to add to their stable.

At least, they would have him soon, once Peter's wound healed enough for him to revive. The rock had done an impressive job on his skull, and that kind of an injury would take time to heal. Not that that helped me a whole hell of a lot.

Alexis's searching eyes found me, and his lips twisted into an expression somewhere between a grin and a sneer. Now would have been a good time for me to run for my life, but I stood there frozen by his gaze, horrified by my failure.

"I was just starting to have fun," Alexis said with a mock pout. "But then *you'll* be more fun to play with anyway. I'll show you everything I did to your sister, and everything I *would* have done if that interfering faggot hadn't showed up and spoiled everything."

I'd never asked Blake how he'd managed to run Alexis off that night, but now I had a good guess. The air crackled with electricity, raising the little hairs on my arms. I could have turned tail and run, but with Alexis so close, I didn't see how he could miss if he threw a lightning bolt at me. I was superstitiously reluctant to turn my back on him.

Dean squatted beside Peter's limp body, frowning down at him. "Umm, Alexis?"

"What?" Alexis snapped, obviously annoyed to have his gloating interrupted.

"He doesn't seem to be healing."

"What?" Alexis said, and this time he sounded

more surprised than angry. He turned to look at Peter's body.

I'd have taken advantage of his distraction to run like hell, only I took one last glance at Anderson first. His eyes, instead of staring sightlessly at the sky, were focused on the two *Liberi*. As I watched, a smile curled his lips, the expression so sinister as to be almost evil.

Anderson reached out with one leg, hooking it around Dean's ankle and yanking him off his feet. With a cry of surprise, Dean fell, and Anderson rolled until he was straddling him. His hands were still cuffed behind his back, but Anderson leaned back and tucked those hands just under the waistband of Dean's pants, making contact with his bare skin.

Dean let out a shriek of pain, his back arching as he tried to buck Anderson off of him. But Anderson held on tight, bracing himself with his legs and using his grip on Dean's waistband as an anchor.

When Anderson had used his Hand of Doom against Jamaal, Jamaal had passed out after only a few seconds, and I expected the same thing to happen now. The surprise and his friend's screams had momentarily kept Alexis from attacking, but surely a lightning bolt would be on its way any moment.

Figuring that even in the handcuffs, Anderson had a better shot of taking out Alexis than I did, I decided to take one for the team. With an incoherent battle cry, I launched myself at Alexis. If he was busy fighting with me, he couldn't electrocute Anderson. Surely Dean would be unconscious any second now, and then Anderson could turn his attention to the greater enemy.

Dean was still shrieking, his voice high and thin with agony. If he weren't already starting to go hoarse, Alexis might not even have heard my own cry.

Alexis whirled toward me, and I knew the lightning bolt was coming. I'd semi-resolved myself to taking it, but at the last moment I threw myself to the side. The quick dodge kept me from taking a direct hit, but even a near miss with that kind of power was enough to stun me.

I hit the ground with a thump, too disoriented to soften my fall. My limbs felt like jelly, and my head hammered and rang with pain. I wanted to just lie there, maybe slip into soothing unconsciousness so I wouldn't have to hear Dean's piteous screaming anymore.

I blinked away the afterimage of the lightning, expecting another blast at any moment but unable to muster the strength or coordination to get up. I looked over my shoulder, thinking maybe Alexis was going to strike at Anderson now that he'd temporarily disabled me.

Alexis was indeed staring at Anderson, but he showed no sign of tossing a lightning bolt. Instead, he stood there in slack-jawed horror, his face a mask of fear. Muscles still weak and quivering, I forced myself to sit up and see what had put that look of terror on Alexis's face.

Dean's body was glowing cherry-red as Anderson continued to straddle him, teeth bared in a truly savage snarl. A thin, keening wail rose from Dean's throat, but the sound was growing thinner by the second as the glow intensified. Anderson was glowing, too, his skin radiating a white light that made me squint.

"You're next," he growled at Alexis, the snarl turning into a smile that was no less savage.

Alexis looked like he was about to wet his pants. I know I would have if Anderson had looked at me like that. Of course, I'm pretty sure that in spite of my fear, if I'd been in Alexis's shoes I'd have mustered the courage to throw one more lightning bolt in an attempt to save my friend from agony. But Alexis always chose to look out for number one, so instead of trying to help Dean, the cowardly bastard turned tail and ran.

Anderson turned to me, no longer looking anything like the unprepossessing normal man I'd first met. He seemed to have grown in size behind that white glow, muscles bulking up as he put on what I'd guess was another six inches or more in height. His blah-brown hair was now snow white and shoulder length, and his medium-brown eyes were like twin white stars in his face.

"Stop him!" he ordered me, his voice resonating differently in that suddenly deeper, broader chest.

I wasn't in any shape to chase after bad guys, but I wasn't crazy enough to defy an order given by a crazed immortal.

I forced myself to my feet, considering my options as Alexis fled toward the house. Fear had given his feet wings, and even at my best, I wouldn't have been able to run him down when he had this much of a head start. If he made it through the house and to a car, there would be no stopping him.

It was only a slight detour for me to dart to the shore of the pond and grab my backpack before I sprinted after Alexis, but in that time he'd put even more distance between us. I ran as fast as I could, one hand digging blindly in the backpack until my fingers found another rock.

Puffing with exertion, I drew that rock out of my backpack. Alexis was almost to the back door. If he got inside the house I'd never get a shot at him. So even though I was still a good fifty yards away, and it was so dark I could only make out his shape because he was moving, I pitched the rock with every ounce of strength I could muster.

Alexis's hand closed on the doorknob, and he twisted it while banging into the door with his shoulder. He took about half a step inside before the rock made solid contact with the back of his head.

I was too far away and too weak to do the same kind of damage I'd done to Peter, supernatural powers or not. But the blow was hard enough to drop Alexis to his hands and knees. He didn't lose consciousness, but he was clearly woozy, his body swaying as he tried to regain his feet.

My own knees gave out then, and I collapsed onto the grass. As I lay there panting, I dug through my pack for another rock, pushing myself up into a sitting position. Even with the power of Artemis, I wasn't sure I could hit Alexis again from this distance, especially not while sitting down, but I was willing to give it a try.

It turned out I didn't have to. A glowing white

pillar of fire—Anderson—ran by me at an easy lope that seemed to cover about ten yards per stride. Alexis screamed in terror when he saw what was coming for him. He lurched to his feet, still visibly unsteady, and stumbled through the doorway. He tried to slam the door behind him, but Anderson had already closed the distance.

I turned my head and covered my ears when Alexis began to scream.

TWENTY-SEVEN

Covering my ears didn't help, at least not enough. I didn't care *what* Alexis had done—I couldn't bear to hear a human being suffer like that.

Sobbing with the effort, I got to my feet once more and, still covering my ears, ran back toward the pond, putting more distance between myself and the house in hopes the sound would be muffled. I made it all the way back to the edge of the water before my legs refused to carry me anymore and I had to sit down. The screams were fainter now, but I could still hear them, and I knew the sound would haunt my sleep for years to come.

Peter lay where we had left him, his head still caved in from the impact of my rock. There was no evidence of any healing whatsoever, so he'd clearly failed in his quest to become *Liberi*. I didn't see how, though. He'd shot Anderson in the freaking head. I'd seen the bullet come out the other side, seen the life drain from Anderson's eyes. Anderson had died, I was sure of it.

Maybe Peter hadn't really been a Descendant after all, though I wasn't sure how one could make a mistake about that. The glyphs were pretty clear indicators.

And then there was Dean.

Actually, there *wasn't* Dean. Where Dean had lain, there was a shirt, a pair of jeans, and a pair of sneakers, all empty. The air smelled of sulfur and ash, although as far as I could tell there wasn't even a speck of ash or dust to mark where the *Liberi* had once been.

He was dead. And not the kind of dead a *Liberi* could get up and walk away from. He was an immortal being who could only be killed by a mortal Descendant. And yet Anderson—clearly *not* a mortal—had killed him.

Footsteps approached me from behind, but I didn't turn to look. Alexis's screams had finally stopped a couple of minutes ago, so I guessed Anderson was through with him. There was no eerie white glow lighting the night now, but that didn't stop the chill of fear that traveled up and down my spine. I'd been coming to think of Anderson as a friend, but after the savagery I'd witnessed tonight, I couldn't force myself to look at him.

In my peripheral vision, I saw him come up beside me and then sit on the grass, just out of arm's reach. Even just seeing him out of the corner of my eye, I couldn't help noticing he'd lost the handcuffs and the underwear somewhere along the line. Likely when he'd morphed into that humanoid pillar of fire.

"They're dead, aren't they?" I asked in a choked whisper when the silence became too heavy.

"Yes."

"Permanently."

"Yes."

I shook my head, trying not to remember the sounds of their screams. I couldn't be sorry they were dead—especially Alexis, though for all I knew Dean was just as bad—but their suffering sickened me. Worse, I wasn't a hundred percent sure I wasn't about to face the same fate. It didn't take a rocket scientist to realize I'd witnessed something I shouldn't have. Anderson seemed to be a nice guy most of the time, but even before tonight, I'd seen ample evidence of the ruthlessness his genial manner hid.

Trembling, I wrapped my arms around my knees. "Are you going to kill me, too?"

He turned his head to face me, and I reluctantly met his eyes. "Are you going to tell anyone what you saw tonight?" he countered.

I shook my head, unable to trust my voice. How could he possibly believe my denial, though? What kind of idiot would admit they were planning to run around blabbing in this situation?

His expression was grave, though not especially menacing. "You know what fate awaits you if you talk. And the same fate awaits anyone you talk *to*. I trust that will motivate you to keep quiet."

There was another long stretch of silence, but

silence gave me too much room to think, and that was the last thing I wanted to do right now, so I hurried to fill it.

"You aren't *Liberi,* are you?" I asked.

One corner of Anderson's mouth tipped up, though I wasn't sure what he found funny. "No, I'm not *Liberi.*"

"Then what are you? If you don't mind my asking . . ."

I thought at first he wasn't going to answer. Then he shrugged, perhaps deciding it wasn't necessary to be coy when I knew too much already.

"I am the bastard child of Thanatos and Alecto." I gave him what I was sure was a blank look. "The Greek god of death and one of the Erinyes, or Furies," he explained. "I am Death and Vengeance, rolled into one."

I swallowed hard. "So what you're saying is . . ." My throat tightened, and I considered the possibility of panicking. "What you're saying is you're not *Liberi,* you're an actual . . . god?"

He gave me a small smile. "Is that really so hard to believe after all that you've seen?"

I stammered like an idiot, making his smile broaden and bringing a mischievous twinkle to his eye. The expression further widened the chasm between the Anderson I knew and the terrifying creature I'd seen him turn into.

"There are a few of us left on this earth," Anderson said. "We were abandoned here by those who thought themselves our betters. We keep our existence a closely guarded secret."

"But Konstantin knows who you really are, right? That's why he made a deal with you?"

Anderson nodded. "Yes. He saw me kill one of his people, back when we were at war. He escaped, but immediately abducted Emma so that if I killed him, I'd never be able to find her and I'd doom her to an eternity of suffering. That was when we made our deal. He's made sure to abide by it, knowing that as long as he didn't provoke me unbearably, I would let him live in hopes that he would one day lead me to Emma."

"And no one else knows who you are. Konstantin has kept your secret."

"To tell anyone who and what I am would be to acknowledge that he isn't the most powerful being to walk the Earth, something his ego will never allow."

A number of facts lined up in my mind, and something clicked. "That's why Konstantin was so desperate to recruit me, right? Not because he wanted me to hunt Descendants—or not *just* because of that, anyway—but because he didn't want me to help you find Emma."

Anderson nodded.

"And you didn't bring any of the others tonight because you knew you were going to end up killing *Liberi*, and you didn't want any witnesses."

Another nod. "I am as anxious to keep my identity a secret as Konstantin, only for different reasons. I had no choice but to risk letting *you* find out, but I did have a choice with the others." He shrugged.

There was more to it than that, I knew. I didn't

really matter to him, so if I saw something I shouldn't and he had to kill me to silence me, it wouldn't break his heart, not like it would have if he'd had to make the same decision with one of his own people. I was still an outsider, an interloper, and I probably always would be. I told myself I was used to it and that it didn't hurt a bit.

I turned to stare at the pond. "Is she in there?"

Something sparked in his eye, an expression that held no hint of mischief and screamed of fury. "She's there. If you've settled down enough that I can trust you not to bolt, I'll go get her out and we can all go home. And then Konstantin and I are going to have a long talk."

I suppressed a shudder. Right now, I was really, really glad I wasn't Konstantin.

"Then go and get her," I said. "I want to get out of here."

Without another word, Anderson rose gracefully to his feet. And wouldn't you know it, despite everything I'd learned about him that night, despite all the fear and awe and horror, I couldn't help taking a moment to admire his naked backside as he walked to the water and once more plunged in.

It took the better part of forever to get Emma out of the water. She was chained and weighted down, and god or not, Anderson didn't have the strength to break the chains that bound her. It occurred to me that Alexis might have been planning to haul her out and maul her in front of Anderson as part of the slow, torturous death he'd had in mind, so I reluctantly went back to the house. Shuddering the whole time and trying desperately not to think, I searched through Alexis's empty clothes until I found a ring of keys. I brought these to Anderson, and sure enough, one of them was the key to the shackles. Anderson brought Emma's body to shore and laid her on the grass.

She was naked, naturally. Her skin was ivory pale (or corpse white). Her hip-length black hair and her rosy lips gave her the look of a sickly Snow White, and I knew that alive and healthy she would be a stunning beauty. Which I supposed was only appropriate for the wife of a god.

"Does she know?" I asked Anderson as he knelt beside the body, brushing his wife's hair from her face as we waited for her to revive.

He spared me only a brief glance. "No. And it's going to stay that way."

I raised my hands in a gesture of surrender. No way in hell I was going to mess with him, not with everything I knew, although I kind of thought his wife had a right to know exactly who and what she was married to. Still, that was their problem, not mine.

Naked and wet in the frigid air, his teeth chattering, Anderson was almost blue with cold. I fetched his clothes from where he'd discarded them in the woods, but for the time being, at least, he ignored them, all his attention focused on Emma. She wouldn't be in much better shape when she came to, and I figured we were past the time for stealth by now. Even so, I stayed near Anderson, giving him ample chance to veto my decision as I called the mansion. I got Logan, and asked him and Maggie to come help us. I provided zero details beyond the address and the need to bring something warm to wrap Emma up in.

It was at least twenty minutes before Emma suddenly sucked in a breath, then started coughing. Anderson turned her onto her side and supported her head as she expelled the pond water from her lungs.

Embarrassed by their mutual nudity and wanting to give them time to get reacquainted without an audience, I wandered off into the woods before Emma finished retching. I sat heavily on the ground as soon as I was out of sight, drawing my knees up and resting my forehead on my folded arms.

I'd seen too much pain and misery in the past few days, endured too much fear. I couldn't contain it anymore, and I finally let it all go at once. Muffling the sounds with my arms, I cried for everything Steph had suffered at Alexis's hands; for the multiple deaths Jamaal was suffering in punishment for his disobedience; for all the abuse Emma must have suffered over the years she'd been Konstantin and Alexis's prisoner; for the normal life I'd once taken for granted; and for the uncertain future, which I had no doubt would expose me to even more life-altering traumas.

TWENTY-EIGHT

I let Anderson do all the explaining when the cavalry arrived. I tried to make myself concentrate on the answers, thinking it was a good idea if I actually paid attention to the "official" story, but I was a little too shocky to manage it. Certainly I knew Anderson made no mention of Alexis's demise, or that of his crony, Dean. We'd weighted Peter's body down in the chains that had once held Emma, then dumped him in the pond, where hopefully he would never be found, at least not by any human authorities. We'd disposed of the empty clothes, as well. No one except Konstantin could possibly guess what had actually happened here tonight.

Emma was alive and conscious, but that's about the best you could say for her. Her eyes had a glazed, shell-shocked expression, and she didn't react to anything anyone said to her. Anderson cradled her in his arms, and while she didn't resist, she didn't cuddle up to him, either. For now, at least, there seemed to be no one home. My heart broke for both of them, and if I hadn't already cried my eyes dry in the woods, I probably would have done it again on the ride home.

As far as I could tell, Emma was no better the next day, although she would move around and eat and drink if prompted. She wouldn't make eye contact with anyone, and forget about talking or changing her facial expression. Still, Anderson seemed confident she would recover, if perhaps not all the way. I didn't know if that was the wisdom of the ages speaking, or just wishful thinking, but I certainly wasn't going to argue with him or try to take away his sense of hope.

I'd really hoped that Emma's presence would inspire Anderson to commute Jamaal's sentence, but when I tentatively made the suggestion, he silenced me with one cold look. Before I'd seen his true form out at Alexis's mansion, I might have tried to argue or cajole him out of it, but there was no pretending he didn't scare the crap out of me now.

"What really happened last night?" Maggie asked me when we were alone. "It's obvious Anderson didn't give us the whole story."

I would have loved to have told her, to unburden myself and talk the situation through with another human being. But of course, I couldn't, not without risking my own life and hers.

"Don't ask," was all I said, though I could see that the way I'd shut her out hurt her.

Not being able to tell Steph the truth was even

worse. According to Anderson's version of events, we had run Alexis off, but there was no mention of his slow and painful death. Blake was still sticking to Steph like glue, and I didn't dare even hint at what had happened to Alexis when Blake might hear me. I trusted Steph to keep a secret, but not Blake.

Eventually, I managed to get her alone for all of about five minutes. I was worried enough about Anderson's threat that I dropped my voice to a bare whisper even though we were alone.

"Alexis is dead," I told her. "I can't share details, and if anyone gets a hint that I told you, we'll both join him in the grave. But I thought you should know."

Steph's eyes misted with tears. Of the two of us, I'd been by far the most bloodthirsty, so I was a little surprised when she whispered back, "I hope it hurt."

I shuddered, remembering Alexis's screams. "It did," I assured her, then hugged her tightly as she burst into tears.

When sunset rolled around, I seriously considered finding somewhere in the house to hide so I could avoid having to witness Jamaal's third and final execution. I was scared to death of defying Anderson, but I honestly wasn't sure my psyche could survive one more horror.

In the end, though, I pulled on my big girl panties and headed out to the clearing with the rest of Anderson's *Liberi*—minus Emma, thank God, because even hard-assed Anderson had *some* compassion, at least for his own wife. I figured Jamaal was being punished in part because of me, and therefore it was my moral duty to stand witness. In hindsight, I think I was still fighting a boatload of guilt over having killed Emmitt and started Jamaal down the self-destructive path he'd chosen.

What courage I'd managed to muster completely failed me when I stepped out from between the trees and into the clearing, however. Jamaal had warned me that Logan would choose something "heinous" for the grand finale, as he termed it, and he hadn't been kidding.

In the center of the clearing, illuminated by the light of many torches, was a wooden stake, driven into the ground and surrounded by firewood and kindling.

"No fucking way," I said, coming to such an abrupt halt that Maggie bumped into me from behind and almost knocked me over.

There were winces and gasps of sympathy from the other assembled *Liberi,* but no one else reacted as violently as I did. I whirled on them, my outrage reaching epic proportions.

"We are *not* going to just stand here and watch while . . ." I couldn't even say the words, but Maggie was frantically shushing me anyway.

"You're going to do exactly that," Anderson told me coldly as he stepped into the clearing, followed by Logan and Jamaal. Jamaal staggered when he saw what was awaiting him, but he regained his composure and his courage in a heartbeat, visibly steeling himself for the ordeal.

Earlier in the day, I'd been unable to shake the vision of Anderson in his true form, an avenging god of death with pitiless eyes. Memories of Alexis's and Dean's screams had silenced me better than any gag ever could. But this was too much. Jamaal's actions had been misguided, but not truly evil. He hadn't meant to harm anyone but me, and he'd thought he had good cause. He didn't deserve this torment—and I didn't deserve to have to watch it.

I took a belligerent step in Anderson's direction and opened my mouth to tell him exactly what I thought of him, ignoring the steely threat in his eyes.

"Shut up, Nikki!" Jamaal snapped at me, surprising me into silence. "It's my choice whether to submit to this or not, and I choose to submit."

I wanted to argue, but he had a point. He could walk away if he wanted to, high though the cost might be. But he wasn't going to walk away. "Fine. Be a martyr if you want to. But I am *not* watching this."

I didn't wait for Anderson's reply, instead turning and plunging into the woods, running full speed toward the house, hoping I could get inside and as far away from the clearing as possible before the screaming started. If Anderson insisted on punishing me for my act of defiance, I'd deal with it when the time came. I just couldn't bear to see or hear any more suffering.

I wasn't thinking when I ran, but once I entered the house, I found myself pounding down the stairs toward the basement instead of heading up to my room. I didn't analyze my instincts, just went with them, and soon found myself in the cell I'd been locked in the very first night I'd set foot in the mansion.

Slamming the door behind me, I threw myself onto the narrow cot and pulled the pillow over my head.

I lay there for a long time, listening to the thrum of my pulse and the harsh rasp of my breath, my body so tight my muscles ached. Even when I was sure the execution was over and done with, I couldn't relax a single muscle. I figured I might take the whole rest of the night to pull myself together. I was sure I'd have as much time as I needed, because no one would think to look for me here. But I was wrong.

There was a soft knock on the door. I ignored it, not remotely ready to face anyone just now. The door opened despite my lack of invitation, and I did a double take when I saw Jamaal step into the room.

I sat up abruptly, shoving the pillow aside. I didn't know how much time had passed, but I was sure it wasn't enough for Jamaal to have healed from being burned to death.

He closed the door behind him and leaned against it. "He didn't go through with it," he told me. "They tied me to the stake and he had Logan bring a torch over, but he never lit the fire."

My shoulders sagged in relief, although I wanted to punch Anderson's lights out for putting us all through that. The build-up had been bad enough that even failing to light the pyre didn't lessen the horror.

Jamaal pushed away from the door and sat beside me on the cot. Not so close as to be intimate, but not giving off his usual keep your distance vibes, either.

"The point of the whole exercise was for me to prove myself willing to submit," Jamaal said softly, staring at the floor. "There is nothing I wouldn't face to avoid going back to the way I lived before Anderson found me and brought me here. I was so upset about Emmitt that I lost sight of all the good things I still had. I'd forgotten how important being part of Anderson's crew was to me. The punishment sucked, but it also woke me up. So don't, uh, feel bad about all this shit, okay? I'm in a better place than I was before."

I looked over at him, and it was all I could do not to smile at the patent discomfort on his face. I didn't know if it was because he was unused to speaking words of comfort, or because he didn't like speaking to me so civilly, but whatever it was, it made him adorably awkward. I suppressed an urge to reach out and touch him, having learned last night that such overtures would not be welcomed despite our truce.

"Thanks for coming to talk to me," I said, giving him a tentative smile. "I'm glad to know he didn't go through with it. And I'm sorry—"

He cut me off with an abrupt hand gesture. "No. No apologies. Even if you're Konstantin's spy and you killed Emmitt on purpose, you aren't responsible for what happened to me. I made my own decisions, and I'm enough of an adult to own up to that."

I sighed. "I wish I could convince you I don't work for Konstantin."

He cracked a smile that reminded me for the zillionth time just how mouthwateringly gorgeous he was. "If it makes you feel any better, I'm less convinced now than I was a couple days ago. You *did* find Emma, after all." The smile faded into a thoughtful expression. "And Anderson is no fool. He trusts you for a reason. That's good enough for me for the time being."

I rolled my eyes at him. "Wow, what a ringing endorsement."

He smiled again—I think that made three times in two days, which might be a record for him. "Ask anyone—coming from me, that *is* a ringing endorsement."

He stood up, and I felt obliged to stand, too, if only because I didn't want to have to crane my neck to look at him.

"Now if you're finished sulking in the basement," he said, "Anderson's called a meeting for about thirty minutes from now to discuss our future relations with the Olympians now that we have Emma back. You don't want to miss it."

He turned his back and skedaddled out of the room before I could tell him what I thought of his "sulking" comment.

When I'd come down to the basement, I'd been halfway thinking I needed to make myself disappear. How could I consider working for a terrifying god of death and vengeance who could kill immortals with a touch and had no qualms about burning one of his own people to death in punishment for disobedience?

Jamaal's words, however, gave me serious pause. Not only had Anderson not followed through on his most dire threat, but Jamaal was clearly feeling better. Before, he'd been like a wounded animal, snarling and biting without any rational thought. "Borderline crazy," I'd labeled him, and I suspected it was the truth. Now, he seemed human. Still in pain, and still a dangerous man, but not plunging off the deep end anymore. It made me wonder: how much of Anderson's "punishment" had truly been punishment? And how much had been a demonstration of a particularly harsh version of "tough love"?

I wasn't yet convinced that staying with Anderson and his merry band was the best way for me to deal with my uncertain future. They were likely soon to be at open war with the Olympians, and that spelled more ordeals and more trauma for me if I stayed with them.

But maybe, just maybe, if Anderson could take an alienated loner like Jamaal and make him into something like a member of the "family," he could do the same for me.

And that was something I'd gladly brave the terrifying future to achieve.

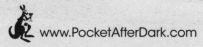

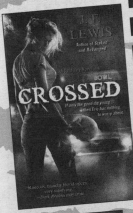